To Maryann, my wife of fifty-eight years. You are the love of my life, and I look forward to triple digits with you in the future.

For Barbara,
Hope you enjoy
my second novel.

Carl Mitchell

ACKNOWLEDGMENTS

No book is the product of just the author. Getting this novel ready for publication benefitted again from the super critiquing and copy-editing strengths of William Greenleaf, who also provided support that greatly improved point-of-view continuity, sharpening suspense levels, and for suggesting which specific characters needed additional background detail. Six readers of the first novel in this series, *Sundown*, were contacted and submitted eighteen Bill of Rights and Obligations. Their submissions and names are listed in the last five pages of *Friendship City*.

As with the first novel in this series, Denice Hunter again led a very focused Covenant Books team of super copy editors and page designers. Robynne, from Damonza handled my story-to-design requests, delivering an outstanding cover. They all contributed to the book you hold in your hands or in your electronic library. Publicity was part of the last author imperative. URlink, various webinars, and books on fiction publicity were helpful. Marketing was the toughest and last hurdle. I had been following the BookMarketingBuzzBlog since early 2018; and its creator, Brian Feinblum, was the most positive marketing force I encountered. I enlisted his help. All above had strong hands in improving this novel and getting it to market.

1

---◆·---

March 19, 2058

Nick Garvey and three Secret Service agents were the only passengers on Air Force One. Nick fixated on one fact: his NYPD captain and his detective partner of ten years both had been shot. Captain Gilmore was dead. His partner, critical condition at best.

Three more agents were waiting just off the tarmac when the jet touched down at New York's Kennedy Airport exactly three hours after leaving Houston. They accompanied Nick into a waiting limousine.

"Mount Sinai Hospital," the lead agent instructed.

"Does it look like Tim Branson will survive?" Nick asked.

The lead agent shrugged. "The doctors said Detective Branson mumbled your name several times. I'd take that as a somewhat positive sign."

"I saw the video on Air Force One. Tim and our captain, Kevin Gilmore, sitting in a diner. Captain Gilmore takes a bullet just above his eyes. It didn't show where or how Tim was shot, just that he fell to the floor."

"Three shots, I've been told."

Nick remembered the reporter announcing, "Captain Gilmore was pronounced dead at the scene. Detective Branson is reportedly clinging to life in Mount Sinai Hospital."

He replayed President Allison's comments during her phone call to him about Tim's mumbling of his name and that Nick's presence might help keep Tim alive. He would have traveled anywhere in the world to help Tim live.

The limousine pulled up to Mount Sinai. The doctor who had performed Tim's six-hour surgery stood waiting for Nick.

"Your detective friend is super resilient," Dr. Joseph Dillon said. "I expected at least a week to pass before he regained consciousness. He awoke not three hours after the operation. He's asking questions about his own shooting. I see minimal problems resulting from your visiting him. My understanding is that you were his partner. As such, he might welcome talking to you. In fact, he mumbled your name several times as he regained consciousness."

In Tim's room, a metal table with a stand holding a pulse and blood pressure monitor stood at the far side of the bed. Beside the monitor, an IV bag hung from a hook with a tube running down to Tim's right arm. He was lying down but watching TV.

Nick shook his head, shrugged, and walked in. "Anything good on?" He plopped down on the bedside bench, taking care not to block Tim's view of the screen. "If so, should I go get some popcorn?"

"Don't make me laugh," Tim said, raising his left hand to point down at his abdomen under the covers. "They told me to keep my stitches in one piece."

Nick was relieved. Tim had managed to exchange banter for banter, just like in the old days.

Tim extended his right hand. "How's your sorry ass been, old buddy? Better than mine, I hope."

"Slightly." Nick shook Tim's hand.

"Your daughter, Sandra?"

"Still in the induced coma."

"She'll come out of it okay when the doctors figure it's time."

"What in hell happened to you? President Allison said you'd been shot to pieces, and I had to get here in a hurry."

Tim shook his head. "No reason to rush. Just this morning, the doctors said I'll survive."

"Good to hear, but the president said to get here pronto."

"Pronto? I was only shot up about"—he looked over at the wall clock—"twenty-three hours ago. How did you get here all the way from Texas so fast?"

"Air Force One."

"No justice in the world at all. I get shot up by a bunch of third-class thugs, and in response, you get gifted a first-class seat on the president's jet."

"No champagne, though." Nick's eyes narrowed as they always did on receiving his first clue. "Who were these third-class thugs? President Allison wasn't sure who shot you."

"Three of the creeps from El Camino's old gang. The boss and I were at a circular table having lunch, both of us facing the door. They came in with some dandy in a prissy business suit topped off with an atrocious tie swirled with every color in the known universe."

"Did you recognize Mr. Dandy?"

"He looked vaguely familiar. Thinking back now, I saw him a day earlier, maybe two days, lifting two empty beer kegs into his sedan."

"Empty beer kegs?"

"Well…kinda weird-shaped kegs. About the same height, but fatter, with a flat top with clamps."

"Who started shooting?"

"When they were about to sit down, Mr. Dandy pointed at me, or at least in my direction. One of the thugs turned toward me, and I could tell he recognized me. He pointed his finger at me, then pulled out a handgun and pumped four bullets into me…and I don't know how many into Captain Gilmore. I was told later that Mr. Dandy and the other two whisked Pistol Pete out in one hell of a hurry."

Nick nodded. It matched the information told by the TV reporter. "The doctor said you mumbled my name a few times as you were coming out of anesthesia. What was that about?"

"I saw you standing over me, telling me to hold it together, and that you would make those bastards pay. In an hour or two, I realized I was imagining you were here when you were still down there in Happy Town."

Nick chuckled. "It's Friendship City, not Happy Town. I haven't been there myself. Houston is as far south as I've been."

A nurse came in with a tray of medicines, bandages, and other stuff. She put it on the metal table on the other side of Tim's bed, studied the monitor's numbers, and started writing in a pad.

Nick gathered from her expression that she needed some alone time with her patient. "I'm going out for a bit, but I'll be back. Get some rest."

He found the three Secret Service agents still in the waiting room.

"Where you go, we go," the senior agent said.

2

———◆———

Nick waved at Brian McKenna, tall with a full head of red hair, as they entered the abandoned convent used as a set of meeting rooms.

"Good to see you, Nick," Brian said, raising his arms and flexing his muscles as if showing off to a crowd prior to a boxing match. "Almost back to normal, thanks to you."

Nick pursed his lips and gave the young man a thumbs-up. He remembered carrying the kid through the subway tunnels six months ago while trying his best to stanch the flow of blood from the gunshot wound in his chest. Another half hour, and Brian would have been six feet under. Now, he was his neighborhood's leader—or guardian, as they called it—until his father returned from what Tim called Happy Town.

"My partner was shot in a diner yesterday. He's in the hospital, recovering. He recognized the shooter and the shooter, him. He said there was some fancy business suit with the three street thugs. Said the thugs were part of El Camino's old gang. Does that combination ring any sort of bell?"

Brian paused, then nodded. "About a week ago. A block or two south of our neighborhood. One of our men was walking his son back from school when he noticed a group something like you described. He recognized two of the scruffy-looking men as gang members. Didn't say El Camino's or anyone's, just gang members. The suit guy he said looked like he felt out of place."

"Can I talk to your man?"

"Most definitely. You're one of us. Remember, you passed the Vote of Acceptance. You're a resident now." Brian wagged his head. "Well, not a twenty-four-seven resident, but an accepted one nevertheless."

Brian told the three Secret Service agents not to follow too closely, then took Nick six blocks toward the Hudson River to a storefront with a sign over the door that proclaimed *The Capable Cobbler* in large purple letters on a gold background.

Inside were six padded chairs against the left wall. The rest of the small store contained three long workbenches, each littered with hand tools, shards of leather, and a dozen or more shoes.

Brian introduced Nick to Kenneth Malloy, about Nick's own six-foot height with white hair and wearing a denim apron. The name tag on his apron read *Cobbler Ken*.

Nick asked about the thugs.

"Saw them two more times," Ken said. "The last time yesterday in a restaurant without the tall man in the suit. The first time was eight days ago, and the suit was with the other three. The first thing I noticed was a man wearing a flashy suit with worn and crusty shoes. Then I noticed the three grubbies he was with. Two I recognized from a year ago. Street thugs, both. I saw the same group two days later. Same three thugs, same crusty shoes."

Nick got the restaurant's name and location, then took off, followed from a block and a half away by the three agents.

He intended to case the diner and the surrounding neighborhood so as to pick out a place where he, or one of the agents, could watch for the group. He would have to get back to Houston and Sandra in four days for Dr. Charles Johnson's weekly update. Nick figured finding the shooter would take at least those four days.

Four days shrunk to zero seconds as soon as he turned right at the last corner before the diner. Even at a football field's distance, he instantly recognized the group. Three strutting street thugs and one prim and not-quite-proper businessman, all four headed in his direction. He recognized the one on the outside, nearest the road, having interrogated him a year earlier about his gang connections.

Nick paused and looked in the window of a barber shop. He hoped the three Secret Service agents weren't too far behind.

The four men kept walking toward him.

He stroked his chin as if trying to assess his need of a shave, hoping his hand to his face would prevent recognition. He watched the group's reflection in the window.

The four men passed him and were about to turn the corner when one of them stopped and spun around. "Detective Nicholas Garvey," the thug said. "So good to see you again after all these months."

The other three hurried around the corner.

Nick turned to face the man.

The thug was pointing his right forefinger at him, his middle finger pressing an imaginary trigger. His left hand reached into his left pant pocket, the one with the pistol-sized bulge.

Nick reached for his pocket revolver. He raised his pistol a tenth of a second after the finger-pointer.

"It's been nice to know you," the thug said, leveling his gun and smirking. "So long."

3

---◆---

Before either Nick or the thug could take aim, two Secret Service agents each shoved a pistol hard against the back of the thug's head.

"You squeeze one, we squeeze two," the older agent said. "Drop your weapon now!"

The thug complied.

The third agent raced around the corner. "They jumped in a car and sped off," he said, not quite out of breath.

The thug was cuffed and hauled off to Rikers Island. He spoke not a word from capture to being placed in his cell. Facial recognition software revealed only his street name: Sure-Shot Tompson.

A full-face picture of Sure-Shot was sent electronically to the NYPD detail guarding Tim. Within ten seconds, the response came. "It's him."

Sure-Shot remained silent throughout four hours of interrogation. By midnight, Nick, the agents, and senior Rikers Island interrogators had exhausted all avenues and decided to reconvene midmorning.

Nick texted Brian and sent him the mug shot of Sure-Shot. He followed up with a call. "I hope I didn't wake you. I just sent you a mug shot of the thug who shot the police captain and my detective buddy. Do any of your contacts know where the fellow lives? He's locked up but won't answer a single question."

"Someone probably does. I'll call you back either way in about a half hour."

Nick's cell rang in less than ten minutes. "That was quick!"

14

Brian gave a chuckle. "I would have called back in less than two minutes, but I wanted to verify with three other contacts. Sorry for the delay."

Nick wrote down the address, roused his Secret Service detail, and headed out.

The landlord said nobody used the apartment except Mr. Tompson. He unlocked the door.

Nick thanked him and suggested he return to his own quarters.

Sure-Shot's apartment was just short of plush: four large TV screens, an ebony dining room table capable of seating twelve, a curio cabinet with at least thirty figurines, an ornate chandelier, plush and colorful carpeting, and drapes that hung from ceiling to floor. Nick figured the only thing needed to qualify for inclusion in some *Decorators of the Decade* magazine was a marble fireplace.

Nick and the agents started searching through every drawer or shelf in every kitchen counter, every closet, every dresser, and every night table. He went into the master bedroom.

The top-left drawer of the desk was stuffed with envelopes, most of which contained bank receipts showing large deposits every other week from some foreign source. The center drawer was empty except for a large folded paper—a commercial-type map of the United States probably taken from some travel brochure.

Two pen-drawn oblongs caught Nick's attention. One encircled the west coast from San Diego and half of Nevada on the south up to the north, where the red ink crossed right through Vancouver, Canada. The red line on the right coast encircled the top half of Florida, leaning to the right all the way up through the Carolinas; Washington, DC; New York; and most of Maine.

Nick pulled out the drawer full of envelopes and brought it with the map to the dining room table.

Two of the agents checked through each envelope.

Nick and the third agent tried to fathom the intent of the two circles drawn on the map. "Something was in the works." Nick shook his head. "But what? There is no writing, just the two hand-drawn circles."

The agent nodded. "I'll take it to the lab. Maybe they can determine where it came from, how old it is, if there are any slight impressions, fingerprints, or whatever."

Nick shrugged.

The four of them put the door latch on lock and left.

*****

Midmorning found Sure-Shot dead in his cell, suspended by a metal hanger wrapped around a huge nail pounded into the wall. The curved part of the hanger used to hold the unit from a rod was inserted into the back of Sure-Shot's neck. Fully four inches of his tongue had been cut out and was taped, bloody side up, to his prison shirt.

Nick left with the three agents to return to the hospital with two face shots of Sure-Shot, mouth closed.

Tim took the news with an attempted shrug. "It's him. Got what he deserved. I'm sure Captain Gilmore's wife would have liked to do more cutting and slicing. I know I would've."

Nick shook Tim's hand. "Gotta get back to Houston."

Tim squeezed Nick's hand. "Tell your granddaughter, little Nicole, I asked after her." He grinned. "And Nathan, the little black boy you adopted—" He feigned a moan. "I keep forgetting Nathan adopted you as his replacement father." He paused for a moment, then shrugged. "And Half-Penny too. Can't forget our young kidnapper."

*****

The three agents ushered Nick to a waiting limousine. President Lenora Allison awaited him in the back seat. Sam Kirby, the president's lead Secret Service agent, sat behind the wheel.

Nick climbed in next to the president.

"What's your assessment?" she asked.

"He had to have been butchered by one of the guards, not an inmate."

"Is it safe to assume that a message was being sent? A message to us? A message that the World Council is somewhat alive, if not alive and well?"

"There was that map I called you about."

"You said it had a circle drawn around each coast, but nothing else. He was planning something."

"Definitely not a trip. At least not with a family. We don't know if the drawing was about something in the future or in the past."

President Allison agreed. "The safest path is to assume it portends something happening in the future. Something nefarious. Something we have to discover. He wasn't a nice person, so the map won't relate to anything less than evil."

"Madam President, after your terms in office, you could find gainful employment as a detective."

President Allison nodded. "If you promise to be my detective mentor, I couldn't fail." She waved for Sam to start for the airport. "You're getting an Air Force One round trip. I checked with Dr. Johnson. Sandra is getting stronger but should remain under medication for not more than another week or so."

"Thank you," Nick said, feeling closer to his daughter.

"I will try not to pull you away from Sandra, but this map has me worried. If something unfolds, something really bad, you will be one of my first calls."

"Understood, Madam President. I'm worried as well."

"I want to give you an early heads-up on an announcement coming out tomorrow. Carter Johnson has been confirmed as my new vice president."

Nick's eyes popped wide open. "But he's from the opposite party. You're Republican and he's a Democrat. Who thought that was a good idea?"

President Allison smiled. "I did. Still do."

"Don't appointments have to be approved by both houses of Congress?"

"It is just the Senate, but I involved both houses. Got three-quarters of each. More than enough."

"Well, you did need a vice president. You've been without since Wellsley was murdered seven months ago. Did Carter have any reservations?"

"Not that he conveyed to me. He agreed to support all laws and bills enacted to date but assured me he would argue his point of view on future proposals. I have no problem with that. He is the most qualified and most experienced candidate. I trust him to work for the good of the country."

*****

Sam pulled right up next to Air Force One. Two Secret Service agents escorted the president, Nick, and Sam aboard. The agents then returned to the limousine and drove off.

*****

Air Force One landed in Houston just past noon.

When President Allison told Nick she had no doubt Sandra would soon awaken and things would return to normal, Nick succeeded in not flinching. He had never told President Allison that his daughter truly hated him, mistakenly blaming him for killing her beloved uncle Joey and for her mother's subsequent death by alcohol addiction. He hoped Sandra's recovery returned her to anywhere *but* normal.

"Thank you for your helpful words," he said to the president.

"I'll keep in touch with Dr. Johnson while I'm in Mexico City."

"Nice sunny vacation?"

"I wish. Mexico's president and I have to finalize a few outstanding issues regarding Friendship City and the rest of our common border."

"Any big problems?"

"No. Pretty well everything is set. Just have to get it down on paper so it can be presented to the citizens of Friendship City for approval. The people of Brownsville, Texas, and of Matamoros, Mexico, have been pleading for years to be allowed to join the two municipalities into one self-governing unit. They were continually terrorized by thugs of the World Council and decided that by working together as one entity, they could protect themselves. President Emilio Lopez and I granted them autonomy eight months ago—an autonomy we tried to keep secret from Jason Beck and his World Council." President Allison gave Nick a nudge. "By the way, when I asked you for a recommendation of someone who could help steer the city to productive independence, your suggestion of Robert McKenna was outstanding. Even the mayor and all the district officials have nothing but praise. Apparently, he was most helpful in straightening out their Bill of Rights."

"I figured he would be a positive influence."

President Allison smiled. "Detective Garvey, after your tour with the NYPD, you could find gainful employment as a chief staffer to any government entity, national or local. I'll even volunteer to be your mentor."

Nick chuckled and shook the president's hand. "I'll add that skill to my résumé."

He departed Air Force One and got into a waiting limousine, which was to take him directly to Houston's Methodist hospital.

The limousine dropped him off and waited.

4

◆

D r. Charles Johnson had just finished his noon rounds of the neurosurgery center when Nick entered his office.

They took their seats at the desk as Dr. Johnson dropped several folders atop a metal rack. He picked up a folder from another rack and gave it a quick glance.

He nodded, then looked up at Nick. "Sandra is progressing a bit better than we projected. Instead of the two months of our last estimate, I expect we can pull her out of the induced coma in just two or three weeks."

"When you say she's progressing a bit better than projected, what does that mean?"

"It means that we project a complete physical recovery. Physical *and* mental." He checked the folder again, shuffling the pages. "It says here that Sandra was beaten comatose by her boyfriend."

"I wouldn't call him a boyfriend," Nick said. "More like a really bad and, eventually, regretted choice. She told him to get out, and he beat her senseless."

"I hope you made him pay."

"Somebody did. He ended up stuffed inside a garbage can. Appropriate place for him."

Nick was shown into Sandra's room and stayed for almost an hour, saying silent prayers. He prayed for her to emerge from her seven-month coma fully healed. Interspersed now and then was a prayer that her heart would shed her hatred of him, hatred that had festered since she was a little girl when she blamed him for the killing of Uncle Joey. To this day, she refused to accept that her uncle was shot by his criminal cohorts.

Nick looked up when a nurse came in to check the flow of medications through the IV. When a technician entered as well, Nick decided it would be best to leave.

The limousine took him to his apartment. The agents accompanied him inside, checked that everything was secure, returned to the limousine, and drove off.

As requested, he called President Allison and verified he had gotten home and that Sandra was expected to finally rejoin the world within the next two weeks or so.

"Glad to hear that, Nick. Glad for you and glad for Sandra. Keep me apprised."

Nick assured her that he would.

He made himself a coffee and sagged down into the one easy chair. Hopefully, the news would get better. It couldn't, he felt, get any worse.

He wasn't as sure about those who had killed Sure-Shot Tompson. Maybe it could get worse. He remembered the president's question after Sure-Shot's death. Was his murder "a message that the World Council is somewhat alive, if not alive and well?"

He was convinced that they hadn't destroyed every single cell of the World Council, but they had brought it close to destruction. He shook his head. What could the council do, thrashing around in the ashes of its former self? How could it make the world any worse?

5

◆

April 12, 2058

The death countdown had reached its final stage.

Dr. Horatio Baumberger paused from studying the forty-eight patients on the other side of the protective glass and double-checked his watch. In exactly one hour, he expected the twenty-four strapped-down patients, writhing and struggling on the left side of the white-walled barrack, to expire. Only the closest six of the twenty-four on the right were still writhing and struggling. Each was hooked up to three different monitors. In all cases, struggling didn't begin until twenty-four to thirty-six hours before death.

Baumberger raised his right hand as a signal to the six men inside wearing biohazard suits. The two-stage antidote was administered to the closest six on the right. The other eighteen patients on the right, still strapped but not struggling, had received the antidotes, six at a time, at scheduled intervals going back ten days of the fourteen-day infection period.

The twenty-four on the left had been given nothing.

Dr. Baumberger allowed himself a small smile. The two little bottles of antidote in his left hand represented the power to save half the human race. Half, that is, if the World Council wanted even *that* many to survive.

As he watched the antidotes being administered, he projected all twenty-four in the right group would survive, only one or two with lasting effects.

Exactly one hour and two minutes later, the monitors attached to the last patient on the left all indicated absence of life. All the monitors on the right showed functional improvement in each patient.

Each, except one. That patient had indicated poor circulation at the start of the proof.

After another hour, when twenty-three of those in the second group showed even greater improvement, Dr. Baumberger turned to six intensely interested young men who had been watching with him. "As you can see, the antidote is quite effective. In the one case where poor circulation impeded quick infusion of the antidote, the patient has stabilized, albeit at a non-improving state. You have all been screened for, and have, excellent circulation." Dr. Baumberger scanned the faces of all six men, noting only mild concern. "As you know, this plague takes at most two weeks to kill and is contagious after only one day, with late-stage transfers very aggressive in bringing the noninfected quickly to the same point as the one infected. No painful or disabling effects will present themselves for at least four days. No body part—heart, lungs, kidney, liver, blood…or whatever—is harmed throughout the fourteen days. Your nerves would be agitated should you go without the antidote beyond those four days.

"You will each be infected one day before your departure. The itineraries with which you have been provided, and which you will memorize, detail your travels for two days subsequent to your arrival. You will then complete your missions, take the antidotes, and return. Upon your return, you will go back to your previous lives, none the worse for your commitment." Dr. Baumberger again scanned each face. "Any questions?"

There were none, as expected.

Introduced to them only yesterday, Baumberger knew none of the six. The World Council had provided them, all volunteers.

He smiled to himself. *Whatever or whoever is thrown against it, the World Council will survive.* He tapped his clipboard with a pen. *Not only survive but thrive!*

He made some quick notes for his records. Supreme Director Jason Beck might have died in a helicopter crash, but his World Council would live on.

For the council to live on, there were a few *sub-humans* that had to be dealt with: Chris Price, the traitor who stepped up to claim Jason Beck's position; President Lenora Allison, the eternal enemy; and Detective Nicholas Garvey, that insignificant little...

Baumberger shook his head and mustered another smile.

Protocols had been established years ago, and after a few months of confusion and panic here and there, normalcy was about to return. This plague test was the first promise of the World Council's return to greatness. He called it Project Restore.

*****

Baumberger's Project Restore, already approved by the new supreme director of the World Council, started two days later.

Along with the approval, the new director had demanded that each of the volunteers be fitted with an encrypted body camera. Should anything or anybody interfere in any way with the project, the supreme director insisted Baumberger and he be in the loop.

Baumberger turned on the six display-and-record units. It was about an hour before the first planeload of three carriers would land in the New York area. He wanted to be ready. He had not yet met face-to-face with the new supreme director, but the man had transmitted all the proper code sequences, and Baumberger wanted to be on the man's good side. Jason Beck had frequently bounced medical ideas off him, and he hoped the new director would do the same.

The plan: use the six infected volunteers to introduce a modified bubonic plague into the United States and wait for two weeks. Two weeks would be sufficient for the plague to infect between one hundred thousand and one million people. Most of those infected would appear outwardly normal but would be besieged by ever-increasing nerve pain until heart failure.

The sweet part for Baumberger was that most of those infected would make it through to the fourteenth day before embracing an excruciating death. A few with previously compromised immunity would react more quickly.

Locations of antidote sufficient for all 210 million US citizens would be communicated to the government at the end of that two-week period. The end game of the plan was the United States agreeing to a specific set of conditions to be communicated within a month under threat of activation of a more severe plague infection—an infection with no antidotes.

Small vials of this more severe pathogen would be placed with the initial antidotes. Analysis of these vials would convince Lenora Allison and her advisers to meet any and all World Council conditions.

Baumberger checked his watch. It was time. He leaned in toward the screens.

The first three of Baumberger's plague-infected carriers deplaned from the international flight at the recently reopened Newark Liberty Airport. He watched the screens as they exited the plane with 138 fellow passengers and crew, all now new carriers of the plague as they walked beside the three along the dimly lit mobile passenger boarding and exit walkway into the arrival and customs area. Cloth taping stretched between pole stands compelled the passengers to snake back and forth in single file. Within twenty minutes, all the customs agents became carriers as well. The passengers hailed the few cabs available while others caught buses to various points on the compass. The agents and baggage handlers finished their day and returned to homes in New Jersey, where contagion would continue.

He watched and took notes as the three primary carriers took the PATH into Manhattan, then to Penn Station, where they each boarded a separate train to a different east coast destination.

Baumberger spaced his bathroom breaks and sandwich-making to coincide with the expected travel times. Within a few hours, he watched the remaining three primary carriers deplane at San Francisco International Airport and scatter for transportation to the states of Washington, Iowa, and Nevada.

Each of the six men carried two small, numbered vials of bluish liquid. They had instructions to take the first vial by mouth three days after landing and the second exactly six minutes later. Baumberger wrote down the two landing times so he would remember to verify and record each team swallowing the liquids.

The six each roamed their assigned destinations for two days, took their two-vial antidote, and returned to Newark Liberty and to San Francisco International, where they boarded their return flights.

Each of the six had completed one final instruction before returning to their assigned airports. Three abandoned warehouses on the west coast and three on the east coast each contained six fifty-five-gallon barrels filled with blue liquid, half with several stickers with a huge *1* marking, the other half with a *2*. One of the *2* barrels in each warehouse had a small, opaque vial taped to its side.

Baumberger had watched as each man activated a homing device in the warehouse and adjusted the alert date and time to read *04-28-2058, 12:00 noon Greenwich Mean Time.*

The next twelve days would allow for all the infected airplane passengers to encounter their morticians. Individual countdowns would begin anew for each person encountering one of the thousands of follow-on infected.

The six homing devices were keyed to the same date that an Internet alert would be sent to the president of the United States. The alert, already set in web-based stone, detailed the location of each abandoned warehouse and how to use the two-stage, stop-the-plague-in-its-tracks antidote and cure for all citizens, infected or suspected exposed.

6

───◆───

Nick Garvey swore he had paced every second-floor hallway in Houston's Methodist Medical Center. His daughter, Sandra, was still in a coma induced eight months previously when President Lenora Allison had Air Force One bring them to Houston on her way to California. President Allison had suggested Sandra would be up and around in weeks, but Dr. Charles Johnson said recovery from her injuries was best accomplished at a slow and measured pace. Yesterday, Dr. Johnson had said the next day or two would tell the tale. He had added that the tale was certainly going to be good.

"I'll believe good when I see it," Nick said to himself.

He was at one of the hospital's coffee machines when a nurse hurried up to him.

"There you are," she said, puffing as if just completing a 5K run. "Dr. Johnson wants you in his office."

Abandoning his coins in the machine and the blinking *Select* button, Nick spun around and followed the nurse to the elevator. His heart was thumping. He had just left Sandra's bedside. Although still in an induced coma, his daughter had appeared okay. His mouth turned dry. *What happened?*

He followed the nurse through Jones Tower's second floor. He knew this hallway by heart: the Neurosensory Center of the hospital. Sandra's progress and life signs were all positive. So he had been told. What had happened?

27

They came to the door with the legend *Dr. M. Charles Johnson, Chief of Neurology* on its frosted glass. Nick entered just as Dr. Johnson walked in from an inside door and dropped a folder on his desk. Nick tried to inhale normally but couldn't. He couldn't read the doctor's expression.

"Sit down, Nick," Dr. Johnson said. "It's good news. Sandra is awake."

Nick's sudden exhale caught the doctor's attention, and he nodded reassuringly.

"Can I see her?"

"We took her down for several scans and tests. She'll be back in about two hours. I just wanted to tell you the news as soon as I was sure."

"She'll be okay?"

Dr. Johnson nodded.

Nick sank into the nearest chair. He had visited Sandra every day, but the one President Allison had called him away to review some plans and give her and her team advice.

Dr. Johnson nodded a second time. "This is a significant positive step on the road to full recovery."

"Can I have her daughter brought in to see her?"

"Definitely."

*****

Nick glanced at the other four he had brought into the waiting room. Nicole, Sandra's seven-year-old daughter, was sitting attentively opposite the entrance where she could see any activity in the hallway. Julia Ramirez, the only other adult sharing their four-bedroom apartment, had brought in Nicole and two others: her grandson, seventeen-year-old Half-Penny (or Julian, as she insisted on calling him), and almost-twelve-year-old Nathan Williams, who had accomplished a reverse adoption of Nick after the death of his father, William.

Julia Ramirez, responsible adult in Nick's absence—or as Nicole claimed, even when he was *not* absent—was the first to speak. "You said Sandra was awake and okay," she said, referring to his hurried phone call.

"Yes. Dr. Johnson said she had been taken down for some tests and should be back in"—Nick glanced at his watch—"well, about any time."

"Did she speak?"

"Johnson didn't say."

Nicole jumped up. "They're wheeling someone down the hallway."

A procession appeared—at least seven nurses or attendants, the patient on the gurney, and, bringing up the rear, Dr. Johnson. The group made a right turn along the hallway to Sandra's room.

"It's Mommy!"

Dr. Johnson gave a follow-us wave as Nicole broke into the hallway.

Everyone followed Nicole into Sandra's room and waited as she was hooked up to the various sensors and fluids.

Dr. Johnson nodded to Nick and took several steps backward, allowing Sandra's family to surround her bed.

Nicole was on her right side, standing by her head. When after almost a minute, Sandra's eyes fluttered open, Nicole smiled and jumped once, straight up and down. "Mommy! You're awake!"

Sandra wrinkled her brows, then moistened her lips. "Nicole?" she said just above a whisper.

"Yes, Mommy. Yes!"

Sandra hugged her.

Nick, trained by his granddaughter in the art of reading lips, was able to make out the whisper into Nicole's ear. "I love you."

Sandra slowly rotated her head to take in the remaining four. "Who are these people?"

Nick, on the opposite side from Nicole, reached his right hand out and placed it lightly atop his daughter's bandaged left hand. "You've never met these people, but—"

"Who are you?" she asked.

Nick's head quivered. He assumed this was another of his daughter's ways to show her hatred of him. Whatever would help her to get better. "Sandra, you don't know these people because—"

"Sandra? Who is Sandra?"

7

---◆---

Peter Meddleson was the owner of the eighty-five-meter yacht *Runner*, with two crossed assault rifles before its name and two more after. It had just steamed through the Strait of Gibraltar and was heading out into the North Atlantic. Sitting around a small conference table were multibillionaire Meddleson, Dr. Horatio Baumberger, and a tall, lightly bearded man wearing a Western-style suit.

Meddleson felt off-kilter. Dressed in a gray business suit with a colorful neck scarf and brown shoes crusted from the salt water, he ran the fingers of his right hand through his thinning, dyed-blond hair. "I've been told by Dr. Baumberger that all twelve of the antidote drums have been activated and will transmit their alarms in nine days."

"Per plan," Dr. Baumberger said. "Our research indicates that if they administer the doses within twenty-four hours, they will lose less than five percent of the remaining infected but still-alive individuals."

Meddleson turned to the third man. "I assume this timetable is to the master plan, Mr...." he paused, waiting for a name to be proffered.

"I'll take Melville's advice. Call me Ishmael." The man's facial expression changed not a bit. "The master plan is comfortable. At the moment."

Meddleson continued to feel uncomfortable. The man had been brought aside *Runner* in a small, high-speed cruiser, had effected radio contact via the exact, supposedly secret frequency, and had informed the captain he was coming aboard. Once aboard, he had insisted on this three-way conference. As they were sitting down, he had given the two verbal passwords and the one keyed-entry password on Meddleson's own cell phone.

Whoever this Ishmael was, he was now the order giver.

"When the drums have been located," Ishmael said, "portions of the contents will be rushed to hospitals in each affected area. Portions sufficient for ten million immunizations in each city."

Meddleson was impressed. He had not yet received such detailed information. "I have a team of four engineers en route to the secure location of the five follow-on plague containers to relocate them to the locations you requested. I understand that Jason Beck's master plan was to give President Allison two weeks from the first plague-antidote discovery to unleash this more severe version."

"That plan is to be put on hold," Ishmael said.

"But we can't—"

"Can't what?"

"We can't change the plan. We can't—"

"The plan is not being changed. An additional week or two must pass before we implement."

"But...the plan isn't open to change. There is no authority that—"

Ishmael lowered his head slightly and glared at him. "I am the authority. The plan is on hold."

"There's probably a very good reason to change the plan," Dr. Baumberger said. "We are on the same team. If you tell us the reason, perhaps we can be of help."

Meddleson searched Ishmael's face for any reaction. Nothing.

"We *are* on the same team, and to make your cooperation less problematical, I will apprise you of the goal."

Baumberger nodded.

Meddleson allowed himself to breathe evenly.

"The goal," Ishmael said, "is to attack through Texas."

"Texas? President Allison has border agents all over that state, especially the southern part. That area is protected around-the-clock by all sorts of federal police. Even Secret Service agents."

"And I own a workable portion of the federal police and several of the Secret Service agents. Besides, Texas is the first target. After bringing many to their knees, we will also be hitting other targets, cities."

Meddleson shrugged acceptance. "I guess that's what Jason Beck meant when he said something about us all being cattle and some have to be slaughtered."

"His direct quote was, 'The people of the world are all cattle and have to be herded.' He said nothing about slaughter, but rather, 'Sometimes the herd needs to be thinned.' His final words on that particular analogy were, 'The world must have a single, enforceable philosophy and not be allowed to stray. Straying puts all others in danger.'" Ishmael paused for a moment, then continued, "Not everyone is part of a herd. The select beings—us and those we appoint—are keepers of the herd. And we must decide if any thinning is required. Sometimes even those previously appointed must be part of the thinning."

Meddleson was well aware of Ishmael's pointed glance in his direction. He tried to keep his breathing even.

8

◆

N ick sat quietly in the waiting room. Seven days had passed
since Sandra awoke from her induced coma and didn't
know her own name.

Dr. Johnson had shared some details and plans with Nick. He
had said her physical progress was excellent. Her inability to remember major portions of her life would, he felt, be able to be resolved.
"Resolved in time," he had added.

The doctor was scheduled to meet with Nick in about twenty
minutes.

Nick picked up the TV remote, deciding some form of distraction would keep him somewhat on the rails. He chuckled, asking
himself if he had any rails left. He pressed the power button.

Network programming was struggling to recover from years
under the control of the World Council. News was the first to regain
a strong footing.

As the screen popped to life, a young news anchor with dark
eyeglass frames matching the color of his hair was reacting to clips
of various news items, commenting as events unfolded. He had just
finished something about boating on a river as a new clip faded in.

The upper left banner read *Downtown Spokane, Washington:*
10:27 a.m.

The anchor informed the TV audience that the following clip
had been recovered from a drugstore security camera in Spokane. He
glanced down to his script. "Nineteen-year-old Jessie Goodman, hav-

ing just picked up a prescription at the local pharmacy and without turning to leave, suddenly fell writhing to the floor in front of the counter."

Nick's eyes widened.

The anchor didn't have to tell about the girl's grandmother screaming.

The anchor continued after the video clip snapped forward in time. "Paramedics arrived in seven minutes," he said as emergency equipment was unpacked. "The grandmother of the thrashing young girl told the paramedics that they had just come to get medication for the girl's parents, told them that four days ago her son, the girl's dad, had come down with identical symptoms just a few days after driving up from the San Francisco airport. She said that the girl's mother had come down with the same symptoms just one day later, prompting the daughter to leave college and come home. She, herself, had arrived just three days ago from Casper, Wyoming."

Another clip advance.

"After two minutes and a multitude of quick checks, the paramedics shook their heads and told Grandma she was to accompany them as they took her granddaughter to the hospital."

The image on the screen, obviously enlarged in the studio, focused in on the grandmother's face as she screamed, "My God. What's wrong with Jessie?"

One of the paramedics held the grandmother by her left arm and guided her out behind the gurney. "Right now, only God knows the answer to that."

Nick felt nowhere near being on any rail. Sandra was a bit older than the young girl, but the only rail he could hold on to was the one where he fully understood the grandmother's panic.

The upper left banner changed to read *White Plains, New York: 11:47 a.m.*

The screen showed a shopping plaza.

The anchor apologized for the lack of sound. "Forty-two-year-old Johnathan Cryer fell to the ground, twisting and turning, just inside the entry doors to the recently reopened Galleria at White Plains. Of the two dozen adults nearby, only four closed in to offer help. Later, when an ambulance arrived, many of those that kept their distance told the medical personnel that they had either seen similar incidents or had heard about them.

"It was later determined that Mr. Cryer had visited his son at Columbia University, where the younger Mr. Cryer, Patrick, was close to wrapping up his junior year. Upon contacting Columbia, it was reported that the son had been hospitalized two days earlier with very similar symptoms. No diagnosis had yet been arrived at in young Cryer's continued thrashings, which were persistent and unrelenting."

Nick shook his head. "What the hell's going on?"

The banner changed again: *Bangor, Maine: 12:23 p.m.*

"This is a video taken by cell phone," the anchor announced.

The screen showed a vertical video frame of a golfing green, then the video of a golf ball racing toward a flag-topped pole held by a caddie.

The anchor slowed his delivery to match the actions on the screen. "After sinking a forty-two-foot putt on the seventh hole of the Bangor Municipal Golf Course, Ryan Pitts, fifty-one, threw up his hands in jubilation, smiled, then fell writhing and thrashing to the green. His wife, Ingrid, stood quiet for a few seconds before chiding her husband that his celebration was getting out of hand." The video stopped, and the screen returned to the anchor, who glanced down again at his script, then up at the camera. "It was right after she gently prodded his stomach with her own putter, both the others in the foursome said later that Ingrid herself fell whipping about to the green just feet from her husband.

"A doctor who happened to have finished the sixth hole tried to stabilize both Ryan and Ingrid. Within a minute, he called his hospital and requested an emergency ambulance." The anchor tapped his forefinger atop his script and looked straight at the camera. "It was later discovered that both husband and wife had visited two days prior with one of her cousins, who was hospitalized just hours after they had left."

Nick shook his head again, blinking. Something was destroying people. He took out his cell phone and dialed President Allison.

Sam Kirby answered, telling Nick that the president was in a very tight trade negotiation. "She won't be available for several hours unless there's a national emergency."

"I just saw on the news that there are at least a dozen people being gripped by some strange and debilitating seizure. Doesn't strike me as a national emergency. Not yet."

"Where is this happening?"

Nick told Sam what he had seen. "It's definitely not local," Nick added. "I suggest the health community watch these events like a hawk."

He was about to suggest more when a nurse asked him to follow her to Dr. Johnson's office.

Johnson was already seated behind his desk. Nick sat opposite.

"Again, Nick, Sandra continues to make excellent, improving strides in her physical condition. Her memory of recent events is clearing somewhat. Events before her coma continue to elude her consciousness. With your permission, I plan to bring in several specialists in cognitive reconstruction to give her a series of monitored tests. Nothing they do will be at all invasive."

Nick nodded his permission. "How long before they reach a conclusion?"

"About a week."

Nick signed the three papers Dr. Johnson pulled from a folder on his desk.

9

◆

April 26, 2058

Ishmael called a short meeting with Baumberger and Meddleson just after the yacht *Runner* finally docked at Puerto Cortes, Honduras. He looked Meddleson square in the eyes. "Before I leave, I would like you to tell me if your four engineers secured all five containers of the follow-on plague liquid." He studied Meddleson's reaction.

"They have, sir." Meddleson looked guarded but anxious. "And I personally transferred the remaining two to my engineers, who then transported them to the destination you provided."

Baumberger coughed and raised a hand. "I assume you have a way of getting however many additional containers of that second plague you need into your target location."

Ishmael seemed to decide an extra tidbit or two would not hurt the plan. "We currently have the two containers in position with one soon to be relocated into Mexico. One container will be enough for its present location. In fact, one container will take care of half the state of Texas. But to answer your question, I do have a way."

"Are you going to release it right off?" Baumberger asked. "The president will know it's part of the earlier threat. Maybe we should work up a different release date. That way—"

Ishmael raised a hand. "It's under control."

"Do you have a plan for the target?" Meddleson asked.

"We'll start small over the next few days with a few supposed malcontents mocking opposing citizens and leaving messages of hate.

Then there will be muggings, brick throwing, and the like, which should result in several people being locked up. The next day, we'll quickly graduate to sending a few to the hospital. By that time, I feel we can count on citizens from throughout the area joining in. If conflicts don't exceed the off-to-the-hospital level, we'll make sure a few from all sections are sent to the hospital DOA. But getting back to the first plague, what about the incubation period of the antidote, not to mention that of the plague itself?"

Baumberger stated the timetable. "Sixteen hours for the antidote to offer full protection lasting for three weeks. One twenty-four-hour day for the plague to fully mate with any unprotected individual and to begin the lead up to two days of agony and pain, followed by death."

"So we have two days before the alert goes off exposing the container locations," Meddleson said.

Ishmael nodded and called the meeting to a close.

1 0

◆

April 28, 2058

Nick paced back and forth in the waiting room. Over the past thirteen days, Dr. Johnson had monitored Sandra closely, and over the last six days, he had called in several cognitive reconstruction specialists. In addition, he had brought in two psychiatrists to spend many hours with her and to provide detailed, written evaluations.

Dr. Johnson had shared a few details with Nick and had assured him he would provide all results, with a prognosis, in the very near future.

Today was that future. Dr. Johnson said he would bring Nick fully on board right after he received the final evaluations scheduled for one o'clock in the afternoon.

Nick checked his watch. Almost 11:00 a.m. He had been in the waiting room since 9:00 a.m., knowing he could be nowhere else while he waited to learn his daughter's fate.

His mouth was dry, his hands twitching. He had to sit down and try to collect himself.

He picked up the TV remote. As he pressed the power button, he remembered that President Allison and World Council Director Chris Price had scheduled an important broadcast to start in—he checked his watch again—three minutes.

He slouched back and tried to relax.

The screen brightened to a man with a microphone describing a bridge construction. Nick remembered when, thirty-plus years ago,

40

commercials would take up at least the final three minutes before the start of any and all broadcast hours. The two networks, recovering from the edicts of the old World Council, were still trying to pull in sponsors.

The bridge construction bit ended.

A female reporter from Manhattan, Nick's old stomping ground as a cop and detective, was next, commenting on a bunch of citizens who had caught some strange sickness and either died or had been taken to various hospitals and were in intensive care. Standing outside Mount Sinai, the reporter related that seven people had died in their homes and twenty-seven more, as old as seventy-four and as young as thirteen, had been brought to various Manhattan hospitals. She noted that similar deaths had been recorded elsewhere. California and Massachusetts had the most.

Two doctors were interviewed, each commenting that the patients seemed to have the same symptoms, primarily thrashing about and losing consciousness. Nick noticed that both doctors avoided the word "disease."

It was becoming clear to him that something was happening, something that not too many people seemed to be concerned about. He recalled the news story a week ago of several people dropping like flies and thrashing about, then nothing for a week. Now some were dying and being rushed to hospitals.

The reporter ended by telling the camera that her team would keep atop developments.

The screen switched to Houston's local news anchor, who alerted the audience that the next hour would be a live broadcast hosted by World Council Director Christopher Price in cooperation with President Lenora Allison.

Nick remembered working with Price and Allison to bring the World Council to heel. He still cringed whenever he reflected on the blood spilled to keep Jason Beck, that council's SOB leader, in power.

This broadcast was coming almost nine months after the helicopter crash that "officially" ended Supreme Director Jason Beck's villainous life and, with his demise, the end of the World Council's exclusive control of the world. It had been decided by Director Price and President Allison that the depth of Beck's depravity would be modified to be seen as "leveling the playing field" so as to initiate positive growth through implementation of many "dream plans."

The first dream plan to be implemented was the elimination of the population controls restricting the number of children allowed per couple to just one.

Another dream plan was the relocation of the New York City rectenna power grid. Jason Beck's hatred of the grid was portrayed as a plan—most successful, it turned out—to prove its viability before dismantling it and relocating it to the middle of the Sahara Desert.

Nick marveled at the convincing nature of Jason Beck's whitewash.

Television was now in much wider use, with a couple of former networks slowly regaining profitability. The broadcast today was to be beamed worldwide. Its title was "Dreams Fulfilled, Part 4," and it listed two points of origin: New York City and Houston.

The "Dreams Fulfilled" logo filled the screen.

Nick sat upright.

He wondered if any official would mention the multitude of recent deaths.

11

$\spadesuit$

As the screen faded from logo to black, Nick glanced at his watch. 11:17 a.m.

"Citizens of the world, welcome!" World Council Director Christopher Price sat behind a generic desk in front of a bank of windows that revealed a panorama of Manhattan buildings. It was early evening. All the building lights, power supplied from restored generating stations, were on full display.

"The World Council is announcing the actualization of one of the many visions Supreme Director Jason Beck left behind for us to complete."

Price's image squeezed to the left while the right half of the screen blossomed forth to show an older man wearing coveralls and mopping his forehead with a colorful kerchief while surrounded by tubing and wires.

Price waved at the right screen. "It gives me great pleasure and honor to introduce one of this century's great minds: Dr. Owen Pendleton."

The man in overalls bowed to the camera.

Nick remembered Dr. Pendleton from his agriculture experiments atop a penthouse in New York City. He was a world-renowned bioengineer whose death was faked to keep him from the clutches of Jason Beck.

Price continued, "Dr. Pendleton, please tell those viewing what you and your team have accomplished."

"Clean coal, Director Price."

43

The right half of the screen stretched out, revealing a rather large, brightly lit, and clean industrial-type room with a group of men turning dials and reading meters.

Pendleton waved at the camera. "Follow me."

The camera followed Pendleton for about thirty seconds when he stopped beside a chute filled with black irregular rocklike chunks. Several men were pushing the chunks down the chute. It led into a metal enclosure, inside of which was a very visible fire.

Pendleton pointed at the enclosure. "A furnace." He then pointed at the black chunks. "Microbe-treated coal." He smiled a toothy grin. "I tell people that it's cleaner than bathroom soap, but no one wants to shower with it." Chuckling, he reached down, picked up a single piece of coal, rubbed it hard against his right cheek, then turned his cheek to the camera.

There were no traces of contact. Not a single mark.

"More importantly, this coal is clean in its emissions. This coal cannot produce carbon dioxide, a gas most useful and essential to the planet if you are looking to grow flowers, vegetables, and forests. The byproducts of the burning of this microbe-treated coal are pure carbon and pure oxygen. No CO_2."

Nick chuckled as he watched Dr. Pendleton almost bouncing up and down, betraying an abundance of enthusiasm.

"In fact, the carbon solidifies and falls to the floor of the furnace. If the company still existed, we could get De Beers to clean the furnace floor and make diamond rings." Pendleton's grin was now at its widest as he waved his hand and his screen black-holed into nonexistence.

Christopher Price emerged from the darkened swirl. He stood and approached the camera. "As you see, we are implementing many of Jason Beck's visions. We are also moving beyond those visions in many ways. The most recent..." He paused, visibly taken aback by something he could see but the viewers could not. "Well, I think Vice President Carter Johnson should be the one to explain."

The screen again split into two vertical halves, Price on the right this time, with the vice president standing just to the left of what looked like the edge of the desk in some business or medical office in Houston. Framed diplomas covered the wall behind Carter Johnson.

Price extended a hand toward the vice president's half of the screen. "Vice President Carter Johnson, this is your first appearance since receiving Senate approval of your appointment. How does it feel being a Democrat appointed by a Republican president? Has there ever been such a cross-party pairing in our history?"

Carter Johnson smiled. "To answer your first question, my feelings are that I must be up to the challenge twenty-four-seven. President Allison and I have been working together, and at odds at times, for well over twenty years. As to your question of this ever happening before, the answer for the last century and a half is no. When Vice President Jerome Wellsley was murdered last year, there was a growing divide in the country. When President Allison approached me with the vice president offer, I was intrigued, to say the least. Within two days, I accepted and was appointed. It took the past eight months until this Sunday morning, today, for the Senate to confirm. I am most honored, and as I said, I must do my best to be up to the challenge." Carter motioned to his left.

The camera shifted.

"It was President Allison who wanted me to introduce your newest vice president," Price said. Then he chuckled. "Madam President, please tell the world about the most recent event relating to Friendship City."

"With pleasure, Director Price," she said, motioning Carter Johnson to take a nearby seat.

The left half of the screen zoomed slowly to the president's head and shoulders.

"I'm sure you all remember eighteen months ago when President Emilio Lopez of Mexico and I announced to the world the establishment of Friendship City. The citizens of Brownsville, Texas, in the United States, and Matamoros, Tamaulipas, Mexico, had for years petitioned both governments to support their joining into one community open to controlled immigration."

Nick checked his watch again. Only 11:22.

He glanced back at the screen. President Allison was recounting the evolution of Friendship City, an evolution in which twice in the past nine months since Jason Beck's supposed death via copter crash, he had had a front-row seat. He remembered how Friendship City, once endorsed and sponsored by both governments, got off to a rocky start. Citizens from both ethnicities were at a total loss on how to create a cohesive city government. After nine months, President Allison had called him up to Washington, DC, to join a group of about twenty individuals chartered to advise her on how to rescue Friendship City before it split apart at the seams.

After almost a week with no viable plan, Nick had offered a wild card suggestion. "I dealt with the most functional neighborhood in Manhattan. It comprised a diverse group of people with leaders but with each person required to assist in enacting laws. One of those leaders, Robert McKenna, would be an excellent choice to bring some amount of cohesion to Friendship City."

After an hour of back-and-forth discussion, his suggestion was accepted, approved, and, within days, implemented—all without him ever having set foot in Friendship City.

What to this day had confused the hell out of him was the World Council and its leader, Jason Beck, even allowing the formation of an independent city-state, let alone the construction of a bulletproof forty-foot-high glass wall over 140 miles in circumference to control entry and exit.

Nick looked back at the TV.

Christopher Price was about to ask a question. "Madam President, will you—"

He was cut short as the president was interrupted by someone on her right. The camera zoomed back. Nick recognized Sam Kirby, President Allison's lead Secret Service agent. The president had cut the sound, but both faces were close enough for Nick to use the lip-reading skills his granddaughter had taught him.

Sam was telling the president that the CDC had just reported something about "a monumental medical emergency on both coasts."

The president stood, and the screen went blank.

Nick shook his head. Was this the reason, he wondered, for all the recent deaths?

Before he could formulate anything more than that question, a nurse came into the lounge. "Dr. Johnson asked me to bring you to his office."

It was only 11:37. The news couldn't be good. Nick's knees felt weak.

12

---◆---

The nurse took Nick into Dr. Charles Johnson's office and told him the doctor would be just a couple of minutes. This was the thirty-fourth weekly meeting since Sandra had been admitted, and he was used to the wait.

Dr. Johnson walked in, took a seat across from him, and dropped a folder on the desk.

Before he could say anything, Nick congratulated Dr. Johnson on his brother, Carter, being confirmed vice president.

The doctor thanked him, then patted the folder. "Nicholas. Sandra, as we know, has made positive, albeit slow and measured steps in regaining and maintaining her new memories. Per our agreement of the past two weeks, I have had specialists give her cognitive tests every day, with a scan once a week. What I've found is that her retrograde amnesia, the inability to recall events before her physical attack and resulting coma, has not improved to any noticeable—"

"Is there any way—" Nick broke in. "Any treatment that can restore those memories?"

"I was about to suggest a program. It's experimental and totally safe. But as it is experimental, there is no guarantee of even partial recovery."

Nick's only fear was that Sandra would fully remember her hatred of him, her unfounded conviction that he had killed both her mother and Uncle Joey. But for the sake of Nicole, his seven-year-old granddaughter, he dared not succumb to his fear. He had lived with his daughter's undeserved scorn and hatred for years and years before, and he would do so again. For Nicole.

Nick nodded his understanding. "Do I have to sign anything?"

"Just the three forms I have here," Dr. Johnson said, patting the folder again. "I have marked where you are to sign." He eased the folders toward Nick. "Once the treatment begins, you will find—"

"Dr. Johnson!" A young man in a suit and tie burst into the room, waving a single sheet of paper. "You're the only senior doctor I could find. I don't know if the president wants us to shut the hospital down or what."

"The president?" Dr. Johnson reached for the extended sheet of paper. "President of the hospital?"

"President Allison. It's her signature at the bottom."

Dr. Johnson's gaze raced back and forth as he digested the paper's contents. "Holy shit!"

"What is it?" asked Nick.

"A plague has been released along both the east and west coasts of the United States. Intentionally released. More than twelve hundred people have died. Large caches of antidotes were found in locations near the various ground zeroes. Holy shit!"

Nick winced as he remembered the image of the Chinese premier, twenty years earlier, looking down at the body of his dead, plague-ridden son. Jason Beck, the World Council's personal devil incarnate, was responsible then. *Who now?* he asked himself.

13

———◆———

With *Runner* still moored in Honduras, Peter Meddleson offered his latest guest a gin and tonic. The athletic man sat across the wood captain's table from him.

"Thank you, no," said six-foot-three Bart Donovan. "Let's just talk business."

Meddleson had hoped to share a drink and ease into discussing his financial difficulties. Bartholomew Donovan was the key holder of Meddleson's corporate debt, which had grown at a monster rate since he had to fund various undercover activities for Jason Beck's World Council. When Beck died in that helicopter crash, his debt could not be repaid, as all World Council funds were frozen, with every current and future payment controlled by President Allison and Christopher Price, the replacement council figurehead.

Bart placed both hands on the table. "You claim you're involved in a program that will soon enable you to begin repaying your debts." His fixed gaze under furrowed brows, Meddleson was quick to realize, signaled a question which had better be answered in the positive.

Meddleson nodded. "I have obtained new commitments that will soon result in restoring my portfolio."

Bart rested his chin on his right fist, its elbow braced on his chair arm. "Good news. I've never asked what your past commitments were, and I won't presume to begin now. However, you can appreciate how…*invested* we all are in your financial restoration."

Meddleson's eyes twitched.

Bart smiled. "I do need one sliver of information as to when these new commitments will begin to provide returns."

Meddleson watched Bart's smile fade and his eyes become fixed and intense.

"We need an approximate date we can expect repayments to begin," Bart continued. "Will that be immediately after your commitments are discharged, or sometime after? I will be asked for many details. My goal is to pass along as little as your commitments allow. I am sure you appreciate I have to give some time frame assurance."

Meddleson nodded.

"Good. I just need a ballpark time frame, albeit a somewhat tight ballpark."

Meddleson nodded again.

"Will your commitments bear financial fruit within the next two or three days?"

"More like six to ten days, subject to delays."

"Keep me informed of any movement one way or another, especially when we get within those two or three days' time to make market adjustments." Bart raised his chin from his fist, splayed the palm open, and lowered it to the table. "Are we clear and in agreement?"

Instead of nodding a third time, Meddleson vowed to keep Bart up-to-date, and through him, the other five investors whom he had never met and whom he hoped he would never have to meet.

14

◆

April 29, 2058

President Lenora Allison motioned for her cabinet members—the nine she was able to round up at 2:37 a.m.—to take their seats. "I believe you have all seen the communique I sent to all major hospitals throughout the country stating that the plague that suddenly gripped both coasts yesterday and the day before was not a natural event. The fact that it arose on both coasts at the same time was most suspicious right from the start. It was when we were boarding to return from Houston that I received a communication stating the plague was perpetrated intentionally."

"Do we know who did this?" Josh Cabrera, attorney general, asked.

"No idea," said Secretary of Homeland Security Peter O'Malley.

The names of at least a dozen culprits were shouted out by those around the table. President Allison waved her hand. The room fell silent.

She looked around the room. "Twelve large drums of supposed antidote have been located using instructions in the communique. Initial evaluations indicate they are not poisonous."

Secretary of State George Pinter raised a hand. "How much antidote is there?"

"More than enough," President Allison said. "It's a two-part antidote, and we calculate there is enough for twice our country's current population. The infected and uninfected."

Health and Human Services Secretary Serena Clayborn cleared her throat. "I'll put our scientists on a full three shifts to prove the effectiveness and safety of the antidote. It should take no more than—"

"No!" President Allison said, her fist not quite slamming the table. "We do not have any time to waste."

"But—"

"I plan to authorize immediate administration of the antidote to those just minutes from death, then, working backward, to those with an expectation of twenty-four hours of life remaining. We will continue working backward."

Secretary Clayborn frowned. "I feel that—"

"I understand. I *do* want your people to go full bore on determining the safety of the antidote. At the same time, I want your team of medical scientists to evaluate each person receiving the antidote." President Allison arched her eyebrows. "Each person. Surviving or not. Those that survive are to be monitored to evaluate their progress. Do they get better or do they stay in whatever state they were in when given the antidote? If any of those further back from death are found to get worse, we stop."

"I'll get my teams on it."

"One of the drum sets included a small vial of a supposed super plague that will be unleashed if we do not reply favorably to a forthcoming request. I want the vial contents analyzed ASAP. I want to know everything: spreading mechanism, incubation period, possible antidotes…everything."

Secretary Clayborn nodded.

President Allison turned to Josh Cabrera. "I need the Justice Department to analyze the communique I received and to work with the men bringing in the antidote drums. Find what can be found: country of origin of the drums, any scrapings found on the drums, any chemicals in one drum not found in the others, any—"

"I've already had my people approach the retrieval team," Cabrera said. "We'll find anything that can be found. Anything and everything."

President Allison pushed back her chair and stood. "Let's get started."

The room emptied.

President Allison pulled out her cell phone and paged Sam Kirby, her senior Secret Service agent.

By the time she got to her desk, Sam was waiting. "Madam President," he said.

"Take a seat, Sam. Health and Human Services will be administering the antidotes to near-death individuals, then working back. Justice will be going over everything with several fine-tooth combs. Their job is to find where these drums came from."

"They'll do a thorough job, Madam President."

"I'm sure they will." She drummed the fingers of her left hand on her desk. "I just don't have a good feeling about this. Time is of the essence, and time is what we have precious little of available. You said last week that Nick Garvey called you about earlier problems?"

"A few. Not as many as the CDC has reported."

"The last part of the communique suggested we check passengers arriving on two specific international airline flights. I've given the flight numbers and dates to the FBI. Have someone keep tabs on them, Sam."

"Will do, Madam President."

"I haven't told the cabinet yet that the communique also described possible targets as landmark locations." The president shook her head.

"What, Madam President?"

"We've been set up to thin our ranks by covering a multitude of locations. 'Landmark locations' is an intentionally vague term on the perpetrator's part."

"I'll see how many agents the FBI can put on this to work with the local police in any city or location we feel qualifies as landmark."

"A start, Sam, but they're still rebuilding after the removal of the World Council Guard and may need assistance. I insist you brief only the agents you *personally* trust."

Sam Kirby nodded.

President Allison's drumming fingers paused in midair. "We have politicians and bureaucrats working full tilt. What we need are productive people. The FBI is almost there, but we need more than *almost*. We need someone who lives and breathes solving problems." Her fingers relaxed. She paused and looked down at the desktop. "Yes. I like the way he thinks."

"The way who thinks, Madam President?"

"We need a detective." The fingers folded into a fist. "We need Nick Garvey. I know his daughter is just starting to recover, but the country needs him here now."

15

---◆---

N ick had asked Dr. Johnson for the use of his small conference room after Sam Kirby had called him and outlined
the president's request: that he come to DC to help track
down the perpetrators of the plague. Sam had told him a senior agent
resident in Houston would meet with him and explain the request
in more detail.

"I can't decide on my own," Nick had told him. "I have family here, one of whom, my daughter, is recovering from the coma
induced in New York. That family has to be part of the decision."

"Fine," Sam had said.

A time was agreed upon.

As an afterthought, Nick had recommended Owen Pendleton
be brought into the plague analysis team. "He's got extensive insights
into all things biological."

Now Nick looked around the conference table. Nicole, now
seven years old, was sitting opposite him, looking quite serious and
mature; Half-Penny, who still preferred that nickname, and his
grandmother, Julia Ramirez, who supervised the family when Nick
was by Sandra's bedside, were both highly attentive; and Nathan
Williams, almost twelve and almost a genius detective, was the most
attentive of all.

Five feet to Nick's right, Senior Secret Service Agent Jonathan
Bellamy sat, rapidly keying on his laptop. Nick cleared his throat.
The keying stopped, and the laptop closed.

Nick glanced at each person in the room. "The president has
requested my services in Washington. I told her I was willing but had

to check with you." He looked each of his family eye to eye. "*Each* of you."

The younger members of the family turned to look at Julia.

"We agreed you should go," she said.

"I need to ask each of you. It may be dangerous and—"

"The plague," Half-Penny said. "President Allison needs your help finding out who started it."

Nick's mouth dropped open. "Who told you that? That information hasn't been released."

Half-Penny answered, "Nathan figured it out. He explained to us how the plague had to be set up by someone, that only six cities were the starting points. He figured the president would need all the help she could get. It made sense to all of us that she would want a super-smart detective at her side."

Nicole stood. "We already took a vote, Grandpa, four to zero that you should go help the president."

Nick swallowed and tried, unsuccessfully, to look stern. His smile betrayed his effort. "I thank you all. I do expect you to keep visiting Sandra. Dr. Johnson says she continues to improve and that her memory will slowly get better. Agent Bellamy will be at Dr. Johnson's beck and call and will communicate with me when needed, day or night."

Agent Bellamy nodded confirmation. "I've got your flight booked already."

16

◆

Nick sent his duffel through the scanner and dropped his watch, phone, and wallet into a plastic bowl and sent it after the duffel.

He was ticketed for the 7:00 a.m. flight, number 1729, Houston to DC. It was just shy of 6:00 a.m., so he had a good half hour till boarding. The nation's airports were beginning to recover from twenty-five years of minimal travel during the dark-glory years of World Council control. The waiting area was the first on the right side of a long corridor and was at least thirty feet deep by sixty wide. The corridor itself was dark after just four active gates. Looking around, Nick figured it would be at least another two years of economic growth before flights would approach anywhere near full booking. Right now, it was bring-your-own-lunch time as nothing was served on board and food shops in airports were close to nonexistent. Only one newspaper and souvenir shop was open.

Nick took a seat in waiting area 42 and hefted his duffel up onto the seat next to him. He chuckled to himself that the departure board had shown just seven gates out of 120 were scheduled for use for the next ten hours. He revised his estimate of full booking from two years to four. Maybe ten.

Not having a book to read and having yesterday sent messages to the president and to Julia Ramirez alerting them what flight he would be on, Nick spent his time checking out each passenger and uniform in sight. He shook his head; old police habits die hard.

One disheveled young man wearing sunglasses, denim trousers, and a shirt with bright, blotchy colors—Nick remembered the term *tie-dyed* from a hundred years ago—approached him asking for money to buy a plane ticket.

Nick gave him five dollars. "Maybe that'll help. Where you wanting to go?"

The young man shrugged. "Anyplace but here. Just gotta be on the move. Thanks, man." He pocketed the bill and drifted away.

Nick went back to observing. There was one group he didn't see: children. Thirty years ago, children would have been everywhere. Now almost nonexistent incomes coupled with years of one-child laws resulted in no children in airports.

Of the first seventeen individuals he observed, twelve were men, all seemingly alone. The five women all kept in one group. An occasional uniformed male would traverse some corner of the corridor for a few seconds, then disappear.

Nick shook his head as the back of his neck began its old red-flag itch. He noticed that one of the uniformed men appeared more frequently than the two others. *Much* more frequently. Nick began to pay particular attention to the man's frequent comings and almost-goings. He had been a cop for almost forty years and had practiced similar back-and-forth moves when he was on a patrol stakeout, the goal being to keep a subject under observation while not attracting the subject's attention. One key was to have an apparent reason for movements: getting a coffee, helping an elderly individual cross the street, replacing a light in a sign while dressed as a repairman, or a dozen other blending-into-the-background moves.

Nick nodded to himself. The uniform he had been studying had reasonable motivations for his frequent sweeps of the immediate area, but not reasonable enough for an experienced cop. The man would glance around: side to side, up and down, nodding at people, but he never glanced directly at Nick. When the disheveled, tie-dyed ticket grubber approached, the uniform waved him off without telling him not to bother the other passengers. The uniform was essentially doing nothing even halfway useful. Nick scratched his itch, strengthening his suspicion he was being watched.

He glanced up at one of the clocks in the waiting area. Seventeen after six. Enough time left to change suspicion into confirmation. He stood, grabbed his duffel, and headed for the restroom two empty gates back toward the main terminal.

He assumed a leisurely gait, giving him the opportunity to check several shiny and reflective advertising signs for any movement behind. The uniform, headed in the opposite direction, stopped, paused as if checking his pocket, then reversed course, following Nick at half Nick's speed.

Nick entered the restroom. He went into a stall, counted to ten, flushed, and fiddled with the faucet for another count of ten. He left the restroom, paused to check the nearest advertising sign, then turned right toward the main terminal.

The uniform had been standing half a waiting room behind him and was probably starting to follow. A glance at a second sign confirmed this.

Nick, feigning confusion, stopped in his tracks, shook his head, turned back around toward his seat, and started walking.

He had given his uniformed follower enough time to alter his presentation of disinterest. The man was bent down, checking an electrical outlet.

Suppressing a smile, Nick retook his seat.

The boarding announcement came at 6:22. Nick gathered his duffel and stood. He made a big production of fishing his ticket from his right pants pocket, snagging it several times, shaking his head with each snag.

The uniform was just then walking down toward the next waiting area.

Nick hoisted his duffel straps over his left shoulder and sauntered toward his gate. Then, as if on impulse, he turned and went into the newspaper shop.

*****

The man in the uniform caught his target's sudden change in direction and crossed to an unused ticket-taker podium and started to fidget with a nonexistent problem. Whichever way he turned and twisted, he kept his eyes on the dimly lit shop. He eventually glanced at his watch and headed for the newspaper shop.

After only two steps in that direction, Nick Garvey exited the shop with newspaper in hand and heavy duffel almost squashing his shoulder. The uniform watched his target move to the podium and hand his ticket over for validation and kept watching as Garvey moved through the gate, descended the steps, crossed the tarmac, and boarded flight number 1729.

He waited until 7:12 when 1729 taxied off, and then until 7:42 when the plane raced down the runway and ascended into a cloudless sky. At no time did anyone get off the flight.

He reached for his cell phone and keyed a two-digit code. Two gates away, the bum in the weird shirt and sunglasses was still hassling people for cash. When the call was answered, the uniformed man lowered his voice to a whisper. "Tell Ishmael the target is on board."

The next command caught him off guard.

"You want me to go to Friendship City?" he repeated.

"You heard me." The connection was broken.

Frowning, he shook his head, then shrugged. A command was a command. He headed to the baggage security door.

17

◆

President Allison's cabinet meeting had started at 7:15 a.m. The president and twelve others were seated around the conference table. First up was Secretary of Health and Human Services Serena Clayborn.

President Allison was hopeful that Clayborn's initial slow response, dotting all the i's before crossing any of the t's, was a thing of the past.

Serena Clayborn opened a folder and read from a report. "We have administered antidote sets to all 132,067 infected parties still alive. We were unable to save six, as they were in the process of being shifted to life support and died as the antidotes were administered. Another nine were so close to death. They responded but did not improve, remaining in a comatose state. The remaining 132,052 individuals have improved, 97.6 percent to pre-infection levels."

"Excellent," President Allison said. "And your safety analysis?"

"As claimed in the attachments to the antidote."

"Good. Keeping tabs on all relatives and coworkers?"

"Yes, Madam President. We are administering antidotes to all."

President Allison took a deep breath. "The vial of the super plague. What have you learned?"

"It is first a gene adapter, then a DNA splitter-cum-modifier. Our scientists have exposed it to seventeen different human DNA samples in separate, enclosed petri dish environments, and have found it not only splits apart selective DNA but modifies itself to infiltrate and pollute entirely different blood samples."

"Keep on it, hard. Very hard. If you need anything, you ask, you will get."

Again, Secretary Clayborn assured President Allison that her team would work full steam to find the solution.

President Allison decided that Clayborn was now on a productive fast track. She turned to Homeland Security Secretary Benjamin Laughton. "Border security, Ben?"

"Tightened up several notches from the previous impassable. Our intent is to keep crossings down to zero."

"And how have you been doing?" Actual numbers rather than intents were key.

"Nine days since last crosser, whom we immediately sent back."

The president nodded approval. She looked across first to the secretary of state, Jules Harmon, and then to Secretary of the Interior Jean Morgan. "Friendship City…are our controls…still in control?"

Secretary Harmon took the lead. "No problems have been reported. Secretary Morgan has listed several procedures in the Friendship Constitution upon which we will be increasing our focus." He nodded at Secretary Morgan.

Interior Secretary Morgan opened a small sheaf of papers. "We will abide by the constitution items agreed to by the United States and Mexico. We will, however, increase attention to the following items:

- "If any family member has been convicted of a violent crime in either Mexico or the United States, that family member will be sent back. If it is the principal who was convicted, all family will be sent back.
- "No guns to be owned or held by incoming individuals until establishing residence.
- "Residence will be established once a home has been lived in for six months.
- "All principal members employed in Mexico or the US continue to physically report back each month.
- "Patrols checking all sections of the border wall have been increased in frequency."

Interior Secretary Morgan grabbed her glass of water, took a quick sip, and continued, "We have imported enough antidote for protecting two hundred percent of the present population. We have alerted local—"

Sam Kirby hurried into the room, moving straight to President Allison's side. He placed a sheet of paper in front of her.

Her reaction took less than three seconds. She pounded the table. "Damn bastards! They will pay dearly, whoever they are."

Secretary Morgan flinched. "What happened?"

"Flight 1729 has crashed, just minutes after takeoff. No chance of survivors."

"Flight 1729?"

"Nick Garvey was on that flight."

Sam nodded. "He was family. Like a brother. A lost brother"

President Allison looked across the room at the wall clock. Sam's phrase "a lost brother" raced through her mind, and the second hand appeared to stand still.

Ancient memories rippled over her. She saw her nine-year-old self, an only child, jumping joyfully up and down when her mom, a second-grade teacher in her daughter's previous school, hugged her and said she was pregnant with twin boys. Her mom then guided her hand to her large belly, where she felt young feet moving about.

The next six weeks flickered through her mind. Six weeks of smiles as she worked with Mom to get the extra bedroom ready: bringing in and setting up two cribs with blue mattresses; figuring out how to stabilize a folding changing table; buying and placing several stuffed animals, none in the cribs; helping paint the walls a light blue; decorating those walls with large stickers of pandas, penguins, peacocks, and a couple of giraffes.

The view of the second hand still holding was overlaid with the image of her dad pulling her from class and telling her that Mom had been shot by some crazy kid and was dead. Before she could ask, Dad said both twins were lost. She knew then that she would never have brothers.

When she asked her Sunday school teacher if she went to heaven, would she meet her two brothers, her teacher said she would get the answer. But she never did.

When she saw the second hand finally click, she remembered Dad helping her recover, helping her become strong. He hugged her for using her karate club skills to protect others when she stood up to high school bullies. He hugged her when she graduated from college with a degree in engineering. He also hugged her five years later when she decided to get into local government.

He had said, "You have a strong instinct to protect the weak. You also know how things work and how to repair them. Your instincts and knowledge will keep you on your true path."

The second hand ticked again, shaking away the memories.

President Allison took a deep breath. "We need to tell Nick's family."

"It's all over the news, but I'll check in with Julia," Sam said, then turned and left.

18

◆

Julia Ramirez and Nicole had just cleaned up the breakfast dishes when the TV erupted with news of the crash of flight number 1729, emphasizing there were no survivors.

Julia turned to Nicole in time to see the young girl's fingers splay open and the dish she was holding clatter to the floor. Julia bent down and pulled Nicole to her. The whole family knew Nick was on that plane.

Nicole shook her head and pulled free. "Grandpa is alive," she said, her tone measured, sure. "Grandpa is alive!"

When Nathan and Half-Penny heard the news, they were immediately deflated.

Julia decided no one was going to school today.

"Grandpa is alive," Nicole repeated and marched out of the kitchen.

19

------◆------

Alone in the men's room, the tie-dye shirt came off first. Next, the hastily applied eye shadow was wiped from cheeks and jowl. Next, he put on the shirt he had taken from his duffel along with a couple other items.

The clock at the exit read 7:52.

He had little chance of catching the sneaky uniform, but thanks to his granddaughter passing along her lip-reading skills learned from a nun, Nick knew where the uniform was headed: Friendship City.

He checked his wallet. Not enough to rent a car but maybe a motor scooter with enough in its tank for over 350 miles.

Nick found a very old scooter at a rental price, which after haggling, he could afford.

He motored off minutes before the announcement of the crash of flight number 1729.

*****

The dilapidated scooter chugged for almost nine hours to bring Nick within sight of the reinforced glass-and-steel walls of Friendship City. After pulling the scooter about a hundred yards into a wooded area, he brushed the road dust off his jacket and headed for the city's northern entry portal, the sole entry gate this side of the US and Mexico border.

Two miles later, he arrived at the first of what he knew were three concrete gates. This first gate was built into the massive transparent glass superstructure, which resembled a giant, forty-foot mushroom that in cross section started as an almost thirty-foot-high stem. That stem, hollow after the first gate for at least thirty more feet to the last gate, billowed out in the last ten vertical feet, expanding both outward and inward to a fifty-five-foot mushroom cap. At the first gate, he was asked to show identification for comparison to records of individuals having recently exited with intent or requirement of returning. Nick always carried fake identification. He displayed it this time. When no match or alarm was encountered, a call was made to the second gate, inside, and he was ushered through after the first huge gate slowly swung open.

At this second gate, he was again asked for his identification as well as his reason for requesting entry.

"My entry has been requested by an individual inside who is supporting community services."

"Individual's name?"

"Robert McKenna. He was assigned by President Lenora Allison to help both sides work together. He may not recognize my name. If so, tell him I'm Nathan's adopted dad."

After two minutes on the phone, the guard walked Nick to the last of the three gates. "Mr. McKenna said he will be here within ten minutes. Please wait."

Nick nodded as the guard returned to his post, then looked out the gate's reinforced glass to the wall, marveling at how it stretched away in both directions. Averaging thirty-five-plus feet above the ground, from such a sharp angle, the wall appeared twice that height.

Pressing his left temple against the glass to see up to his right, Nick could just make out a couple of hawks flying over the wall and into Friendship City.

"Hey there, Wesley," came a familiar voice behind him. "Pressing against the glass won't get you inside. The guard has to press some kind of button."

Nick turned. "Mr. Robert McKenna. I wasn't sure you'd remember my name. It's one impressive glass wall you have here."

"It was erected to keep out the World Council thugs. Once they are eliminated, the wall will come down."

McKenna brought Nick back with him to the guard's station. "I'll sign the papers while you get scanned."

"Scanned?"

"Of course. One cannot just *walk* into Friendship City. Three scans are required on first entry: iris, fingerprint, and face scans."

Nick shook his head and grinned. "Why don't they take a pint of my blood?"

"You laugh," McKenna said. "The city council is considering a requirement that if you brought a young child which you claimed was your biological offspring, they'd require just a gram or two of blood from both you and the child for later validation."

Nick stepped up to the scanning station and underwent all three scans.

McKenna then motioned Nick to follow him through the last gate into the city. "For the first month, I cursed you for suggesting President Allison have me mentor the citizens of Friendship City. Well…maybe for only the first *week*. The people here are super eager to make this concept work. I gotta admit, I get a charge out of helping them. Helping everyone from the leaders on down to small kids and newbie citizens."

"I figured you would." Nick tapped McKenna's left shoulder. "When you accepted, I calculated you wouldn't be able to curse me longer than seventeen minutes."

"Why are you here? Why the Wesley name?"

"I was called to DC by President Allison. A man in a security uniform was spying on me for almost an hour at the Houston airport. I was suspicious as hell. Snuck behind a newspaper stand and gave my ticket to a guy who was apparently happy to be going anywhere on a plane. Traded some clothes with him too."

McKenna raised an eyebrow. "Houston airport, you say?"

Nick nodded. "He whispered on his cell phone to tell someone called Ishmael that I was on a plane. Then he was ordered—I guess ordered—to go to Friendship City. So here I am. I figured it all had something to do with why President Allison wanted me in Washington, and I should return the favor and check him out."

"What was your flight number?"

Nick told him. "Why do you ask?"

McKenna nodded, frowning. "I don't know if his being ordered here had anything to do with spying on you. I think whoever he was talking to just wanted you dead. Flight number 1729 crashed soon after takeoff. Crashed into a huge fireball. There were no survivors."

Nick sank down onto a nearby bench. He stared at the ground between his feet, thinking only of the man he had sent to his death.

2 0

◆

Nick had a hard time shaking off the guilt of having persuaded the tie-dyed young man to accept his plane ticket, swap clothing, and after he removed some items, take his duffel. He had sent the man to a fireball death in his place.

When they arrived at McKenna's house, Nick went straight to the kitchen table and slumped into the nearest chair.

"How about some lunch?" As McKenna opened the white fridge door covered with photographs, he added, "There may be a thing or two in here that can pass for lunch." He grabbed some cold cuts and took a loaf of bread from a cupboard. "Coffee, water, soda, beer?" He stopped again at the refrigerator.

Nick shook his head. "No, thank you."

McKenna shrugged and took a chair across from Nick. "We've got to call President Allison and let her know you're alive."

Nick was about to agree when his back-of-the-neck itch started. He raised a hand. "Not right now. Let's give the call a minute or two."

"Why? You have family that—"

"I need to figure out why the bastard who set me up to die was ordered to come here."

"Could be they didn't want you coming here." McKenna squinted for a moment. "I know you weren't told to come here, but maybe that was to be your next assignment, and—"

"And someone on the inside passed along the information."

McKenna nodded.

Nick slouched further into his chair. It was his turn to squint. "Could be. But *something* attracted them here, not me."

"Maybe they just want to stir up trouble."

Nick felt his itch kick into overdrive. "Exactly! I was an item on this Ishmael's list. For some reason, this city is also on the list. Maybe a different list, but a list, nevertheless. What makes this city more list-worthy than…say, New York City, Chicago, Denver, San Francisco, Miami, even nearby Houston? What?"

"We're a focal point in the national psyche."

"But why? Why not any other of the cities I mentioned? They all have problems. They all have vulnerabilities. They're all struggling. They're all—"

"For all those reasons, Nick. Those cities probably see this city as a beacon of light, a beacon of progress and recovery. I know I do."

"So maybe Friendship City is at the top of the 'Turn Off the Lights' list."

McKenna nodded. "Possible."

"Or maybe the correct list is the 'Turn the Light Toward Failure' list."

"Failure could well be the goal."

Nick sat upright. "Robert, what makes this city unique? Besides the walls."

"Bonds."

"Bonds?"

"Yes, bonds. The bonds of neighborhood and the bonds of family. The bonds of self-government probably factor in."

"Examples, please."

"Neighborhood and family go a long way to making sure there are zero gangs within our 146 square miles."

Nick allowed an appreciative whistle.

McKenna continued. "No controlled drugs are allowed in. Should any be found—and there have been three such discoveries since incorporation almost a year ago—the culprit *and family* are subject to being expelled to their sponsoring country. All three were allowed to remain, as their intent wasn't criminal.

"Education: all children up to the age of eighteen are required to attend school, pre-K through twelfth grade. Language classes are available for all adults to satisfy the requirement that everyone sixty years and younger be able to eventually speak the two common Friendship City languages, English and Spanish. Assimilation is important, but understanding and communication more so.

"A broad spectrum of vocational training is provided for all adults, male and female, as they are each required to contribute to the physical and economic growth of Friendship City.

"One of the bonds that include both family and neighborhood is in the city charter: all children must be cared for by family or by trusted neighbor. If children are brought into the city, their parents should be married. Divorce is allowed, but the city will then assign a family monitor to ensure that any child's physical and mental health is not jeopardized. We have no set of rules how a child should be cared for, but basic health is the neighborhood's concern."

"That's one hell of a list. A lot to consider. I'm sure old Ishmael, whoever he is, has many options from which to choose."

"Without a doubt, but he's had more time to make his plans."

Nick scratched the back of his neck.

McKenna shook his head. "Still get that neck itch whenever you can't figure something out? Shall I call and tell President Allison you're alive?"

Nick lowered his head as if studying the floor between his feet. His *yes* came out with a reluctant tinge. "Let her know all I told you. About Ishmael, about my being a target, and about Friendship City being some kind of target. I think we should suggest she tell as few people as possible."

"My thought as well," McKenna said, reaching for his cell phone.

21

---◆---

P resident Allison had just taken her seat behind the Oval Office desk when her private cell phone buzzed. Only five people had the number. All calls into and out of the White House on this phone were double-encrypted, but there was no way to keep wireless calls from being captured. Even with double-encryption, doublespeak was essential.

"Hello?"

"Sheffield? Brian here."

President Allison nodded. McKenna was calling. Long before schedule. "Your call is unexpected. Is there a product defect or missing part?"

"Definitely missing, Sheffield, ma'am. One extra part was delivered to me, not listed in the manual. I checked the forwarding, and it is definitely listed as missing. I just wanted you to know. It has some sort of mailing label with your address with delivery scheduled for today."

"Any other addresses attached?"

"Above, my old hometown, ma'am, and below, my current workplace, of course."

President Allison placed both elbows atop the desk and tapped an open palm against her forehead. One problem with doublespeak was that it took more than double the time to pull out any sense. *What did McKenna just send? Something listed as missing started in New York City. That something was supposed to come to me. But it ended up with McKenna in Friendship City. What...listed as missing... was supposed to come to me...but ended—of course! Nick Garvey. Fits exactly. He was the only missing "item" scheduled for arrival here today. How to verify?* "Was the part delivered in good shape? Any scratches?"

"Only in its neckpiece, ma'am—a scratch that probably prevented its expected shipping."

President Allison chuckled to herself. *Everyone should have such an itchy neck to save them from a flaming disaster.* "How did your address get attached?"

"Handwritten, ma'am. Maybe a spur-of-the-moment scribble by the delivery man before leaving. Since he made the change, no need to contact the shipper."

President Allison now had the complete picture. Nick didn't get on the plane because some person struck him as questionable. He then followed that person to Friendship City. His survival was not to be publicized.

"Thank you for the information, Brian."

"You are most welcome, Sheffield, ma'am."

22

◆

Before President Allison could put the cell phone down, it buzzed again.

"JC here," was the greeting. Apparently, Josh Cabrera had some information on the antidote drums.

"JC, good to hear from you. It's been a while."

"On vacation. Sunny California. I was taking a photo of the hillside where the old Hollywood sign used to be, and I almost fell into a manhole after taking a little more than three giant steps. I ripped my right pant leg, but I'm okay now. Shook off the dust."

"JC, I think your vacation needs to be cut short. Your family needs you in one piece."

"I plan on catching a train in a few days."

As she turned off the phone, she smiled. There was no double-talk better than colorful, exaggerated double-talk. Josh and his team had found a lead to where the plague drums came from. To indicate distance, one step would be one mile. A little more than three giant steps would be a bit more than thirty miles. Pulling up a map of the region, President Allison figured ripping the right pant leg indicated stepping left while facing the Hollywood sign. That would lead you in a northwest direction. She estimated that just over thirty miles would land you in the neighborhood of Castaic, near a large dam.

After deciding that Josh and his crew had the drum location narrowed down and under control, she dialed Sam's number. She knew that Sam had arrived in Houston over an hour ago and had been with Nick's family all that time. He answered his phone, also in double-talk.

President Allison conveyed the news that Nick Garvey was alive and in Friendship City.

Sam's single-word, non-double-talk response was "Super!"

He also passed along information from Half-Penny. Half-Penny had, several times, recognized two thugs from the old El Camino gang checking up on the comings and goings of house members. Also conveyed was Half-Penny's fear that the thugs might make some type of vicious move against them.

It was agreed that Sam would take the whole household to Friendship City, not informing them that Nick was alive. President Allison and Sam agreed that it would be best if Sandra could be moved from the hospital in Houston to Friendship City's Valley Regional Medical Center, which Dr. Charles Johnson had recommended.

She closed by conveying that Nick would be immediately informed of their impending arrival.

Then, wanting an update on the CDC progress of decoding the biological behavior of the new plague molecules, President Allison called for transportation and for her security detail.

2 3

———◆———

"Take us to the CDC lab," President Allison told the agent driving the limousine.

The CDC had been fully reconstituted only nine months ago. Its previous lab had fallen into disrepair after twenty-three years of closure by the World Council. Until a new facility could be constructed, the CDC's lab was the one previously built and used by the World Council in Dallas, Texas.

President Allison figured turnabout was only fair. Fair, and the only alternative.

It took her and her lab handlers forty-two minutes to suit up and test.

Her five Secret Service agents were not allowed inside the lab. Three doors controlled entry to the inside testing area. The doors and the surrounding floor-to-ceiling walls were of clear and super-strong glass. Between the first and second door was six feet of tile flooring. An identical stretch of tile floor came after the second door before one encountered door number three, which, when opened, provided access to the lab. Five monitor machines were lit and monitoring each of the two tiled areas so as to assure absolutely no contamination of the work area inside.

The suit each entrant wore was their sole protection and was to be worn full time.

President Allison saw at least twelve individuals inside, each wearing protective suits identical to hers. Those individuals were hunched over workbenches. She could see the exit door at the far end of the lab.

"Another three doors for exiting," the director told her. "You will go through decontamination at that point, which will take about ninety minutes."

President Allison said she was ready and stood in front of the first door as it opened electronically. She stepped inside and followed the detailed instructions announced by loudspeaker as to how she must connect herself to each of the first set of monitors. After twelve minutes, she successfully completed the monitoring and stood in front of the second door, which was again opened remotely. The next set of machines was slightly different. The second analysis went more quickly, and the third door was opened after nine minutes.

President Allison stepped into the lab. The pocket door slid closed.

Two lab workers turned and moved toward her.

"Welcome, Madam President," came the slightly electrified female voice.

"Thank you," she replied, assuming her voice would transmit.

The lab worker raised her fully wrapped right arm and hand, extending an upward thumb. President Allison was at first impressed that a completely clothed thumb could be so mobile, then realized that a thumb without such mobility would be useless in this laboratory.

"Follow us," the voice requested, the owner's right hand indicating the other lab worker.

President Allison followed to the near end of the first of four benches. She estimated the bench extended at least fifty feet into the brightly lit room. She counted twelve transparent glass or plastic boxes; the first she guessed to be about two feet square and two feet tall. The nearest box had two manipulator handles protruding from the sides. A worker stood in front. Five small, test-tube-like vials were evenly spaced front to back up top, with each tube's bottom section protruding slightly into the box.

She saw the same two manipulators on both sides of the next three boxes and similar test tube vials.

The first worker motioned her to move to the third box. Inside was a rectangular petri dish about ten inches by five, the ten inches running parallel with the table along the middle of the box. Liquid covered the bottom of the dish to a height of maybe a quarter inch. The liquid had a faint purple tint. To the right of that dish was a smaller glass dish. It appeared empty at first glance, but upon bending closer, she could see a thinner film of liquid in a lighter purple color. A binocular microscope was clamped atop the box.

President Allison glanced at the dishes inside the boxes on each side. Their large dishes also presented with a shallow liquid, but of a different tint. No microscope was attached to either box.

"Both dishes in each box have the same DNA from an individual that does not match any other DNA in any other box," the worker said, her voice echoing slightly in the president's helmet. "In these forty-eight boxes, we introduce one drop from the plague vial into the large dish. We do not introduce any drop of the plague into the smaller dish. It is difficult to see, but we have a thin membrane completely separating the two dishes. This membrane is continuously drip-swabbed with a chemical combination used worldwide to prevent transmission of all known bacteria and viruses. Think of it as a vaccine."

President Allison spoke before the worker could continue. "The smaller dish appears to have a similar color as the large one."

"Because we have found that our vaccine does not work in any of the forty-eight cases, no matter the DNA makeup."

President Allison's shoulders sagged inside her bulky suit. She knew what that meant. There was no protection against this plague.

A sudden memory flash almost prompted President Allison to slap her right hand against her forehead. She remembered just in time that she was wearing the second cousin to a spacesuit. The memory was Sam reporting that Nick had suggested Owen Pendleton be brought into the plague team. Nick had claimed that Owen could be the team's ace-in-the-hole biotechnology expert.

Of course. There is no protection against this plague…yet.

2 4

◆

May 1, 2058

President Allison's call the previous evening had brought Nick to an emotional crossroads. He was excited and concerned at the same time. Excited that his family would soon be close enough to hug. Definitely excited but concerned that they had been stalked.

Nick was up first, not rested from his tossing and turning all night. Robert McKenna eventually joined him, and they went out for breakfast at the Happy Holster Restaurant, a classic diner with padded seats along the front window and tables with chairs in the back around the front counter. Waitresses brought loaded trays to customers while busboys wiped down tables and loaded empty china onto similar trays to disappear behind swinging doors.

Nick repeated his concerns across the breakfast table.

Robert McKenna assured him for at least the tenth time that his family would be safe in Friendship City.

Halfway through their meal, McKenna waved at two men approaching the table. As they both took a seat, he introduced them. "Wesley Martin…" he said, using Nick's cover name. He nodded toward the Hispanic man opposite Nick. "This is Daniel Perez and…" He indicated the native-born Texan sitting next to Nick. "Warren Parker."

All nodded and shook hands.

A waitress, order pad in hand, stopped and asked if the two new men wanted anything.

Both Daniel and Warren declined.

McKenna took a quick sip of his coffee. "These two gentlemen are considered the unofficial mayors of Friendship City. Although not holding a formal position in the city council, their views and positions are widely respected."

"Widely respected does not equal one hundred percent," Daniel Perez said.

"Not even close," Warren Parker added.

McKenna shook his head. "They have their little routines. I told them you had some concerns that security here might have been breached."

Both men leaned toward Nick.

"Is there immediate danger?" Daniel asked.

"I don't believe any danger is immediate. I do have information that an individual with a most nefarious set of connections has been ordered to get inside Friendship City."

"By sneaking in?"

"Whichever way has the least chance of getting caught."

"You've seen the walls surrounding the city," said Warren. "The only way to gain entry is via one of two checkpoints. I assume you entered the checkpoint on the US side."

Nick nodded.

"The Mexican side also has a similar, single checkpoint."

McKenna finished his coffee, and the four men rose and left the Happy Holster, turning left onto Matamoros's Heroico Colegio Militar, an old auto road now a pedestrian walkway. In the near distance, they could see the Brownsville and Matamoros Expressway with its many people and just a few automobiles crossing both ways.

Daniel raised a forefinger. "We do have twenty-four-hour video at each checkpoint. The resulting files are saved for at least six months. If you have a picture, we can find a match using facial recognition in less than a couple of hours given a specific entry day."

"I have nothing to match with. Yet." Nick knew where he could find useful video. "Do you keep track of new entrants for some period?"

"Somewhat," Warren said. "Friendship City now has close to seven hundred thousand people. Thirty-five years ago, our two separate areas had reached one million five hundred thousand. World Council rules, restrictions, and outright interference brought us down to under a hundred eighty thousand."

McKenna turned to Nick. "We went from a hundred eighty thousand to seven hundred thousand in nine months. Shows the power and magic of Friendship City."

Daniel nodded. "It's the human rules and common sense obligations that have driven that growth. Once in a great while, we have some issues with sudden occurrences of young men turning into street thugs. Happened the past two days, yesterday a bit more violent, but citizens intervened, and no one had to be incarcerated. Citizens stepping up and in when police are not yet on the scene to calm things down is one of our keys to keeping Friendship City safe."

As they approached the expressway and headed to the Brownsville side, they saw two groups of about twenty people each confronting each other as they waved signs they were holding up. Neither group was directly engaging the other, just waving signs and being vocal.

"What is that?" Nick asked. "Doesn't look like citizens calming things down."

Warren shook his head. "Just Donna and Doug doing their thing. I seldom know what they are disagreeing about, but it's always something. They wave homemade signs, shout at each other, then go home. Some call it political activism. Others, performance art."

Daniel smiled in agreement. "It is interesting to watch. Many people take pictures of them. No one has ever been hurt."

Warren pointed across the street. "See that woman?" he asked, indicating an aristocratic-looking lady walking ahead of them. "She is the source of most of Friendship City's code."

"Absolutely," Daniel said. "When the people of the two towns reached a fever, clamoring for a common city, she was the key to unlocking the two governments."

Nick guessed her to be about fifty. "What's her name?"

"Elise Carpenter," Warren said.

Nick squinted. "She has the shiniest big earrings I've ever seen on a woman."

Warren chuckled. "She wears them all the time."

Nick watched the woman bend down to scoop up a soccer ball kicked toward her by two young boys. She held the ball in front of her, then dropped it, and just before it hit the roadway, kicked a straight shot back to the boys. Nick chuckled to himself. If the two boys had had a net between them, Ms. Carpenter would have been one goal up. As it was, they both had to turn and chase after the ball.

Nick turned to Warren. "Is she the official mayor of Friendship City?"

Warren and Daniel shook their heads.

"No way," Warren said. "She was more adamant than even we were. She wouldn't even allow her name to be credited as the major author of the Friendship City codes."

"I'll have to read the codes," Nick said.

McKenna gave a thumbs-up. "Everyone should read them."

"Everyone," Daniel chimed in, "believing in peace, family, opportunity, and earning your own way."

Warren nodded. "All those apply here in Friendship City. Everything we have reinforces that first one: peace. We have no gangs, no addictive drugs, a robust educational system, a growing manufacturing base—"

"And a political system," McKenna interrupted, sweeping his right forefinger in a left-to-right arc, "that keeps leaders on a short leash. Short enough that they know and follow the interests of those who elected them. The citizens in this city hold that leash and can yank them back if they wander astray. All that keeps the streets safe."

They turned right onto the expressway, heading toward Brownsville. Less than thirty steps along, Nick noticed Ms. Carpenter, still a good forty or so steps ahead, start loping toward the two soccer boys.

Nick watched as she herded them to the right behind a small wooden work shed.

As Nick wondered what she was up to, he saw six hooded men race onto the far end of the expressway less than a quarter of a mile off.

Five seconds later, another group of hooded men dashed from behind Nick himself and the others, heading toward the first group. Nick counted seven men in the second group. All struck him as under thirty years of age.

The back of Nick's neck itched furiously. He'd seen action like this but never on streets touted as safe.

Suddenly both groups stopped. Hands dug into pockets and threw rocks and small bricks. Nick and the three other men dropped flat to the roadway.

Both groups pulled out baseball bats and metal pipes. They swirled around and at each other, swinging bats and pipes in wild and deadly arcs. Thumps resounded as shoulders and chests were whacked and whacked again. Grunts and screams of pain filled the area.

Nick heard police whistles behind him. Still flat on the roadway, he watched both groups disengage and run off the far end of the expressway, all disappearing in the same direction. One of the men had a pronounced limp but was able to keep up with the combined group of hooded thugs.

Nick and the others pulled themselves up slowly, checking all around them. He glanced over at the wooden shed. Ms. Carpenter and the two boys were still crouched between the shed and the guardrail.

Still glancing all around, he moved to the shed and extended a hand down to the closest, still-cowering boy. Ms. Carpenter patted the boy on the shoulder and muttered something. The three of them stood.

As they inched out in front of the shed, Nick walked over to where McKenna, Daniel, and Warren were checking out the battle scene. Two pairs of shattered eyeglasses, quite a few blood-splattered rocks and bricks, and several abandoned bats and pipes were strewn about the roadway. Daniel and Warren stooped over, checking the scattered debris. Seconds passed. Both shook their heads.

"So much for a safe Friendship City," Warren said, echoing the thoughts of the other three.

Nick checked back at the two boys still standing just in front of the shed. Alone. He saw the back of Ms. Carpenter retracing her steps, leaving the expressway without looking back.

What had possessed her to head back to the unknown? Even the two boys recognized that safety, for the moment at least, was where they were.

Nick's itch returned to full furious. Plus.

2 5

◆

aniel and Warren scrambled about checking the scene for any pointers to the identity of even one of the combatants. McKenna already had his cell phone out and was calling police headquarters. Daniel and Warren stood, shaking their heads.

"Nothing," Daniel said.

Warren nodded agreement.

They waited the three minutes it took for the police to arrive.

Questions were asked, answers given and compared. What little forensic evidence remained, mostly blood, was captured, and the two boys were escorted home, each by two police officers.

The soccer ball was nowhere to be found.

A police van arrived. The officers placed anything that looked even remotely suspicious in bags they put into the back of the van, which drove off. The nine remaining officers thanked them and left. Nick, Daniel, Warren, and McKenna traded stunned looks.

McKenna shook his head. "We should meet with the city leaders."

Nick was about to agree when his cell rang.

It was Sam Kirby. Nick's family was waiting with him at the US portal.

2 6

◆

Nick didn't want his family to see he was alive until they were all behind closed doors. He didn't yet know what to make of the street brawl, but it was obvious to even a blind man that Friendship City could no longer boast of being safe.

Robert McKenna said he would go to the portal, get Sam and the others scanned, certified, and admitted, and bring them all back to his house. He and Nick had made ready several extra bedrooms for their use. McKenna lived alone in a large house and assured Nick that he would enjoy having some company for a while.

Warren and Daniel agreed to go with Nick to McKenna's house. On the way, they saw that news of the gang fight was spreading quickly. Men were no longer sitting on front stoops; women were scurrying about corralling young kids and babies in strollers and taking them inside houses and apartments. Those few men and women still on the streets kept glancing left and right, forward and back, even up and down as they walked quickly and purposefully.

Ten minutes later, they arrived at McKenna's house and took seats around the kitchen table. Nick realized his cover name of Wesley Martin wouldn't survive the presence of Nicole, Nathan, and Half-Penny. Julia, maybe.

Nick told Daniel and Warren his real name. "I'm bringing my family into a war zone." He raised his eyes to look at the other two. "I've seen gangs before, seen how they operate, seen the situations they avoid. This was not typical, not to any script I'm familiar with. This was a planned event. Planned by someone other than the partic-ipants. I'm not even sure they were gangs. Both gangs ran off together, all previous head-banging and rock-throwing forgotten as if they had been caught stealing hubcaps and wanted to split the booty."

Daniel and Warren hadn't said a word.

"What do you guys think?"

Warren took a deep breath, his hands shaking slightly. "It's been years… I haven't…" Another deep breath. "I'm forty-seven, and I haven't seen anything like this anytime in the past twenty years."

"Me neither," Daniel said. "When I asked you if there was any immediate danger, was this an example?"

"I have no idea. If neither of you have seen anything at all like this in Friendship City, maybe the man I followed here is part of what seems to be a new and very dangerous problem. Will the police keep them from escaping the city?"

Daniel shrugged.

Warren held up two crossed fingers.

"Until now," Daniel said, "we've been excellent in regulating who comes in, and it's been our belief, controlling who goes out. We will have to find out where these two groups of thugs came from and when."

"And how," Warren said, raising his right fist with elevated thumb.

The knock on the front door brought all conversation to a halt. Nick rose and went into the nearest bedroom so no one coming in would see him.

The door opened, and Robert McKenna announced, "We're home!"

Following that, Nick heard all the familiar voices. He stepped out into the living room. All conversation halted.

Julia Ramirez, Half-Penny's grandmother, was the first to see through his disguise. She smiled. Nathan and Half-Penny just stood, their mouths agape.

Nicole pursed her lips and nodded, almost to herself. She walked across the room and stood directly in front of Nick. After two or three seconds, she raised her right forefinger and shook it at him. "And you didn't tell us. Why, Grandpa?"

Warren and Daniel grinned and announced it was time for them to leave.

Sam stayed and helped Nick explain why they had been kept in the dark. "Your grandpa was concerned for your safety," Sam said. Seeing their confused expressions, he added, "The plane explosion was not an accident. We suspect it was an attempt to kill him."

Nick took over. "Fortunately, it didn't work. I noticed a man in uniform watching my every move. I tricked him into thinking I had boarded the plane." Nick swallowed hard as he decided not to mention how he had tricked the man. He looked down at Nicole. She was no longer shaking her raised finger. "I learned from Nicole how to read lips, and that's how I learned the guy had been ordered to Friendship City by someone called Ishmael. I changed my appearance a bit and made my way here."

Nicole wrapped her arms around Nick's waist and hugged him hard. Nathan and Half-Penny moved behind her and waited their turn. Each shook his hand. No hugging. Julia, sitting on the couch, smiled and gave a quick wave.

The conversation was interrupted by loud, rapid knocking on the front door. Sam checked through the peephole and unlocked the door.

Warren and Daniel, breathless, stepped in and closed the door behind them. Both seemed confused. Warren, still breathing heavily, gave a no-immediate-problem wave of his right hand.

Daniel stepped forward. "Police found one of the gang members who was wearing clothes like the group who came from behind us."

Nick took a deep, measured breath. "Dead?"

Warren nodded. "Shot in the forehead."

"Was his right leg damaged in any way?"

"The police said the right leg was twisted and offset as if slammed by one of the bats or pipes."

Nick and Sam looked at each other.

"Any clues to the whereabouts of the others?" Sam asked.

"No," Warren said. "They said they're looking everywhere."

Nick looked at his just-arrived family members, brought here to escape any harm.

Sam, his voice almost a whisper, turned to Nick. "What do you think we should do?"

2 7

◆

Sam and Nick retired to the bedroom and closed the door, exploring their possible avenues going forward. Sam placed the call to President Lenora Allison on his secure cell. He turned on its speaker mode.

"Sam, are you okay? I just heard there was a shootout in Friendship City. Are Nick and his family in one piece, so to speak?"

"All are fine here, Madam President. It was not a shootout. More a street brawl between two gangs. One dead gang member, shot in the head, was found later by the police."

Sam filled the president in on all that had happened in the last hour, then motioned Nick to step in.

"Sam brought everyone here in good shape, Madam President. I do believe that additional agents should be sent here to assist Sam's investigations. Maybe two or three to keep my kids safe."

"They will be on their way within the hour. Sam, how many and what skills?"

"Just investigative and normal forensic skills. Maybe just three or four. For the moment."

"Understood. Sam, I need you to make sure everything is safe down there, then return to Houston, where a plane is ready to take you and Owen Pendleton to California."

"Owen has a lead on the plague solutions?"

"He's not one hundred percent sure, but…"

"Understood. I should be there in…" Sam glanced at his watch. "Four hours."

"Also, Nick, I want to thank you for suggesting I bring Owen aboard. He has already discovered several unique chemical properties of the plague and its antidote. Those discoveries led him to several guesses as to where it was developed and who developed it."

Sam and Nick exchanged a few more thoughts with the president and hung up. They returned to the living room, and Sam went to the three youngsters and Grandma Julia, who sat at the kitchen table reading books.

Nick joined McKenna, Daniel, and Warren. "Sam said he has some US federal police coming to assist with tracking down that last killer and learning how they got here."

"Good news," McKenna said. "Daniel, Warren, and I are heading off to an emergency neighborhood meeting at the local high school. We figured you might want to attend. We'll bring your extended family with us."

Nick nodded. "Sam has another assignment and will be moving about for the next hour or two."

Julia announced she would stay behind. Nick collected Nicole, Nathan, and Half-Penny, then joined the other three men on the porch.

Sam said goodbye to Julia and pulled the front door shut behind him. Julia threw the bolt, but he checked that it was locked anyway and headed off to the entry portal.

*****

The auditorium, which had to have seats for over seven hundred, was full. Nick and the others took standing positions along the far-left aisle. Nick was even with the second row of seats. He rested his back against the wall as a six-foot-plus man in uniform took to the podium.

McKenna, immediately in front of Nick, turned to him. "Police Chief Antonio Rojas. He's responsible for our section of the city, about a fifth in territory and a quarter in population. Three-H all the way."

Nick remembered McKenna's verbal shorthand for someone hardworking, helpful, and honest.

The police chief called the audience to order. He gave a quick summary of what had happened that morning. "There will be patrols by our police. Also, US and Mexican police agents will be assisting in our investigation. I understand most of you frown upon any non-city police setting even one foot in our city, let alone helping solve crimes, but this situation is critical."

There were almost universal nods of approval.

"Again, we will have many patrols in all neighborhoods, not just ours. There are things you must, or should, do until these gang members and whoever else is a party to whatever crimes we eventually find they have committed have been identified and brought to justice."

Every soul in the auditorium was silent, hanging on every word. A few were jotting in small notebooks.

"Keep all your doors and windows locked. If they don't have locks, get them. Whatever you have to do to keep your children safe, do it! If something you see or hear strikes you as suspicious or just peculiar, communicate! To police or to neighbors. Your input could be vital." Chief Rojas crossed his arms atop the podium. "Questions?"

More than half the audience raised a hand.

Chief Rojas pointed to a blond woman in coveralls about six rows up along the center aisle. A young male officer scrambled to get his microphone to her.

"I have two adopted children in third and fifth grade. Do you have plans to have armed guards at all schools?"

"There will be one armed officer assigned to each of the twenty-seven schools in our district." The chief scanned for the next questioner, then turned back. "That assignment covers all public, private, and religious schools."

The woman nodded and took her seat.

"You asked us to communicate to you anything suspicious," said a Mexican man with a child seated on either side, his delivery slow, his face etched with concern. "Will you be communicating to us? Will you tell us what parts of the city are safe and which parts are not?"

"Most definitely."

"How will you tell us? Face-to-face or by phone text or—"

"By any way you need and we can. We will let you know everything and anything, good or bad, that we feel does not aid these thugs."

The man took his seat, and Chief Rojas pointed at a grandmotherly Mexican lady who was being pointed at by at least ten people around her.

She stood slowly, assisted by the younger man sitting by her side. "Will the portals be closed while you investigate?"

"No one will be allowed out unless they have some type of family emergency and can verify where they were this morning."

"Respectfully, Chief Rojas, that is not my concern. I have a son coming back in three days from his permitted work in the United States. Will he be allowed into Friendship City?"

"Most certainly, ma'am. Most certainly."

The gray-haired lady did not move to sit. "And are you most certain that no more gangsters or killers will be allowed in?"

Chief Rojas turned to one of the officers standing on his left. "Excellent question. I'll have Captain Theodore Martin, the chief of all portal agents staffing both the US and the Mexico ports of entry, respond." Chief Rojas moved several steps back.

A tall man in his forties with a full head of dark hair stepped to the podium. He was wearing the light-blue uniform of the portal police. "Thank you, Chief Rojas." He nodded and looked out at the gray-haired lady. "As the chief said, your son will definitely be allowed to return to Friendship City."

The lady shook her head. "How?" she insisted, almost stomping a foot.

"We have three key biometrics we use to validate each individual entering or leaving the city. They are facial recognition, fingerprint scanning, and iris scanning. If your son was sponsored, our data bank has all three files of everyone who entered through either portal. He will be scanned upon his return. There will be a match. He will be allowed into Friendship City."

The grandmother thanked Captain Martin but wagged her head as if bothered by a question that had escaped her.

A young man two rows behind her stood without being acknowledged. "The question is this: How do you keep killers and other human garbage out of Friendship City? They have never been scanned before. They—"

"When an individual enters the city for the first time, they must be sponsored, *then* their biometrics are recorded and saved. Facial contours can be changed but with great difficulty. Fingerprints have been faked in the past, but we soak the finger in a special solution before recording, preventing false readings one hundred percent. Finally, iris scanning has been absolutely foolproof. The scanner detects any fakery such as contact lenses or coloring eyedrops."

"So?" The young man stomped his foot. "How are thugs and killers kept out? What do first-time biometrics tell us about how many people a man has murdered before getting here?"

Nick almost expected an auditorium full of foot stomping to begin.

"As I said," the captain replied before taking a quick drink of water, "newcomers must be sponsored, and the sponsor or key representative must be at the portal at the time of entry. Those sponsors must be known to us, must have a spotless history. When a criminal or gang member appears, like what was encountered this morning, we will soon know who in the city was the sponsor. That sponsor will bear full responsibility for any and all criminal actions. Should any citizen voice concern at any point that an admitted individual is a danger because of prior acts, we forward our data to the appropriate outside government officials."

"Have you found out who sponsored the dead gang member? Have you sent the dead gang member's data to your outside government officials? Have you even checked your own files?" The young man swept his arms around the auditorium. "There are probably many people in here tonight who really don't belong here at all. You said we should voice our concerns if we feel someone in Friendship City is a danger. I have many such concerns. What would you do about that? Send data to outside governments? Impresses the hell out

95

of me. You guys are idiot turkeys who don't even know how to cook a turkey."

A one-note hum filled the auditorium, quickly morphing into "Ring around the rosy. A pocket full—"

The young man swept his right hand around the audience. "Spare me your nursery rhymes," he shouted and sat back down.

Nick chuckled to himself. McKenna had struck again, introducing nursery rhymes to counter schoolyard name-calling. *Act like a baby, you just might get baby songs in return.*

The gray-haired lady shook her head and looked down, put her hand on the shoulder of the man sitting next to her, and slowly lowered herself to her seat.

Chief Rojas stepped back to the podium. "We'll get to the bottom of this gang-type warfare. That I promise. Until then, remain alert. Keep your loved ones safe. Communicate with your neighbors, your schoolteachers, and, most importantly, your police."

Chief Rojas squinted at the rear of the auditorium. Nick turned and saw a young man in uniform waving both hands up and down—a clear signal to cut everything short.

Chief Rojas nodded. "Again, communication is the answer," he said, pulling several papers from the podium and stepping down to the center aisle. He headed straight to the uniformed hand-waver.

Nick watched Chief Rojas start to speak to the young man, who apparently cut his superior short, as Rojas shook his head. Then his head snapped up, and both of them dashed out of the auditorium.

Nick started for the door, determined to find out what had made Chief Rojas race off. He had gotten halfway to the door when three teens burst in, shouting and waving their arms.

"The Islamic Center is burning down!"

2 8

———◆———

T he auditorium emptied. It took Nick, and the few who could keep up with him, just under six minutes to reach Gilson Road, just past McAllen Road, where huge flames could be seen engulfing the Islamic Center.

Chief Rojas, Captain Martin, and the young policeman were all calling on cell phones while trying to cordon off the site. The heat was intense. There were six houses between the center and McAllen Road. Homeowners with homes near the flames were hurrying three houses away.

Nick and McKenna approached the captain, who was frowning at his cell phone.

"Can we help with anything?" McKenna asked.

"Maybe just keep people back." Martin pointed at the inferno. "The building is too far gone. Cleanup is all we have left."

Two out-of-breath clerics arrived behind the captain. Nick recognized them both from the meeting: Imam Omar Mohammad and Rabbi Steven Goldstein.

Two policemen were running yellow tape along Gilson Road. Chief Rojas motioned everyone to step back.

Nick watched as the imam lowered his head. Rabbi Goldstein placed an arm on the shoulder of the stricken Islamic leader. "Together we will rebuild it."

Nick was just close enough to hear the rabbi's words and to catch the imam's shudder as he put his left arm around the rabbi's waist.

Four fire inspectors caught his attention. One followed close behind a black lab whose mission was to sniff all around for traces of any of a couple dozen flammable concoctions used to start fires. In Nick's experience, this small team would soon get to the source. Accidental or intentional.

Over the imam's shoulder, he saw Elise Carpenter standing three houses down across the street. She was by herself. Others were either clustered around the yellow tape or a full block away.

Captain Martin glanced in Elise's direction, then furrowed his brow and typed into his cell phone.

Elise suddenly turned and walked away.

Maybe Nick wasn't the only one who wondered about the woman with shiny earrings and unexplained actions.

*****

As the Islamic Center smoldered, Daniel and Warren headed off to their own homes. McKenna and Nick herded the three youngsters back to the apartment.

At Nick's knock on the door, Julia Ramirez checked through the curtains and pulled back the bolt. "Finally," she said. "I'll need a half hour to get dinner ready."

Nick motioned McKenna to follow him into another room. "Tell me more about Elise Carpenter."

"What do you want to know?"

"Warren said she wrote or was the source of most of Friendship City's codes. He also said she refused to allow her name to be attached to the codes in any way."

McKenna nodded.

"Why? What is so special or unique about these codes that she renounces any authorship? Are they harmful?"

"Definitely not. The codes are central to the operation of Friendship City, to the government of Friendship City. Without the BORO, there would be no successful Friendship City."

"BORO? What's that?"

"It's like our Bill of Rights, but with an important add-on."

"Like the letter O?"

"Exactly. BORO: Bill of Rights and Obligations."

"Obligations?"

"Yes. I've been told she insisted that rights are never free, most must be earned."

"Okay."

"She apparently insisted that many of Friendship City's rights require certain obligations from its citizens and its politicians." McKenna smiled as if just remembering something. "Especially the politicians."

"How do I get a copy?"

McKenna went to a breakfront, opened a drawer, pulled out a slim volume with a blue jacket, and handed it to Nick. "I have many more."

"Thanks. I'll give it a read."

"Don't wait too long." McKenna chuckled, then tapped his watch. "I just scheduled a quiz for tomorrow. Same time."

2 9

———◆———

Nick had just finished his lunch BLT when McKenna's cell phone buzzed.

McKenna hung up after only ten seconds. He told Nick that the lead agent sent by President Allison the day before had asked for McKenna to meet with him because the local officials were reluctant to share information with outsiders without his presence.

Nick nodded and said that he and Julia would keep everything and everyone on the straight and narrow.

McKenna nodded. "Don't think this postpones your BORO quiz."

Nick and Julia cleaned up the lunch scraps and dishes, checking frequently on the three youngsters playing outside. Half-Penny had assured them both that he would keep Nicole and Nathan in the front yard. He was true to his word; although a couple of times, Nathan chatted with neighborhood boys strolling by.

*****

Robert McKenna returned an hour later with Warren and Daniel in tow. The four of them retired to McKenna's bedroom and closed the door.

"We got tons of Friendship City data that gives us nothing," McKenna said.

"Nothing?" Nick repeated.

"There was no record of the dead gang member. No facial records. No fingerprints. No iris scans. Nothing."

Daniel shook his head. "There's no way to trace how he and the others came in nor who sponsored them."

Warren slapped the arm of his chair. "It's got *insider* written all over it. *Key insider*."

Nick turned to McKenna. "President Allison has to—"

"Already done," McKenna said. "The chief agent said they don't do iris scanning outside the city, so we gave them several pictures of the dead thug's face from several angles, along with prints of all fingers."

"Let me see the photos," Nick said.

"I figured you would want a copy." McKenna handed Nick a large envelope.

"Damn right! Maybe there's a match to my airport uniformed SOB."

Nick spent more than ten minutes scanning and rescanning each set of facial photographs. There were several of the dead man: some with eyes closed and others with the eyes taped open.

"No match," Nick said.

"The agent told me the face photographs would be run through any and all databases. At least we might get lucky and learn his identity."

Nick looked up at McKenna. "But not how he and the others got inside Friendship City."

"No, probably not."

"Has Captain Theodore Martin been made aware?"

"He was there when the president's lead agent conveyed all the information. He looked stunned. Said he would find the answer no matter what and no matter who. I could see his fist repeatedly clenching and unclenching."

Nick wished the back of his neck would start itching again. Even just a little bit. The itch was a signal that there was something to be suspicious about, some sort of clue. No itch, no clue. He packed the papers back into the envelope and handed it to McKenna. *To be a detective*, he thought, *one must have something, anything, to detect.*

101

3 0

◆

Nick brought the whole family to see Sandra at the Valley Regional Medical Center during the hospital's 3:00 p.m. to 6:00 p.m. visiting hours. They got there at exactly 3:00. It was the first time any of them had visited her since Houston.

He was surprised to encounter Dr. Charles Johnson checking a chart at the nurses' desk on Sandra's floor. The chart was Sandra's. Dr. Johnson smiled at the expression on Nick's face.

"I decided to take a little break from Houston and see what Friendship City's all about." He offered a slight shrug. "President Allison also thought it might be a good idea for me to stay with Sandra for a while longer, since I'm so familiar with her case. I agreed that it was a good idea. And Houston's just a short helicopter ride away if an emergency comes up there that I have to deal with."

"Well..." Nick didn't know quite what to say. "Thank you. How's she doing?"

"She's doing much better in the short-term-memory department," Dr. Johnson said. "Still only a bit better in the long-term department."

"Can we all see her at once, or one or two at a time?"

"All at once will work. No problem. Okay if I come in with you?"

Nick nodded and gave a flourished after-you wave of his hand. He was pleasantly surprised to see Sandra sitting in the chair beside her bed.

Nicole ran straight to her mother, reached up, and gave her a big hug. "I love you, Mom."

Sandra, smiling, wrapped her arms around Nicole.

Nathan and Half-Penny stationed themselves two steps behind Nicole.

Nick, standing at the foot of the bed, turned to the right, where Julia stood beside him. "I haven't seen her smile like that in years."

"She's making excellent physical improvement," Dr. Johnson said, moving to Nick's left.

"You said her long-term memory is improving slowly?"

"Yes. Slowly. She does now remember her own name. What initially surprised me was that she remembered her daughter's name long before her own. I guess the old cliché applies: slow but sure. What is good in her case is once she remembers something, it is retained and not lost."

Nick was glad for Sandra but concerned for his relationship with her.

Sandra released Nicole. She looked up at Nathan and smiled.

Nicole ran to Nick, grabbed his hand, and pulled him right up to Sandra. "Grandpa has been worried about you."

Nick watched as Sandra's gaze moved from her daughter to him. He was disappointed there was no sign of recognition. Disappointed, but relieved.

Nicole moved back closer to Sandra and gently placed both hands atop her mother's knees. "Uncle Robert took the three of us to school today to meet with the principal."

Nick chuckled to himself. "Uncle Robert" was Nicole's name for Robert McKenna, a man Sandra had never met.

"The principal, a nice lady with almost-white hair, had a different teacher ask each of us some questions. After the questions, they all talked with the principal for a while. Then she said we could start classes tomorrow, Friday."

Nick could see Nicole's excitement bubbling from her every pore. He smiled as Sandra wrapped her arms around Nicole again.

31

---◆---

Ishmael walked up the plank to *Runner*, which had docked earlier that morning at the abandoned and decrepit mooring posts on the west side of Brazos Island State Park, a US peninsula about five miles above where the Rio Grande emptied into the Gulf of Mexico. The park had been deserted and overgrown for the past twenty years.

Baumberger and Meddleson were waiting for him in the yacht's conference room.

"Heard we're off to a good start," Baumberger said, offering a "well done" nod.

Meddleson remained quiet and stoic.

Ishmael took the seat at the head of the table. "Definitely. As we speak, there are neighborhood meetings being held throughout Friendship City."

"Anything planned?"

"Nothing physical. Now is the time for sowing division."

Meddleson shook his head. "What headline does one get from division?"

"Division leads to discontent, which leads to discord, which leads to disruption, finally ending in disaster," Ishmael said. "Division will ultimately lead to warring factions."

Baumberger pursed his lips. "Which will quickly lead to the failure of the Friendship City concept. Also, we won't have to use up our human resources to accomplish the mission."

"Exactly."

Meddleson appeared unconvinced. "About using up human resources…one of our men was killed. By our own people. And the remaining dozen are now in hiding. That strikes me as a huge waste."

Ishmael assumed from Baumberger's sudden lurch to his seat back that he had tried to secretly kick Meddleson in the leg. Meddleson's startled frown confirmed his assumption.

Ishmael leaned toward Meddleson. "A waste, no. A loss, yes. But not huge. One is dead. Twelve are alive, and with help from key people implanted long ago, they'll be stirring the division pot once again."

Meddleson still didn't look convinced.

Ishmael's cell phone buzzed. It was a brief text: *Following Sam Kirby driving Owen Pendleton.*

He typed: *Terminate.* Then, after a slight pause, typed *Both,* followed by send. Then he stood and left without another word.

32

---◆---

"Come aboard?" came the call from outside.

Meddleson was startled by the request. Baumberger and Ishmael had been gone for less than an hour, and Meddleson at first thought one of them had returned. But neither was prone to ask for permission to board the yacht.

His heartrate kicked up a bit when he stepped out onto the deck and saw Bart Donovan waiting at the plank walkway.

"Welcome aboard. Again," he quickly regretted adding.

"Sorry for showing up unexpectedly," Donovan said as he walked inside and took a seat at the captain's table, not waiting for an invitation.

Meddleson followed and sat in his chair. "I didn't know you were even in the area. It's only been four days since we last talked. Do you come here on a regular basis?"

Donovan's smile suggested his appearance was premeditated. "Additional information," was the short reply.

Meddleson tried not to look confused. "And this additional information couldn't be communicated over—" He stopped at Donovan's raised hand.

"The other five who loaned you money were not happy about your ambiguous payback time line."

Meddleson hoped he suppressed his sudden shiver.

"Three of the five were intent on your immediate payment. I offered to buy them out. All three accepted."

"And the other two?"

"Slightly more patient. Emphasis on *slightly*."

"Which means?"

"They both suggested they would be contacting a collections agency." Donovan put finger quotes around "collections agency."

Meddleson swallowed hard and sagged back in his chair. He was well aware of the medieval methods of payment extraction employed throughout the collections community. He was too young to lose a limb, let alone his life.

Donovan stood, moved to Meddleson's side of the desk, and patted him on his right shoulder. "I'm confident I can hold them off for the six to ten days you mentioned earlier." He nodded, gave another shoulder pat, and left.

33

W hen they returned to McKenna's house, Julia rustled all
the youngsters into the kitchen to help prepare dinner.
Nick grabbed the small book McKenna had given
him the day before. He sank into an easy chair and looked down at
the blue jacket with the gold lettering reading, *Friendship City Bill of
Rights and Obligations*. He opened the cover of the book, which he
estimated held fifteen to twenty pages. Skipping the preamble, he
went right to the starting page. He studied the first ten pages, then
browsed through the remaining seven.

Nick closed the book and was about to put it in his bedroom
when he decided to first ask Julia if she needed any help with dinner
preparations or with the kids.

"Thanks, but no thanks," she said, shaking her head and hand-
ing a plastic spoon to Nicole.

Nick started for the bedroom when he heard the front-door
lock click. McKenna, Daniel, and Warren came through the door.
Each gave him a wave.

"Ready for your BORO quiz?" asked McKenna.

Nick shook his head. "I have more questions than answers."

McKenna motioned Daniel and Warren to take a chair. "And
your first question is…?"

"I like the several BOROs on education," Nick said as he
opened the book. "Requiring those thirty and under without a high
school education to pursue one at the city's expense and with classes
tailored to fit their free time is a good thing. A super right on the
list is allowing parents to request and be granted the right to move

a child to another school should they feel the current education has shortcomings."

Daniel gave a thumbs-up. "I've got two grandchildren in elementary grades. Our grandson wasn't displaying the progress in reading his parents expected. They did request a transfer to another school they researched. The transfer was approved. The new school was almost on the other side of Friendship City, but the city paid for the transportation. He got back on track."

Nick returned the thumbs-up. "What grade is he in?"

"Third."

Nick nodded. "Those initial grades are very important. A miss there could be a miss for life. A miss for the individual student, for his or her family, for the community. A good education delivers good problem solvers."

McKenna leaned forward in his chair. "What do you think about how schooling is paid for?"

"Free to the family through high school gets my vote."

"And college?"

"That particular section asserts it to be the responsibility of the family."

"Does that get your vote as well?"

Nick tapped the book's closed cover. "Except the part where it states that Friendship City will not provide backup to any loans the family might incur."

Warren raised a hand. "The family is not being abandoned. We just want the colleges, of which we have three, to understand that no government is underwriting student loans, that the family has the primary financial responsibility. We know from experience that colleges will most likely raise tuitions if they see the government is guaranteeing the loans."

McKenna nodded. "The city will not stand aside if any family starts to flounder paying back college loans. The city will step up, stand with the family, and open whatever doors are needed."

Nick tilted his head and shrugged. "The sections on immigration seem reasonable. No disagreements there." He scrunched his lower lip.

"But?" McKenna said.

"But the section relating to elected officials and bureaucrats strikes me as not so much a Bill of Rights. To me, it comes across more as a Bill of Restrictions."

The other three chuckled.

"He's definitely perceptive," Warren said.

McKenna and Daniel nodded in agreement.

"The restrictions are intentional, Nick. Each and every elected official is elected to serve the people, not to serve themselves at the *expense* of the people."

Nick chuckled back. "They all get my vote," he said, opening the book and thumbing to a specific page. He moved his finger down to a passage. "However, I don't think any elected official would support any of these restrictions: a city-provided salary no greater than twice the salary of the average citizen; no elected official may serve more than three terms in any one position; the maximum number of terms across several positions to which any one individual can be elected is limited to five terms; no elected official can reside inside a gated community, as such is isolation from citizens in general and impairs the official's perspective; an individual who retains a home inside said gated community can be elected to office if that individual commits to live outside said gated community."

McKenna smiled. "The city will cover the cost of the secondary housing. Any other rights or restrictions of interest?"

"I do like that if a sponsored proposal becomes law and causes growth to decline by two percentage points for over a year, a new policy is requested. Should financial growth decline ten percent or more over a period of one year, all sponsoring officials of record will have their city-provided salary reduced by twice the decline. Should that ten percent decline persist for two years, all sponsoring officials will be ineligible for reelection."

"Elise Carpenter insisted that be included," Daniel said.

Warren smiled. "With the requirement that the next election, for which they are ineligible, must take place within two months."

"A special election," Nick said. "You make a bad call, you get called out. In two months." He flipped the book shut and returned McKenna's smile. "They all get my vote."

Julia emerged from the kitchen followed by the three youngsters. She suggested the four men take a seat at the table. "If you are all through trading wild stories," she added.

3 4

◆

May 3, 2058

Nick's cell phone woke him just after three in the morning.
It was President Allison. "I'm trying to reach Wesley Martin."

Nick gave himself a slow nod. Cover names meant doublespeak conversation.

"Wesley speaking. Is this Loretta?"

"No. This is Brenda from your pharmacy. I called to let you know your emergency prescription has been lost but is in one piece. Its container, however, has been destroyed."

For a moment, Nick was confused, as lost as his "prescription." Then he pieced together that a prescription was important medicine, and that Owen Pendleton was an important medical individual. He concluded that Owen was not where he planned to be but had somehow revealed to "Brenda" that he was "in one piece."

"Should I order a refill?" Nick asked, not wanting too much silence to take hold.

"Refills are not available. That one had the solution."

It took another moment for Nick to realize the "container" had to refer to Sam, who was supposedly driving Owen, the "prescription," in his vehicle.

Nick's eyes widened and a shiver raced up his spine. "Destroyed" had to mean that Sam was dead. "If refills are not available, how do I retrieve my prescription?"

"Don't throw stones at where you live because someone will clue you in."

It took Nick a second or two to decode that not throwing stones at where he lived referenced the glass wall around Friendship City and that he was to go outside. "Thank you, Brenda. I'll take your advice in a few minutes."

He hung up, grabbed a pair of jeans, a shirt, socks, and shoes, dressed, and went into McKenna's room.

After waking McKenna and telling him about the president's request, Nick asked, "Will the kids be safe?"

McKenna, stone-cold alert at the news of Sam's murder, said, "Whatever happens here, I'll have Daniel and Warren by my side. Forgot to tell you they are both excellent marksmen and trained hand-to-hand experts."

Nick paused.

"Go!" McKenna said, climbing out of bed. "Do you have transportation arranged once outside the portal?"

"Apparently."

"Apparently?"

"President Allison spoke in double-talk and incomplete phrases. I think I got more than just the gist."

3 5

◆

As he emerged from the portal, Nick couldn't be sure whether the husky, unshaven man who motioned to him from a dilapidated pickup truck was a Secret Service agent. If he couldn't tell, neither could anyone paying casual attention. Nodding, he walked to the passenger's side of the mud-crusted gray vehicle and climbed inside.

The next transportation vehicle, at a makeshift runway, was not as splattered with mud, but it did have one cracked rear window on the pilot's side. Nick had read about the ancient commercial airplanes named DC-3s and figured this one might qualify as a DC-*point*-3.

Seven hours later, he disembarked in a weed-filled roadway obviously unused for a decade or two. Another pickup, not quite as crusty, brought him somewhere inside the city limits of Los Angeles. He watched the pickup drive away. He stood still for about a minute, checking for the arrival of his next mode of transportation.

Nothing.

Behind him, he spotted a dark-green motor scooter half-hidden in a large shrub. He approached. On the scooter's handlebar was what he recognized as an ancient device used to receive travel directions. Nick decided he now would be traveling alone, pulled the scooter free of its leafy home, and hopped aboard. He decided the scooter was the least crumpled, least crunched, and least battered vehicle he'd ridden so far.

He turned on the motor, checked the navigation device, and charged off—if fifteen miles per hour could be called charging off—in the direction given. His scooter might have been the cleanest vehicle he had been provided all day, but it was without a doubt the slowest. A little over two hours yielded a gain of a little under thirty miles.

Guessing he was somewhere in north Los Angeles, Nick pulled to a stop when his direction-giver noted he had arrived. Off to his right, he spotted an empty bicycle-scooter parking rack. He wheeled up his speedy steed and placed it in the dead center.

Although he could see no one in view, Nick wasn't about to linger. If someone was viewing this location from anywhere, near or far, he had to appear not the least bit suspicious. Suspicious would be loitering as if waiting for someone. Of course, that was the president's last instruction, if he hadn't misunderstood her.

Within less than a minute, a stocky man with orange hair ambled free of the tangling brush to Nick's left. Hair the color of his own granddaughter's did little to disguise the wearer.

"Hello, Owen," Nick said.

"Detective Garvey."

Owen motioned for Nick to follow him back through the brush. After some bushwhacking, they eventually arrived at a clearing, if a ten-foot overgrown grass circle with a pile of discarded lumber qualified as a clearing.

Owen circled around the right side of the lumber pile. "It's in here."

"What's in there?"

"My sanctuary."

Nick frog-walked after Owen into a small cave opening. He was able to stand upright once inside. Only light from outside illuminated the interior.

Nick looked around. "Your TV reception must suck."

"Without a doubt," Owen said, taking off his wig.

"Are you okay?"

"Yes."

"Is there a place to sit?"

"The floor."

Nick squatted. "What happened to Sam?"

Owen grimaced. "He had just picked me up in an old Jeep. I told him where we should go, and he headed out. We had traveled less than five miles when he suddenly stretched his arm across and pressed me back in my seat. 'Hold on,' he said and tromped the accelerator. After a minute or so, we encountered a sharp turn to the right. Sam slammed on the brakes, handed me his phone, and yelled for me to get out and run into the woods as fast and as far as I could.

"As soon as my feet hit the ground and I started running, Sam screeched away. Two cars spun around the curve and roared after him. I heard honking and gunshots. I crept through the underbrush in that direction in time to see six men pull Sam out of the Jeep and throw him on the road. I think he was still alive. They kicked him then shot him at least ten times. I remained still until they left."

"Where the hell did you get the wig?"

"Sam gave it to me when he picked me up. Said it might come in handy. I've worn it since he was killed."

Nick put an arm around Owen's shoulder. "You won't have to wear it any longer. As soon as I get some much-needed sack time, I'm taking you back to the president."

Owen shook his head. "Not yet. I have to follow up on the lead. We have to head north."

Nick knew better than to argue. The mission's down payment had been gruesome, and abandoning it could have meant millions more gruesome payments.

Nick grabbed some leafy branches and arranged them into a cave mattress.

3 6

◆

After almost twenty hours, Ishmael was ready to leave *Runner*. He had worked out most of the next several Friendship City disruptions with Baumberger and Meddleson. He appreciated Baumberger's assistance, as the doctor understood the plague's lead-up scenario. Meddleson was totally another deal. Impatient to get the plague introduced, he dragged his feet at every turn, challenging the value of an enlarged plan. He wasn't quite a pain in the ass. Yet.

Ishmael checked his watch. *Time to verify the terminations,* he told himself. He thumbed the number.

Seven rings elapsed before his man answered.

"Are the terminations complete?"

"Agent Sam Kirby is dead. We're checking for Owen Pendleton."

"Our man in Washington said Owen was to be picked up at a predetermined location. Was he?"

"He was, sir."

"And…?"

"And he wasn't in the Jeep when we stopped it and took out Agent Kirby."

"Find him and terminate him."

"Yes, sir."

Ishmael ended the call, gritted his teeth, and went ashore.

3 7

◆

May 4, 2058

Nick felt Owen squeeze his right shoulder. He slowed the scooter from its indicated seven miles per hour to a just-below-risky four.

"Damn," Owen muttered. "Nobody here."

The house on the right was not only dilapidated but shuttered with plywood top to bottom. Nick kept moving. There remained two empty, overgrown lots, another boarded-up house, two more abandoned lots, and one last house.

He couldn't make out its condition. "We're not stopping?" he asked.

"Not safe to be seen stopping at an abandoned house. Especially if it belonged to Dr. William Burner, who developed the plagues."

Owen had filled him in the night before about having a science class in college where visiting professor Burner had covered for a sick professor for a full week. "He so impressed me that I followed his career from then on," Owen had said.

The last house, still three lots away, looked lived-in. Nick slowed the scooter to two miles per hour. When he saw an elderly man pruning a bush along the far side of the house, he brought the scooter to a stop.

The man turned, checking out the two riders. "Can I help you?"

Nick's request for water was greeted with a positive gesture as the man went into the house.

"Don't see very many people along this road," the man said as he brought out two glasses and a thermos. "Not for the past twenty years." He handed them each a glass and filled them from the thermos. He waved to Nick to bring the scooter well into the driveway.

"You've lived here that long?" Nick asked.

"Longer. Much longer."

"Did you know my old professor, Dr. William Burner?" Owen asked.

Nick sensed his passenger couldn't contain himself.

The man's head snapped upright. He stared at Owen. "Name's Henry," he said. "Come inside. Park your cycle in the back."

Owen and Henry followed Nick as he pushed the scooter into the backyard, kick-standing it upright just behind the attached garage. Henry nodded okay.

Henry sat them at his kitchen table while he refilled the thermos. "Henry Fitzwalter." He put the thermos down. "Would your first name by any chance be Owen?"

It was Nick's and Owen's turn to snap their heads upright.

Nick anticipated his neck itch. "How do you know his name?"

Owen turned to Nick. "I wrote to Dr. Burner over the years. Probably twenty to thirty times."

"Thirty-seven, to be exact," Henry said. He offered a sad smile. "William and I were good friends."

"I wrote him a lot." Owen chuckled. "He wrote me back probably seven or eight times, then stopped completely."

Nick looked across at Henry.

"He never told me how many times he wrote back or if he wrote back," Henry said. Then he drew a breath and added, "He stopped writing because he was killed."

Owen's eyes widened. "When?"

"Late July 2035."

Nick's neck started itching even before he made the connection. William Burner had been killed about a month after the June 2035 plague that hit China, attacking the young men and women of working age and bringing China's industries to their economic knees. Those dates were burned into his memory ever since he read the allegation made by Seth Morris, Owen's nephew—an allegation that cost Seth his life. Now another individual, although tangential to Owen and Seth, had nevertheless been killed a month after the incident, investigated three years later by Seth, which led to his murder.

Nick's itch was in full possession. Owen was close to being on the right track. The question was how close.

"How was he killed?" Nick asked. "And where?"

Henry squinted. "It's been over twenty years, but as I remember the police report..." He squinted again. "The report stated that police discovered William's body in central Los Angeles behind the wheel of his 1969 Dodge Dart. He'd been shot in the forehead." Henry looked straight at Nick. "He loved that car. Even though at the time it was sixty..." Henry paused and quickly counted off on his fingers, "Sixty-six years old, he kept it in great running order and drove it around all the time. Claimed no 340 four-speed ever ran or sounded better."

"Did they ever catch who shot him?" asked Owen.

"No. The police figured it was a random robbery. His wallet was missing. They didn't pursue the case after a week or so. That was the time of growing trouble and growing lack of trust in the police, those still remaining on the force."

Nick tapped a finger on the table. "Owen tells me that Dr. Burner was developing some sort of vaccine."

"So I understood. Bill didn't talk much about his work. We talked mostly about woodworking. We were both into building furniture. He was also into carving wood figurines and tried teaching me the art, but..." Henry held up a shaky right hand and shrugged his shoulders. "He gave me a carving of an eagle the last time he was over." Henry motioned toward his fireplace mantel. "Three days before he was killed. Seemed like it was important to him that I have it."

Nick glanced at the eagle. It was a nice piece of art, he had to admit. But he had more serious things on his mind. He felt positive that Owen's hunch was dead right. William Burner had created the plagues. "Do you know where he worked? Where he did his vaccine research?"

"No, he never told me. Just got in his Dodge Dart and drove off each and every morning. And back each and every evening. Sometimes even on weekends."

Nick felt the lead withering away. "Was there a burial ceremony?"

Henry shook his head. "The police released his body straight to the crematorium."

"Any coworkers or family stop by his house after he was killed?"

Again came the head shake. "Within a week, both his kids left the house. His daughter, the day after the killing. His son, one week later."

Relatives. Things were looking up. "Did they ever visit you?"

"The daughter, Felicia, only once. His son, the younger of the two, maybe three or four times. Never saw either one again."

Nick felt the trail blurring again. "What was the son's name?"

"Jerry."

Nick turned to Owen and shrugged. "Do you have any questions?"

Owen shook his head.

Nick started to stand but paused when Henry raised a forefinger. "Jerry… Jerry was short for Jeremiah."

Nick sank back in his seat. The name Jeremiah rang up the memory of one murderous SOB from almost a year ago, the right-hand man to Jason Beck, supreme leader from hell.

Nick saw similar recognition flash across Owen's face.

Henry went to a drawer in his breakfront, pulled out a picture frame, and brought it back. "Doc William Burner and myself. William's son, young Jeremiah, is on the left."

Just one glance told Nick "young Jeremiah" was their Jeremiah. "Did Jeremiah help his dad develop the vaccination? Did he understand chemistry and medicine?"

Henry shook his head. "Nah. Jeremiah wasn't into the sciences. He did read a lot of books, but none of them schoolbook types."

Nick nodded in Owen's direction. It was the best lead they had. Maybe they could track Jeremiah's history down. Jeremiah had drowned ten months ago. Nick figured tracing a dead man's history was now the best path they could follow.

Nick started to stand for the second time. "Thank you, Henry. I really—"

"*Moby Dick!*" Henry said. "Apparently that was Jeremiah's favorite book. Saw him reading it one of the times he came over with his dad. He kept repeating, 'Call me Ishmael, call me Ishmael.'"

Nick plopped back down. *Ishmael.* Time to tell Owen about Ishmael. The trail was red hot.

But were they any closer to preventing the killer plague?

3 8

———◆———

Peter Meddleson was vouched for at the US portal to Friendship City at 3:37 p.m., local time, by a lieutenant in Friendship City's police force. Lieutenant Lutz was also a World Council agent.

"I was not alerted you were coming," Lutz said.

Meddleson decided to play it as a concerned team player. "Unplanned. I understand two containers of liquid were received yesterday from my engineers. I just wanted to be confident that the transfer was successful. Do you have the tubs under complete control and security?"

"Completely."

"Have you received any time frame of activation?"

"I have not."

Meddleson sensed he was approaching the asking-too-many-questions red line. "Fine," he said and mentioned he had some friends in the city he wanted to meet for a coffee or two for a couple of hours. He needed less than a half hour to determine the location of the building where the two containers were stashed. He had attached a tiny location transmitter to the bottom of each one that would emit five seconds of electronic pulses every five minutes. His own little secret. Within an hour, he figured he could calculate out distance and direction. Given those two pieces of information and another hour, he would know the container locations. He checked his wristwatch. *Another three minutes before the next burst.*

He only needed to know the location. Then he would be only hours away from forcing Mr. Ishmael to repay enough World

Council dollars to keep at bay whatever "collections agency" would soon come for him.

"Take your time, Mr. Meddleson. Call my cell when you're ready to leave."

"Thank you, Lieutenant."

Meddleson turned to go, then felt the lieutenant's hand on his shoulder. He saw Lutz retrieve something from his pocket, then hold out his closed fist. Meddleson reached under. The lieutenant opened his fist. Meddleson watched as the two tiny transmitters dropped into his open right hand.

"Have a good couple of coffees with your friends, Mr. Meddleson. Make sure you take these transmitters with you when you leave."

Meddleson gritted his teeth, figuring that now Ishmael might call up his own "collections agency."

3 9

———◆———

Nick told Owen and Henry all he knew about Ishmael. Since he knew very little, it took less than ninety seconds.
Jeremiah was another story.

"Jeremiah was Jason Beck's right-hand, executive-level thug."

"Jason Beck..." Henry squinted. "Wasn't he..."

Owen jumped into the conversation. "Jason Beck was supreme leader of the World Council. Better known as Slime Dictator intent upon enslaving the world."

Owen was one of the few people Nick knew who exaggerated in the wildest extreme and could still be recognized as telling the truth.

Nick continued to fill Henry in about Jason Beck and how Jeremiah had carried out many bloody assignments at Beck's request. "A key man in our group had a car-to-car shootout, which ended with Jeremiah driving into the Hudson River in Manhattan and drowning. Or so we thought."

Henry wrinkled his brow. "Jeremiah was an outstanding swimmer. Even..." Another wrinkle. "Even underwater."

Nick and Owen looked at each other. Owen was the first to nod. Nick shook his head. Reynolds's report stated he had watched the river site for sixteen minutes, pistol drawn, waiting for any sign of life. Nick trusted Reynolds's version of events.

Nick thought about how the exact site where Jeremiah's car went into the Hudson had to be checked out. Reynolds himself had used a large feeder pipe to pull someone out of the river. There weren't many such pipes, but just maybe, if his old partner, Tim, wasn't still recovering at home, he'd ask him to check out the location. There was no other possibility: Jeremiah was Ishmael, who could survive underwater.

Patting his back pocket, he remembered he had left his cell phone hanging from the scooter handlebar. He excused himself and headed out the back door. He unclipped his phone. Slipping it into his shirt pocket, he spotted three men frantically digging in a backyard way off on his right. His neck itch immediately told him it was the backyard of Dr. William Burner. He decided being inside was better than being seen.

Nick was about to walk back into Henry's house when he saw one of the men point in his direction. The other two dropped their shovels and ran into the back of the Burner house.

Nick decided being anywhere would be better than here.

Hustling into the house, he alerted Henry and Owen to get ready to leave. He tried not to panic as he wondered how they could escape. One scooter wouldn't do the trick.

"What's up?" asked Owen, getting to his feet.

"At least three men were digging up William Burner's backyard. They spotted me and, I think, ran into the house. Does anyone live in the house between this one and Burner's?"

Henry shook his head.

"Then there's a good chance they're heading here." Nick moved to one of the front windows. He saw two black sedans pulling to a stop in front. Two men with guns piled out of the first car. Three more from the second.

4 0

◆

"Do you have any guns?" Nick asked, his own pistol already in his right hand.

Both Owen and Henry stood and started toward the window.

Nick raised his hands. "Keep back. Five men. All armed."

"No guns," Henry said, his expression forlorn.

Nick knew his one firearm could hold off two or three, but not five. "We gotta get out of here." He pointed toward the rear of the house. "You got anything in that garage of yours?"

"One 1969 Dart Swinger. William left it to me in his will. The cops dropped it off. Still runs. Of that I make sure. Take it out for a spin at least once a week."

Nick started to herd Henry and Owen toward the garage, then stopped, turned, moved to the fireplace, and grabbed the wood-carved eagle from the mantel. Henry had said that Burner gave it to him just three days before he'd been murdered. Nick wasn't sure why that seemed important to him, but that itch on the back of his neck told him it might be.

Henry had already unlocked the door to the garage. The green Dart with a white stripe across its rear deck faced outward.

"Get in and start the engine and wait for me," Nick said. "I have to make sure they're all in the front."

Henry nodded and waved the garage door opener as he climbed in behind the steering wheel. Owen climbed into the passenger seat.

Nick dashed back into the kitchen, grabbed the three glasses from the table, stuffed each with a paper towel, and headed to the window.

Three men were busy double-checking their firearms while he could just make out the other two heading down the driveway to the back.

He eased the window open just beyond the width of the glasses, his possible explosives containers. He shoved the glasses out and shot his revolver three times. He made for the garage, figuring the distraction might give him seven to ten seconds. He raced through the open doorway into the garage and threw himself into the back seat of the Dart.

Henry thumbed the opener. The garage door was two-thirds open when Henry, already in first gear, tromped their way into the back driveway, spinning and tire-squealing into a tight counterclockwise turn.

Nick was impressed.

They were halfway down the driveway when two men crossed in front of them. They had no chance to raise their rifles as the Dart sent them and their hardware flying. Henry spun the car to the left again as shots followed them onto the roadway. The shots died away as they passed the closest shuttered house.

"Where to?" Henry asked, the excitement in his voice obvious.

Nick checked the rear window and saw three men scrambling into the nearest car.

"Don't worry," Henry said, checking the side mirror. "Those turkeys'll never catch this sweetheart."

The even acceleration while carving a right turn onto the deserted highway convinced Nick that Henry knew his cars, though the memory of his shaking hand did cause Nick a smidge of concern.

Nick's neck stopped itching. "Henry, when you said you take this monster out for a spin once a week, do you spin it like this?"

41

———◆———

Although his attempt to locate the two plague tubs sequestered in Friendship City had been derailed, Meddleson had decided not to leave before exploring a second option: locating Elise Carpenter. Baumberger had once let slip that a lady with that name was under Ishmael's protection, unbeknownst to her.

Meddleson was both intrigued and concerned. He suspected Ishmael had delayed the introduction of the plague so he could meet with this mystery woman. Each week—each day!—that introduction was delayed gave his own creditors time to increase the pressure that was pushing him closer to either bankruptcy or the grave. Ever since Jason Beck was killed in that helicopter crash, the banks had little fear about putting on the squeeze. A rampant plague would distract them at the least. At the most, it would bring them to their knees before falling apart and into hell.

He suspected Ishmael didn't give the slightest damn about anyone's problem other than Ishmael's.

Meddleson wasn't about to lose his money, his yacht, his women, or his life without finding a solution. He went to the town hall where, hopefully, they kept names of their citizens.

The clerk was adamant that he would not be granted access to the search computer. "Not unless you're a certified citizen," the elderly lady said when he asked the second time.

Meddleson nodded politely as he hid a clenched fist behind him. While muttering to himself, he left the building and, noticing a sign with an arrow and the three words *Friendship City Square*, headed off in the arrow's suggested direction.

In the square, he encountered a paved circle about three hundred yards in diameter. Hundreds of people were entering the square, leaving the square, or just milling about and meeting friends. Situated along the perimeter were dozens of small booths. Some vendors sold foods and ice cream. Others, clothing, hardware, books, postcards. Other booths, a bit larger, announced that they catered to people who had come from specific countries. The day was bright and warm, and the people were in no hurry.

Meddleson was about to turn back and head to the exit portal when he passed a stand selling newspapers. He was two steps beyond the last paper rack when he stopped. He stepped back, picked up the paper that had caught his eye, paid the vendor, and headed toward the square's center and the nearest of a ring of benches.

He sat and held up the paper's front page. A woman's picture, a close-up of waist to face and above, occupied the center two of four columns. Beneath the picture and just above the fold was the name *Elise Carpenter.*

4 2

◆

Julia Ramirez had not really pestered McKenna to take her and the three children for a walk in Friendship City Square, but she came close. Eventually, McKenna relented.

"Everybody and his brother are out on a sunny Saturday," he told Julia. "The kids have to stay with us, and we have to watch them like hawks."

Nicole, Nathan, and Half-Penny stuck close as they walked the mile-plus to the square.

When they arrived, Nicole turned to McKenna. "Why do they call a giant circle a square?"

"City fathers don't know geometry," Nathan said.

McKenna and Julia laughed.

McKenna steered them to the nearest ice cream vendor. Digging into their ice cream cups, the kids were all smiles.

McKenna noticed several city officials, followed by reporters, making their way through the crowd. He also noticed a woman who was in their path hurry to the side, avoiding any of the officials and their devoted press. Elise Carpenter. McKenna grinned. She was one lady who avoided fame at all costs.

One by one, the three kids finished their ice creams and deposited the cups and wooden spoons in the nearest trash bin, just fifteen feet from a man holding a newspaper in his lap.

Nicole was the last to finish her butter crunch. She headed for the garbage can.

*****

After double-checking the front-page picture in his paper, Meddleson decided he would follow Ms. Carpenter wherever she went. She moved away from a bunch of photographers, and he started to stand.

He had taken only two steps when he felt a hand on his shoulder. He turned back and recognized Ishmael's field agent, who was wearing a police uniform. The man's name escaped him, but he used to be a senior security guard on the Meddleson Corp. payroll.

"Mr. Meddleson," the man said. "What are you doing here?"

"Checking on things and enjoying the scenery."

"I was told nobody from the group was to be here in the city over the next few days."

Garret something, Meddleson remembered. That was his name. "Who told you that?"

The man checked his surroundings. There was only a small girl dumping something in the trash.

"Ishmael himself," he whispered. "I got a phone call at the airport telling me to get my ass here immediately. Why are you here, Mr. Meddleson? You're part of the group."

Marshal. That was it. Garret Marshal. "Just checking things out, like I said. Everything here seems to be in order. I'll be leaving."

Marshal nodded. "You should leave within the next two hours."

4 3

◆

Nicole dashed back to the group. "Aunt Julia! Uncle Robert!" She took a moment to catch her breath. "A policeman mentioned the name *Ishmael.* Isn't that who Grandpa said was a bad man?"

Half-Penny moved in to listen.

McKenna gave Nicole a calming hand on the shoulder. "Yes, he did call him a bad man. It's not a common name." He was going to ask Nicole how she overheard the name, then remembered she'd learned how to read lips from a nun well trained in the technique.

"Grandpa said the man who used that name followed him around the airport before that airplane crashed," Nicole said. "Maybe it was the same guy."

McKenna nodded, his attention caught. "You said he's in a policeman's uniform?"

"Yes, he's right..." She turned to point, but the man wasn't there. "He said he was told to get here to Friendship City real quick. He was talking to a man in a tan suit. I heard him tell that man to leave in two hours."

McKenna's brow furrowed. "Did you see where the man in the tan suit went?"

Nicole checked again. After about ten seconds, she spotted her target just starting to walk away and pointed him out to McKenna.

"Okay," McKenna said. "I'll call Warren and Daniel. They will know what next steps should be taken. In the meantime, I'll follow the man and see where he goes." McKenna glanced at Julia and the two boys. Correction. One boy. He glanced in the direction of the retreating man. Half-Penny was already on the surveillance trail.

McKenna motioned to Julia. "I'm going to call Warren or Daniel to come here to the square. I have to follow Half-Penny."

Julia, already aware her grandson was on the hunt, grasped McKenna's hand. "Thank you. He's pretty good at keeping out of trouble, even though he constantly stirs it up."

McKenna reached Daniel, who said he'd be at the square in three minutes. He told Julia, who waved him, to get going.

*****

Half-Penny kept his distance as he followed the mystery man in the tan suit. His skills acquired over years of avoiding detection served him well, even in a strange environment. These skills also informed him that McKenna was sixty to eighty yards behind him.

After the well-dressed man made an abrupt right turn at a street corner, slowed his walk for almost a minute, resumed his previous gait, then turned left at another corner, Half-Penny became convinced that the man was following someone. He crossed to the other side of the street so as not to present a consistent rear view should the man be checking.

After two more intersection turns, his target stopped, leaned against a fence, and took something out of his jacket pocket. Half-Penny guessed it was a notepad, as the man made some rapid back-and-forth hand movements.

Half-Penny turned, walked back to the corner, and waited for McKenna. "I think he was following a woman," Half-Penny said. "She went into that big white house with the shutters."

McKenna raised his right hand, stroking a finger along his chin. "I think the house belongs to Elise Carpenter."

Half-Penny saw the man put his notepad back in his pocket. "Let's head back. He may be starting back himself."

They turned and started walking.

"I could see your grandma was a bit worried you followed that man."

"And I could tell that Nicole was confused and worried that he had talked to a man who knows Ishmael. If Detective Nick Garvey is in any danger and I can help, I'm all in."

They were about halfway back when McKenna's cell phone buzzed. He didn't recognize the number, which made him uneasy. "Hello?"

"Robert McKenna, how goes things in the city?"

McKenna grinned at the sound of Nick's voice. "How the hell are you, man? You haven't been gone even two whole days. That's one heck of a short vacation."

"Ran out of money. On our way back. Should be there in the morning."

"Flying?"

McKenna caught a chuckle on the other end. "We're flying, all right. Not in the air, though. We're in a souped-up car driven by an eighty-something-year-old man who thinks he's a teenager."

"Should I have breakfast waiting?"

"We'll tell you one egg or two when we get there."

McKenna knew no additional information was needed. "We" meant he had Owen with him and maybe a lead or two. "See you then."

4 4

---◆---

The number of people in the square had doubled by the time McKenna and Half-Penny returned. Julia gave Half-Penny an admonishing finger wave, followed by a grasping hug.

McKenna turned to Daniel. "The man Nicole saw apparently followed someone into the neighborhood where Elise Carpenter lives. I think I saw her head off in that direction just before old Half-Penny followed the follower."

Daniel shrugged. "Maybe some squarehead wanted an autograph."

McKenna chuckled. "Be the first she ever gave." He looked around the square and at the many people still coming in. "Is there some event scheduled? Music? Poetry reading? Gymnastic dancing? I didn't hear of anything."

Daniel shook his head. "I was going to ask you."

For several minutes, the group watched people, mostly young males, pour into the square.

McKenna sensed something was amiss. "Let's all head home."

Julia plucked her pocket bag from the bench while Daniel and Half-Penny disposed of a few food wrappers. They were about to leave when at least a dozen fistfights broke out. McKenna could make out additional altercations well into the center of the square.

He and Daniel moved the group to the near side of a concrete arch and faced themselves outward, ready to fend off any and all troublemakers. McKenna noticed that each fight he could see was between several whites and an equal number of blacks. A few seconds

136

later, he noticed several news video cameras being trained on the various combatant groups. "What the hell?"

Although fierce punches were exchanged, none of the fighters fell to the pavement. It almost looked choreographed for the cameras.

A multitude of shrill whistles erupted on McKenna's right. He saw at least a hundred policemen filing into the square from the same direction he and the others had come. All fighting stopped. Without hesitation, all the fighters fled from the officers and out of the square. McKenna noted that the majority of fighters fled together, white and black.

Several police officers mingled with the remaining crowd, assuring everything was under control and no additional danger remained.

Nicole tugged McKenna's sleeve and pointed to a far-off policeman. "That's the man," she whispered. "That's the man who knows Ishmael."

4 5

◆

It took McKenna and Daniel almost forty-five minutes to get back to the house, which was usually a twenty-minute walk. The nervous crowds impeded direct movement.

McKenna and Daniel double-checked each door and window lock. Then they checked each room.

"All clear," McKenna said to Julia.

He saw Nathan and Half-Penny in the living room, watching the television.

Nicole was sitting at the kitchen table with a determined look on her face. "We have to find that policeman before Grandpa comes back."

McKenna nodded. "We'll give it our best shot. I'm sure he wasn't really a policeman." He took the seat opposite her and noticed her frown deepening. "I didn't get a clear look. He was kind of far away with crowds swarming about. Can you describe him?"

"Maybe she won't have to!" Half-Penny called out from the next room. "Come and take a look!"

Nicole, McKenna, and Daniel moved quickly to see. The image on the television was from a different angle than their own in the square. The video switched from camera to camera, catching at least fifteen groups of fighters. In each case, the cameraman took care to show a group of young white men pummeling young blacks. And vice versa.

"Now!" Nathan shouted as the video switched to the entry of the police.

The first several videos were of small groups of police at the opposite end of the square. In each, the fighters ran away before any could be detained. In McKenna's opinion, the police were not very interested in capturing a single ruffian.

McKenna mentally crossed his fingers. Hopefully—

"That's him!" Nicole said, jumping up and pointing.

McKenna immediately backspaced the video to where he was able to display the best view of "him." He took several pictures with his cell phone as he advanced the video frame by frame. He also backspaced and set his phone to video mode, capturing the full section showing the target. "Nick will be here in the morning. He'll know if that was the guy at the airport."

Nicole swallowed and crossed her arms in front but agreed.

4 6

◆

May 5, 2058

McKenna was waiting at the portal when Nick and Owen arrived, driven by an eighty-year-old teenager, as McKenna remembered Nick had said. It was apparent from the mud-splattered vehicle that there had been a fair amount of navigation through interesting terrain. McKenna vouched for all three men and for the 1969 Dart Swinger, whose engine was still rumbling. He hopped into the back, behind the driver, who had been introduced as Henry Fitzwalter.

Nick recounted how, at ten of the twelve gas stations where they stopped to refill, the owner had asked for and received the opportunity to drive the car for about a mile. Henry's smile was wide, and his eyes sparkled. Owen just wagged his head and held up both hands, giving them a prolonged tremble.

When shown the video at McKenna's house, Nick needed no more than a second to recognize the man dressed up as a Friendship City police officer. "He's definitely the guy who followed me around the airport. Definitely the guy who mentioned the name *Ishmael* while on the phone." He reached over and patted Nicole on her shoulder and whispered, "Good job."

McKenna turned the television back to live broadcasting. The three available stations all showed replays of the previous day's fighting. Each channel had its announcer saying how the video showed that race relations in Friendship City were far from friendly.

The announcer on one channel shook his head and said, "A far better name for the area would be Sham City. The propaganda that they all respect one another is just that: a sham."

Another channel reported, "Nothing this despicable has happened anyplace else. Friendship City should be closed down."

The third channel was claiming, "Furthermore, if the police had not intervened…"

McKenna flipped it back to the first channel. He was about to turn it off when Nathan jumped up from the couch. "I know that guy! He's not bad."

"Which guy?" McKenna froze the image as Nathan walked up to the screen and pointed at a young black man.

"He lives just down the street. I talked to him just…just three days ago. Right in front of this house. Said his name was Johnny. He was walking with a man he said was a friend. His friend is white, named Norton…and he's the man he's punching right there." Nathan shifted his finger to indicate the man with whose jaw Johnny's frozen fist was about to connect. "He would not fight someone for the reason they say."

4 7

———◆———

By noon, the full city had been notified of a meeting to be held at 2:00 p.m. in the soccer stadium just south of the city square. This time, Mayor Patrick Riley would be speaking.

Julia, Half-Penny, Nathan, and Nicole came with Nick and McKenna. Nick was not about to leave them alone.

As they approached the stadium, Nick noticed clusters of Friendship City police on all sides. The stadium could hold nearly sixty-two thousand people. Nick sensed the meeting was going to last longer than the neighborhood one four days ago.

They got seats in the tenth row, center. By 2:17, the sound system was tested, and its crew waved the speakers aboard.

Police Chief Antonio Rojas was the first to the podium. He had to raise his hand for silence several times. "Thank you, everyone. I know this has been a difficult day for all of us. As the participants of the fights in Friendship City Square were from all parts of the city, we have held this gathering here. Before I turn the microphone over to Mayor Riley, I will tell you all that we have brought in for questioning, and are holding, twenty-seven of the forty-two fighters. They will be thoroughly interrogated before any dispositions are decided. In each case, a lawyer has presented themselves to the police, stating which participant they are representing. Obviously, all interrogations will be carried out with a lawyer present."

"Do all the fighters have a lawyer?" a man in the third row shouted out.

"They do," Rojas answered. "Now I will yield to Mayor Patrick Riley."

Chief Rojas stepped back, and Mayor Riley moved to the podium. Late-fifties, with dark-but-thinning hair and a muscular build, he grabbed the microphone as if he were concerned it would run away. "Citizens of Friendship City, we have had a most stressful four days. First, this past Wednesday we were confronted with two gangs attacking each other with bats, pipes, and knives. One man was later found shot in the head. That leaves twelve men whom we have no clue how they gained entry to our city. Second, yesterday, forty-two men staged a fight and dispersed before police could intervene." Mayor Riley took a slow breath. "I use the phrase 'staged a fight' because both I and the police feel preplanning would be the only way twenty-one fights could erupt at the same time while, at that same time, nine video cameramen were recording everything for later broadcast.

"The broadcast yesterday evening was of a most defaming nature to Friendship City. It painted our city as totally lacking in friendship, a city where white punches black and black slams white. That is not our city. I know it. You know it. We are therefore instituting a significantly increased police presence in all public spaces." The mayor bowed slightly and took another slow breath.

Hands shot up all around the stadium. Nick was impressed that all those hands, with a few exceptions, had held back until the mayor had been able to conclude his remarks.

Mayor Riley spent the next forty-plus minutes acknowledging and answering questions.

A Caucasian woman stormed toward the stage before being held back by two policemen. "Where is my son?" she shouted. "I saw him in that video fighting our neighbor's son, whom your police captured. As they were taking him away, I asked him what happened to my son, because he never returned. Our neighbor's son didn't answer. Just hung his head. I think he muttered that he was sorry. The police said they had not picked my son up and that he was probably hiding." She glared first at the mayor, then at Chief Rojas.

Chief Rojas stepped beside the mayor and leaned into the microphone. "We will check with you right after this meeting. He *is* probably hiding. We have leads on three of the remaining fifteen not yet brought into headquarters. That leaves twelve not yet rounded up. I'm sure he's one of those."

Nick noticed an elderly black man five rows ahead using his cane to push himself to a standing position. An officer with a microphone reached his side as he stood.

"How dare these stupid newspeople repeat over and over that Friendship City is nothing but a collection of racists! Some of us may be sensitive to color, but we all extend helping hands."

Applause filled the stadium and continued for a minute or two.

Over another hour, questions were asked and answers provided. The crowd deemed many of the answers insufficient. Several mentions of the city's Bill of Rights were presented along with the obligations to which elected officials must abide.

The meeting was finally brought to a close.

In addition to the overwrought mother of the missing son, more concerned parents clustered around Chief Rojas and Mayor Riley. Nick watched as Chief Rojas pointed them to an officer standing apart. They left with the officer.

4 8

◆

May 6, 2058

Ishmael marched aboard *Runner* and into Peter Meddleson's private office.

Meddleson looked up, startled.

Ishmael took the seat directly opposite. "What were you doing in Friendship City?"

Meddleson blinked, then swallowed. "Just making sure everything was working to plan."

"Whose plan? Ours or yours?"

Another swallow. "Our plan, of course."

"Did you get your location trinkets out with you okay?"

No answer.

"And what were you doing following some woman to her house?"

Two blinks, another swallow.

Ishmael stood and glared down at Meddleson. "Do not leave this boat of yours. You are not to go ashore again until the plague is released."

Still no answer.

"Understand?"

A nod.

"Good." Ishmael left the private office. As he approached the sloping plank walkway, Ishmael nodded at the ship's captain, who returned the nod with a thumbs-up followed by a nod of his own.

Ishmael climbed into his limousine and watched four men, all crew, motor away from the *Runner* in a skiff. He checked his watch: 8:17 a.m. The start of a good day.

The skiff disappeared into a walled inlet. *Runner* exploded in a huge fireball.

He checked his watch: 8:18 a.m. Definitely a good day.

4 9

———◆———

Nathan walked down the block and hesitated in front of the house where he knew Johnny lived with his grandmother. He shuffled his feet, then walked up the front steps and rang the doorbell. He counted slowly to ten and was about to turn back when he heard a lock click.

The door opened. Johnny's grandma stood there, her black hand shaking slightly on the doorknob.

"Hello, Mrs. Davis. Is Johnny home?"

The shaking became more pronounced. "He hasn't—"

Johnny stuck his head out, looking left and right. He motioned to his visitor. "Inside, Nathan. Quick. What the hell you doing here?"

"I was in the square two days ago and saw you punching it out with Norton. I wanted to be sure you and he were both okay. The mayor at the meeting yesterday said they were going to round you all up and ask a lot of questions."

Nathan noticed the catch in Johnny's breath. He thought changing the subject might put Johnny at ease. He glanced at the door through which the older woman had gone. "How's your grandma?"

Johnny's eyes widened. "Why are you asking?"

Nathan felt he was definitely overstaying his welcome, if there ever had been a welcome. "Sorry. I was just asking. No reason. I'll leave you alone." He turned to leave.

"And don't go to Norton's house," Johnny said, his tone more an order than a request.

Nathan turned back. "Why?"

"He's dead."

"Dead? You didn't hit him that hard. I saw the two of you live and on TV. I think I've punched my pillow harder than either of you swung at each other."

"He died later that day," Johnny said, waving Nathan to leave.

Nathan only partially turned toward the door.

Johnny frowned, raised his right hand, extended his forefinger, placed it to his temple, and raised his thumb. "On second thought, Nathan, I want you to come inside and go out the back and take the alley to your house."

Nathan, confused and a bit frightened, did as he was told.

5 0

◆

Nick and McKenna went over various possible scenarios leading to the white-on-black fights. McKenna had obtained the names of the participants from the police.

Nick shook his head. "We've gone through about a dozen different schemes trying to make sense of the two incidents: Wednesday's gang-on-gang brawl and yesterday's staged fights. Nothing makes sense."

"I agree," McKenna said. "The brawl was deadly to one participant. The staged fights, far from deadly."

Julia came in from the kitchen area. Nathan was at her side. "He said he needs to talk with you."

Nick and McKenna nodded. Nathan pulled out a chair and sat at the table. Nick waited as the boy took several breaths.

Nathan looked across at Nick. "Norton is dead."

It took Nick a moment to connect the name. "That guy you saw in the fight? How do you know he's dead?"

"Johnny Davis told me. His grandmother was really nervous."

McKenna ran a finger down his list of fighters. "Young Mr. Davis is one of those listed as still missing but one of the three they are currently tracking."

Nick's brow furrowed. "Did Johnny say how Norton died?"

"No. But he did raise his hand to the side of his head. Like this." Nathan repeated Johnny's gesture.

Nick's neck started right in, itching full steam. He looked at McKenna. "We gotta go get Johnny."

McKenna agreed.

Nick stood and put a hand on Nathan's shoulder. "We need you to come with us. Okay?"

51

---◆---

athan led Nick and McKenna out to the alleyway and headed to Johnny's backyard. As they approached, they saw Johnny sneak out his back door. A stubby pin oak tree blocked his vision of them. Nathan darted to the gate as Johnny reached to unlock it.

Nick marched up. "We want to help."

Johnny's shoulders sagged.

"The police have you on a short list of the fighters they're tracking. My thought is for you and your grandma to come over to Mr. McKenna's house before the police knock on your door."

"We can keep you both safe. Do it, Johnny. Do it!" Nathan changed his tone to just short of insistence.

Johnny nodded and flipped the gate open. McKenna stood guard while the others went into the back of the house. Three minutes later, they came out, guiding Grandma down the steps and across to the gate. Another three minutes brought them safely inside McKenna's house, where Grandma was relieved to see a female face.

Nick asked Julia to take Johnny's grandmother into another room for a few minutes. As they disappeared into the kitchen, Nick sat at the table with Nathan, McKenna, and Johnny. He motioned to McKenna to pull out his list of names. "We want to keep you and your grandmother safe," Nick said. "It'll help us to know what we're up against."

McKenna unfolded his paper. "The names of all forty-two fighters are listed here. The top fifteen are those not yet in police custody.

The top three, where your name is, the police say they are actively tracking. The next twelve they state have no reported sightings."

Nick waited until Johnny looked up from the list of names and met his eyes. "Again, we want to keep you safe, and if that means keeping you hidden from the police, we'll do just that for as long as it takes."

Johnny met Nick's steady gaze. "The twelve are all dead."

"How are you so sure?" Nick asked.

"They shot all twelve in front of us."

"They?" McKenna asked.

"The men with the video cameras. There were seven of them. There was one policeman who warned the rest of us to not tell anyone about anything that happened, or we would also be shot. He made a point of telling us that if we spoke up, then everybody in our house would be killed."

Nick decided protection could not be assured while the two remained in Friendship City.

5 2

———◆———

President Allison had just finished a cabinet meeting and had returned to the Oval Office when her private cell buzzed. "Hello?" She recognized Nick's voice and immediately signaled the two Secret Service agents to step out. "Yes, Leroy. How is your trip?"

"Well, Sarah, the weather is a bit turbulent, but we are doing well. Planned to stop for some burgers but could only get one worth eating. About a dozen others were fried to a crisp."

"Sorry to hear that," President Allison said. Knowing where Nick was and what had happened in Friendship City the past few days, she understood that twelve missing videotaped fighters had been killed.

"I'm taking piano lessons, and my assignment is to play the tune 'Indigenous Pond' using only half the black keys. My recital is at dinnertime."

President Allison shook her head. *Indigenous Pond...* She reached for her computer and pulled up a map for the Friendship City area. *Half of thirty-six black keys gives eighteen miles.* She scoured the map. *Indian Lake! Recital at dinnertime. Hmm...m...m.* "Am I invited to the recital?"

"Most definitely, but don't pack your Sunday best. In fact, not even your weekday best."

Decoded: "Come incognito."

"Wouldn't think otherwise. Remember to bring your metronome."

Hopefully decoded: "Bring Owen, who is our overall timekeeper."

"Gotcha," Nick said and hung up.

President Allison checked her calendar. Other than pushing hard on the team looking for a plague solution, there was nothing remotely critical scheduled for the entire week. She'd have Vice President Carter Johnson keep the pressure on in that single most important area.

5 3

◆

Ishmael pounded his desktop. He was looking down at a photograph of a hand-carved eagle, the existence of which his noncommunicative minions had failed to alert him to. He had told them to check everywhere inside and outside his father's house for any wooden animal carvings. They had found none but forgot to tell him about this photo. They had just dropped it into the box of old stuff they found and brought back.

He could tell at a glance that the eagle had been carved by his father, who had told him several times before his death that animal carvings were excellent places to hide important secrets. He didn't know for sure that his father had hidden anything related to the plague, but he wasn't about to ignore any possibilities.

His band of incompetents had also told him about an old car racing out of the house at the end of the block as they parked in front. That house had belonged to Henry Fitzwalter, a close friend of his father's.

Ishmael grabbed his cell phone and dialed his chief incompetent. "What color was the car?"

"Green."

"Was there a broad white stripe running across the rear part of the trunk lid?"

"Yes."

Henry was still alive. And if anyone might have the eagle, which might hold hidden information, it was Fitzwalter.

He dialed on his cell again. *Time to call in a competent minion or two.*

5 4

◆

McKenna presented passes for Nick, Owen, Henry, Johnny, and his grandma to exit the portal. He had agreed to return to his house and help Julia keep the three youngsters safe. Before leaving, he handed Nick two loaded pistols. "You never know," he said.

The 1969 Dart—green with a white stripe across the trunk lid—was waved out just one minute before Garret Marshal got his call from Ishmael. Another minute elapsed before he ascertained the car had just left Friendship City and was headed to Houston.

Nick chose to sit in the front passenger seat, figuring he could use the side mirror to check on any pursuit. Henry's driving was more measured this time, nothing over double digits.

Grandma Davis, squeezed in between Owen and her grandson, Johnny, looked calm.

Nick spotted no cars behind nor ahead for almost ten minutes. Then there were three black sedans, definitely in hot pursuit.

Henry had already spotted them and had tromped down on the gas.

Nick turned back to Johnny. "Make sure your grandma is strapped in." He looked over at Owen and saw the here-we-go-again look in his eyes.

The Dart started pulling away. Two of the three cars lost ground. The one in front tried but couldn't keep up. Nick figured they had another ten minutes at most, and they would hand off Johnny and his grandmother to President Allison.

Eight minutes later, the Dart was speeding up Olminto North Road toward Henderson Road when Nick saw four more sedans wheeling left from Henderson onto Olminto. He spotted a somewhat level patch of grass to a parallel road. He motioned Henry to whip sharply to the right. The area between the two roads was mostly overgrown grassland with their exit path one of the few with almost level access.

Almost.

Nick, bracing himself, turned to the rear seats and warned, "Big bumps ahead."

Henry made the sliding turn just yards before the oncoming sedans and tromped full speed along—Nick checked his phone map—Whipple Road. It intersected Stadium Drive, which led to a middle school and one Leo Aguilar Stadium.

Nick turned to check on their bouncing passengers. Johnny was the only one who seemed to be enjoying the chase. Grandma was wide-eyed, and Owen was slowly shaking his head.

Two of the four pursuing sedans didn't make the turn. One crashed into an abandoned truck; the other ran into the woods, disappearing into the tall grass. The other two had to stop, back up, and—Nick assumed—follow his chosen path.

Henry bounced the Dart right onto Whipple.

"In a little over a mile, make a sharp right onto Stadium Drive," Nick said.

Henry made the turn onto Stadium Drive more smoothly than Nick expected, as his head didn't get slammed against the passenger window. Henry had the accelerator full to the floor as the Dart rocketed toward the stadium, its open end straight ahead.

Nick checked behind for the sedans. They were probably bouncing their way to Whipple. He turned to face forward and, seeing no concrete barriers, signaled Henry to head straight onto the football field and stop at the far end.

It was obvious that the stadium hadn't been used for at least a decade or two. There were only traces of grass with team markings barely visible at each end of what passed for a playing field surrounded by a running track. Beyond the track, rusted metal bleachers ran along either side of the field.

Nick signaled Henry to pull near the bleachers on their right. As soon as they stopped, he told everyone to get out and run to where the bleachers started and halfway down, keeping away from the track.

Nick figured they wouldn't be seen by those approaching in the sedans. He took up station inside the bleachers, a few seats in. He glanced to his left and saw the others were grouped under the seats about twenty yards down. He gripped a pistol in each hand.

Within thirty seconds, the two sedans pulled up to the far end of the field. After another four or five seconds, they drove onto the field and up to the empty Dart.

Seven thugs got out. Four paired up and stood in front of their respective cars. The remaining three split up: one to the left and one to the right bleachers. The last of them inspected the inside of the Dart and then stood, looking back at the others.

Nick decided this one was the crew chief and the most dangerous—and thus the one to take out first. His plan to take out the leader, followed by the thug walking along the bleachers on his side, and then the four car watchers, was just formulated when it fell apart.

"I got him!" the nearest bleacher thug hollered as he pulled Johnny from beneath the seats and, slipping his arms around the young man's neck, dragged him upright.

So much for plan A. Nick slid the pistol in his left hand into his pants pocket. "I'm the one you want," he announced, walking into the open with pistol lowered.

Mr. Crew Chief looked at Nick. "Not really. We're after males much younger and much older." He motioned Nick to drop his sidearm.

Nick decided to follow instructions, for the moment.

Two of the men in front of the nearest sedan followed their comrade's head wave, climbed under the seats, and extracted Johnny's grandma and Owen. Nick followed the leader's hand wave to join Grandma, Johnny, and Owen.

One of the men pulled out a cell phone and took several pictures of Nick and his fellow travelers, now prisoners.

Mr. Crew Chief smiled, wagging his revolver as a signal for the others to group the four together. "We weren't after you, but since you insist, I'll accommodate." The pistol-wagging stopped. "Little Spill-the-Beans Johnny first."

Nick leaped in front of Johnny as the shot was fired. His own handgun was in his left hand as his right shoulder exploded in pain. He pulled the trigger and watched Mr. Crew Chief collapse to the ground, a bullet hole in his forehead. Nick fell to his knees but managed to get another shot off, taking out the thug who had grabbed Johnny.

Before he could even think of getting off another, one of the remaining five thugs kicked the pistol out of Nick's hand. Nick watched as the kicker pointed his pistol at him. He refused to close his eyes. He would stare death in the face right to the end.

The Dart's loud engine started up, distracting Nick's would-be executioner. Before any of the remaining four thugs could react, the Dart plowed into the group, sending three of them airborne.

Nick's executioner didn't know who to shoot first: Nick or the Dart. A shot through his head solved his indecision.

Nick, trying to stand, saw three Jeeps roaring across the field. They pulled to a stop. President Allison was sitting beside the driver in the first Jeep. Standing right behind her was a military man still holding his rifle aloft.

Secret Service agents cuffed the two thugs still standing. An ambulance was called for two of the three writhing on the ground from their encounter with the still-growling Dart. The third was pronounced dead.

An agent with medical experience guided Nick to the nearest bleacher seat and administered first aid before even looking at the two on the ground.

President Allison came to Nick's side. "We saw them take off after you." She looked at Nick's shoulder bandaging in process. "You okay?"

Nick nodded. "The bullet just grazed me. A few stitches will fix it up."

"Sorry we didn't get here a few minutes sooner."

Nick chuckled as he watched Henry checking the prized possession for any damage. "At least the Dart came through okay. I think."

President Allison smiled.

Johnny and his grandma came to Nick and the president. Grandma moved to give Nick a hug but, seeing his bandage, hung back. "Thank you for saving my grandson." Tears streamed from her eyes.

Johnny stepped in and shook Nick's left hand. "Thank you."

President Allison said she was here to take Johnny and his grandma to a safe place. Owen stepped next to President Allison, and the two of them walked back to her Jeep.

Henry was the last to check in with Nick. "You look like you're going to be okay, young fella."

Nick chuckled again and nodded at the Dart. "Does that make two of us?"

Henry snorted and gave Nick both thumbs up.

Johnny stepped back to Nick's side. "I told my grandma I was going back to Friendship City with you. I said we have to keep the other boys and their families safe. She isn't happy, but she knows it's the right thing to do."

Nick nodded, rested his left hand on the boy's shoulder, and pushed himself upright.

5 5

———◆———

Nick, still in pain after receiving a row of stitches at a nearby medical clinic, was instructed to plop down on the easy chair and stay out of everyone's way. He did not resist.

It took Julia only twenty minutes to make a batch of pasta and sauce for everyone's late 9:00 p.m. dinner.

Johnny had been assigned to share the bedroom given to Henry. McKenna had previously moved out of the master bedroom to make room for Julia, Half-Penny, Nicole, and Nathan. Nick and Owen each had the two small bedrooms, or "closets," as Nick referred to his.

The dining room table, solid oak, was able to accommodate all nine eager appetites.

Johnny spent the first six or seven minutes expounding how Nick had jumped in front of him and his grandmother, taking a bullet meant for them. "He took the bullet in his shoulder, and as he started to fall, took out the shooter and the bad man who'd shoved me to my grandma's side." Johnny took a spoonful of bowties and mumbled his next word. "Fantastic!"

Nick noticed that both Nicole and Nathan were beaming. His shoulder pain seemed to vanish, washed away by warm waves of love.

Owen chimed in. "A certain green 1969 Dart 340 made a contribution of dispatching two, maybe more," he said, recounting the three airborne men. "A quick warning: don't stand in front when Henry Fitzwalter is driving."

Henry chuckled.

Julia wagged her head at all the braggadocio and said she was just happy that everyone made it home safe for a good meal. She turned to Henry. "My father owned an old Dart, blue as I remember. I never knew the year. He always checked its oil and battery and washed it, it seemed like every other day. Did you feed your green Dart a good meal? Are you going to give it a bath before bedtime?"

Henry went from chuckle to roaring laughter.

The rest of the conversation was similarly light until ice cream time at the end.

Johnny looked over at Henry. "I noticed your carved eagle in our room. My dad had one he carved of our bulldog. The dog was long dead. Dad kept it in the kitchen we shared with two other families. When there were times he wanted to tell me a secret, he would either whisper in my ear or write a note and hide it inside the bulldog. He always said our dog was good at keeping secrets."

Nick and Owen stopped eating and looked at each other.

"Maybe?" Owen asked.

Nick gave a slow shrug, then motioned Henry to follow him.

Thirty seconds later, they returned with Nick holding the carved eagle. Nick placed it down on the table in front of Johnny. "How did you open the bulldog?"

"There was a rubber stopper on the bottom. All I had to do was twist it slightly and pull it out." Johnny turned the eagle upside down and studied its bottom. He looked up at Nick and shook his head.

With his left elbow on the table, Nick rested his chin against his fist and glared at the eagle. "No stopper to twist," he mumbled. He reached over and picked up the eagle, turned it over head to tail twice, then around several times. No visible ways to twist. He tugged on wings and tail feathers. Nothing.

He was about to place the carving back on the table, then paused and scanned every inch of the eagle's face. He held the eagle in his left hand and pushed back on its short beak with his right forefinger. Nothing.

He shook his head, shot a quick, forlorn look at Owen, and placed the intricate carving back on the table. Then he picked up the carving and motioned to Henry. Before he handed it across the table,

Nick placed his left hand atop the eagle and set his right forefinger once more against the beak. He paused, took a deep breath, and pushed down and in at the same time.

A long, thin rectangle angled up and out from the eagle's backside. The carved section of wood was no wider than Nick's forefinger.

Nick exhaled. "Thought I felt a slight give with resistance." He held the beak in and down. "Is there anything inside?"

Owen reached in and pulled out a rumpled fold of paper. He unfolded and studied it.

"What is it?"

Owen looked up. "A chemical formula."

5 6

◆

Nick dialed President Allison's secret number on one of the disposable cell phones provided by McKenna.

It took seven rings before the call was answered.

Before any greeting, Nick coughed once, said "Sorry," and hung up. He handed the phone back to McKenna for immediate disposal. He nodded to Owen. "Your ride should be here within the hour."

It was.

McKenna took Owen and Henry to the exit portal and verified they were picked up by the correct people. He and Nick had agreed that the 1969 Dart was too infamous to be used. It had been moved into the house's four-car garage.

When McKenna returned, Nick said Johnny had called four friends who had survived the fight in the square and the subsequent murders.

"All four are on board," Nick said, "as long as we don't give their names to anyone. Especially, one of them said, to law enforcement. We told them we'd try to schedule a town meeting tomorrow."

McKenna nodded, grabbed his cell, and was able to get an all-citizen meeting scheduled for 3:00 p.m. the next afternoon.

Nick was relieved he didn't have to reschedule next morning's visit with the doctor treating Sandra.

5 7

◆

I t was past two in the morning when Ishmael finally got around to the photographs transmitted by his group sent to capture a runaway boy who was part of the staged fight.

The first few photographs showed a green automobile in the distance. Most of the pictures were of the rear view of the car being chased. One showed a side view as the car had apparently changed course and was headed into a grassy section off the road. This last view showed the white striping across the car's trunk lid and down the side.

Definitely his father's car. For a ninety-year-old car, it looked as good as new. From what the pursuers said, it ran *better* than new. And from what Garret Marshal reported upon his return to Friendship City, it was still in Henry's hands. A 1969 Dart should be easy for his team to find.

Ishmael thumbed through the next ten or eleven photos. He was about to put them aside when the second-to-last caught his eye. The man standing next to Henry Fitzwalter looked familiar. Ishmael leaned closer. He reached into a drawer and retrieved a magnifying glass. He studied the face for a full minute before reaching his conclusion.

Nick Garvey was still alive. Alive, and in Friendship City.

He shook his head. *Some things take longer than others*, he told himself.

He activated his computer. He keyed down to the folder of reports from his Houston team covering Nick's family, who had supposedly lost their patriarch. As he remembered, the report stated that all four members had left a week ago and had not been seen since. Ishmael nodded. He had a strong—very strong—suspicion.

He tapped into his cell.

Garret Marshal answered on the fourth ring. "Yes, sir?"

"Nick did not die in the crash. He's alive and in Friendship City."

There was an audible groan on the other end.

"I am convinced his family is there as well, possibly including his daughter, Sandra. You are to have your team locate them and report back. Finding the green Dart will give you a leg up. You are not to be involved in that mission. I want you to engineer a chance encounter with the lady I told you about, Elise Carpenter. Find out anything you can while revealing nothing."

"Yes, sir."

58

◆

The whole family went to the hospital to visit Sandra. The rest of them had visited each day for the week Nick was away rescuing Owen. Everyone had missed yesterday, but all intentions were to again visit every day.

Nicole had told him that her mom was remembering more and more each time they visited. This brought Nick both joy and concern. His joy was that Sandra would have a much fuller life if she regained all her memories. His concern: he feared that regaining all memories would refresh her hatred of him.

A male nurse was tending to Sandra as they entered the room. Nick asked him about Sandra's general condition and any recent improvements.

The nurse pulled out his chart. "Dr. Johnson had to return to Houston. Dr. Abram is currently treating your daughter while he's away. She notes that Sandra has made significant improvements in her long-term memory. I have noticed that myself. Her mood has moved from one of disinterest to one of engaging with her surroundings. Strong improvement all around."

Nick thanked him and moved to Nicole, who held Sandra's hand and smiled while unleashing an excitable stream of words.

Sandra smiled throughout.

Nicole suddenly turned and grabbed Nick's left hand, pulling him to her side. "Grandpa always tells me how lucky I am to have a mom like you." She released his left hand and reached across to place his right atop Sandra's left.

Nick tried to swallow. "Nicole is right. She's very lucky you are her mom."

Sandra gave a slight nod.

Nick decided to push on and cross the Rubicon. "And I'm lucky to have you as my daughter."

Sandra's response was muted. No smile, one brow wrinkle, and an inquisitive look in her eyes.

Nick sensed Nicole turning, then felt her squeezing hug.

"I love you, Grandpa!"

He watched Sandra as the hint of a smile developed. It remained just a hint.

Nathan and then Half-Penny stepped in, touched her hand, smiled, and wished her well.

The smile broadened somewhat.

Nick decided to let the youngsters have center stage.

As he stepped back, Julia patted his shoulder.

59

◆

The meeting started at exactly 3:00 p.m., the soccer stadium the venue once again. Sixty thousand of the seats were filled. A makeshift stage with elevated large-screen TVs had been set up at the far end of the stadium, blocking out about two thousand seats. Another five thousand plus attendees covered the field itself, sitting either on folding chairs or on blankets. A few hundred parked themselves directly on the grass.

Nick and McKenna were standing behind the curtains at stage left. With them stood young Johnny, another young man, three Friendship City Special Police officers, and four US federal police. Across the stage from them, Mayor Patrick Riley, Police Chief Antonio Rojas, Captain of Portal Agents Theodore Martin, and another seven mixed-force police stood in single file.

A floodlight flickered on, highlighting the podium with its microphone and several glasses of water. Thousands of conversations halted midbuzz.

Mayor Patrick Riley stepped to the microphone. "Citizens of Friendship City, we have a crisis of biblical proportions."

Nick grimaced at the hyperbole, but it wasn't entirely unjustified.

The mayor, having paused for effect, continued. "We promised we would keep you informed of all we learned." He paused again. "The fight was staged for evil purposes. Staged by evil killers: the men behind the video cameras. The forty-two young men were told they would be part of a scene for a grand movie. They were told the fight would be disrupted and they should run away." The mayor took a deep breath. "Run away to a preordained location. It was at this location that they were told never to tell anyone—never, ever—that the fights were faked. They were told that if they ever did tell, there would be... I've been told the term they used...'repercussions' for them and for their whole families." Mayor Riley paused again and bowed his head. "At this point, the video men pulled out guns and murdered twelve of the boys."

Nick looked out to the stands as many shrieks and wails reverberated. On the grass, he saw a man and woman hugging each other and sobbing.

"Two young men have come forward today to give you more detail. Three others have recorded their stories for playback to you here. The families of these five brave young men have all been evacuated from Friendship City and are under the protection of President Lenora Allison. All other families will be provided after this meeting with three rotating shifts each of three Friendship City police officers and three United States Special Operations Forces. It is our intent that absolutely no harm come to any of the involved families."

Gotta give him credit, Nick told himself. *Not sure I could recite those events to these people without breaking down.*

Mayor Riley introduced Johnny Davis and stepped back.

Johnny told the silent thousands how he and the others had been recruited, how they were told the fight scene was central to a super action movie, how they paired up—most with friends—how they were instructed on the required punches to throw, about fifty-fifty to the face and body, how they were split up into three groups of seven pairs and brought via truck to designated entry roads into the square, and how they were gathered up after the fight and taken to an isolated location, where twelve of their neighbors were pulled out at random and shot. "The leader then said, 'The same will happen to you and to everyone in your family if you ever reveal what happened.'"

Nick was amazed how silent sixty-five thousand people had become.

The second young man gave much the same recital of events with a few variations.

The soccer field remained silent.

The mayor stepped back to the podium. "We will now play three tapes of other young men who have been threatened. As I told you, they and their families have been evacuated and are under protection."

The three tapes repeated the broad outlines of what Johnny and the other boy had said live.

Mayor Riley gave the audio technician a quick thank-you nod, then turned to the thousands of citizens. "These five recounts were most painful for me when I first heard them. I am sure they're much more painful to many of you. Friendship City has a cornerstone of beliefs based on our citizen-approved code or Bill of Rights. What makes these rights workable are their matching obligations.

"We all know all of the rights are in place to protect every citizen, or to provide a playing field that is not just even but stimulates the upward growth of each citizen. Many of these rights pertain to your government: me, our police, and our small bureaucracy. As with the other rights, ours have obligations as well." The mayor paused, then bowed his head. "We have failed in those obligations. Our prime obligation is to be diligent in providing for the safety of all of you, our citizens. We have failed to be diligent. That stops here and now." He motioned Police Chief Antonio Rojas to step to the podium. "Chief Rojas has had jurisdiction over just one section of our great city. As of now, I'm assigning him complete citywide responsibility for resolving our current crisis."

As Mayor Riley stepped back, Chief Rojas adjusted the microphone. "In addition to providing round-the-clock protection to the families described by the mayor, we will increase police presence in all locations mentioned by Johnny Davis, Eduardo Ramon, and in the three taped messages. Our key obligation going forward is to answer the many questions we have received over the past seven days. Namely...how do these thugs get into Friendship City? Reviewing video files of portal entries going back three months, we have found zero facial matches with the eleven men gunned down during or after the gang-style shootout. We also found no facial matches with the over a dozen videographers we have identified." He raised one of the water glasses and took a couple of swallows.

Nick had encountered the same identification dead end.

Chief Rojas continued, "We have come to one conclusion: these criminals did not come in through either of our two portals. They cannot climb over the Friendship City walls. They cannot paraglide into our city without being detected by one of our over five thousand detectors. There is only one other way: tunnels."

The stadium audience was no longer silent. Conversations started buzzing everywhere.

"Captain Theodore Martin, chief of the portal agents, will fill you in on our follow-up plan and actions."

Captain Martin stepped to the podium. "I was on the Friendship City committee that reviewed the several construction companies who responded to the requests for quotes to build our wall. In addition to reviewing their plans, our responsibility was to audit their financial history as well as the integrity of all their projects over the last five years of work. We made our recommendation, and the company was officially contracted. We were assured by our builder that the concrete foundation descends below the surface of the ground for the same forty feet that the wall extends above. Sensors were installed to detect any ground movement, be it as great as an earthquake or as tiny as digging a grave. Nothing has been recorded, but we have no way of determining if all sensors are operational.

"We have requested President Lenora Allison to bring in ten seismic-sensors-slash-deep-ground profilers. Think of these ten machines as being capable of producing sonograms—visual images generated by reflected sound waves—of earth strata to a depth of over five hundred feet. If we find any tunnels, they will be traced backward and forward to both entry and exit. If we do find any, they will be sealed. The ten machines will arrive in two days and will be put to use immediately. We project we will complete scanning the full circumference of the city in about a week." Captain Martin looked for who was next to claim the microphone. "I've been told that Mayor Riley will have a few words next addressing our accountability."

6 0

---◆---

When he answered his cell phone on the third ring, Ishmael was confused. He heard only muffled conversation. Just before he could hang up, Garret Marshal spoke.

"I felt it critical that I call you now, not after I leave the stadium. A plan has been put in place to locate and close all tunnels into Friendship City."

Ishmael nodded. It didn't surprise him that they would expose the tunnels. The only surprise was that it took them so long to even think of tunnels. "When is this program to start?"

"In two days, sir."

"And the expected end date?"

"Five days from the start."

The muffled sounds continued.

"What's going on at the stadium?"

"Mayor Patrick Riley and Police Chief Antonio Rojas have been speaking to at least seventy, maybe eighty thousand people about the street fights from a couple days ago."

"Three days ago."

"Okay, three days ago. Two of the boy fighters have stood up and recounted what happened right up to the murders. Three more were presented via recordings. The stadium erupted with question after question, with threats mixed in."

To be expected, Ishmael thought. "Have you been able to track down any of Nick Garvey's family?"

"Only his daughter, Sandra. She was brought to the Valley Regional Medical Center here in the city. She's in the neurological wing. I arranged for one of our nurses to keep an eye on her room in hopes that we can locate her relatives and start tracking them."

Ishmael paused for three seconds, long enough to explore a half-dozen plans. "Good plan, Garret. I'll be sending in a high-level medical person to review Sandra's condition. Prepare your nurse to be ready to vouch to the neurology desk. I'll pass the name when I'm ready."

"Yes, sir."

Ishmael waited for Garret to break the connection. He smiled. The sounds of muffled shouting and loudspeaker noise came across like a stadium full of angry people.

6 1

◆

Nick watched as Mayor Riley reclaimed the podium. He had to admit, Captain Martin had provided the crowd with words of hope. Now it was the mayor's turn.

"We all understand your feelings of insecurity, your complaints, your expressions of distrust of me and of the police. We understand when you say—repeatedly—that we have not lived up to our obligations. I can assure—"

"What can you assure?" blurted a husky man at the front of the field microphone line. "Can you assure no more of our children will be murdered? Can you assure that even if you find all the tunnels, you'll capture all the evil thugs already inside our city?"

Applause echoed throughout the stadium for, by Nick's count, the sixth time. Nick noticed that the line behind the speaker was thinning out. The berating, it appeared, would soon be over.

"You also have obligations," the man continued. "Not just us, the ones who will be in a murderer's crosshairs, but you and other city leaders who have round-the-clock protection."

More thunderous applause.

Maybe the berating would *not* be over anytime soon.

The man threw his hands up, shrugged, and yielded the microphone.

A woman, probably in her midthirties, moved up. "I have three children all in middle school. You and the chief have told us how you plan to keep our schools safe. What about our neighborhoods? Are you going to modify the city's Bill of Rights to allow all citizens, even new arrivals, to have guns so we can protect ourselves?"

Mayor Riley fielded the question. "That particular right is a restrictive right in the sense that you must be certified as being of sound mind and must also be certified as being trained in the use of the firearm of your choice. I am sure you know that citizens may possess guns for protection. If you need help with either or both of the certifications, my office, and the chief's as well, would be glad to assist. Both certifications can probably be completed within twenty-four hours."

The woman nodded. "Thank you, Mayor Riley." She turned and bumped into two people stepping up to the microphone. They stepped apart and allowed the woman to pass.

Nick recognized the two, a woman and a man. Warren had pointed them out during Nick's first walk in the city. Donna and Doug, he remembered, though he couldn't remember their last names. Warren had said they were influential citizens and frequently spoke up during public meetings. *Maybe the berating is far from over.*

The man stepped to his left, allowing the woman clear access to the microphone. The buzzing crowd noise ceased abruptly. Nick could almost feel the expectation.

Donna leaned toward the microphone. "Doug and I seldom agree on anything." She paused for a second. "I guess 'seldom' should be changed to 'rarely.'"

Doug smiled and gave Donna a strong nod.

"We are, however, in agreement together and with Mayor Riley and Chief Rojas. We are all citizens of Friendship City. The word 'Friendship' is not just to locate our homes on a map. It identifies who we are, how we treat each other, and when our differences are put aside."

Donna stepped to her right as Doug moved in to speak. "Donna speaks not just for herself and for me, but for all of us in this stadium. The mayor and the chief are doing what is best for all of us. We should trust them to devise plans to give us all the best protection possible. We should trust each other to be alert and brave and to warn us all when something seems amiss. If any of you are contemplating resigning your positions per your obligations to Friendship

City's Bill of Rights, please do not choose to stand down. Now is the time for all of us to stand up. Together, we can destroy this evil."

Doug turned to Donna, and they embraced.

Applause filled the stadium.

6 2

$$\blacklozenge$$

May 8, 2058

Dr. Baumberger waited until Ishmael hung up before thumbing off his cell phone. He was not eager to slip into Friendship City, but in his situation, it was something like "In for a million dollars; in for whatever dangerous dime you're told to pick up."

He remembered what had happened to Meddleson. He never believed for a second the police statement that the explosion was "a terrible accident." He grabbed a backpack, then went about scooping up needed toilet articles, extra clothes, and his cyber-encryption watch.

At the appointed time, 8:35 a.m., he stepped outside the house Ishmael had rented for him in Houston. A nondescript black sedan pulled curbside twenty seconds later. Three hours later, the car stopped and waited until a brown Jeep pulled up next to them. Baumberger switched vehicles.

He recognized the driver, Garret Marshal, who handed him a brown paper bag.

"Figured you might need some lunch," was all Garret said as they turned about and headed into a densely wooded area.

Baumberger was soon able to see the outlines of the wall surrounding Friendship City. The dense clusters of tall trees revealed the distant walls in a few quick flashes. He managed to keep his breathing even. Given the mission Ishmael had handed to him, he knew he was headed into territory and situations with little room for escape, should anything go wrong. Meddleson had been liquidated, he felt, because of his frequent and continual questioning of "the *plan*." Whatever happened inside Friendship City, he told himself, he would not question any plan or assignment.

He opened the lunch bag, grabbed the wrapped sandwich, and tried to admire the wooded surroundings. He had finished the ham sandwich and taken his first bite of the McIntosh apple when the Jeep pulled to a stop.

Garret motioned for them to get out. "Tunnel number seven," he announced, pointing to a cluster of trees on their right not more than ten feet tall. "This one is still undetected. They started their sweeps yesterday. This one, however, is the smallest and has zero metal to avoid triggering most of the detectors they're using."

Garret started toward the trees, motioning Baumberger to follow. They stopped about two hundred yards from the glass wall of Friendship City. Garret motioned to their left. Baumberger saw nothing but a few broken branches crisscrossing the ground. He had noticed similar broken branches every few feet since they passed through the first trees.

Garret moved to the spot and brushed the branches away with a sweep of his left foot, revealing a slight depression about six feet in diameter. The young man reached down, wrapped his right hand around an oblong ring, and grunted as he lifted up a wooden hatch. "I'll go down first. Hand down your backpack when I signal. I'll stow it below, then come back for you."

Before Baumberger could say anything, Garret disappeared into the hole.

Almost a minute passed before Garret's head appeared just below the hole. "I'll take the backpack now. Just drop it to me."

Baumberger did as he was told.

Another minute, and Garret was back. He placed a hand atop the edge of the hole. "Sit down here and drape your legs over. You'll have to slide. I'll catch hold and guide you down." Garret was holding a flashlight pointed downward, which minimized Baumberger's trepidation. At least he wouldn't be sliding down into total darkness.

When he reached firm ground, Garret released the grip under his armpits. He allowed himself to breathe again. Garret placed the light on a small boulder and clambered back up to reclose the entrance. The flashlight revealed a very small tunnel with two wooden rails heading into the blackness.

"Three foot by three foot," Garret said as he slid back down. "In most places."

He picked up one of two thick ropes stretching into the tunnel and started pulling.

In the dim light reflected back from the tunnel's earth walls, Baumberger could see a wooden wheel mounted into the rocks behind them. The two ropes were clearly one, rotating around the wheel.

After almost an hour of Garret pulling and grunting, first one, then a second flat, wheeled board appeared.

"Our transportation," Garret said, motioning to the farther board. "These two sleds are linked by a short rope. You get in the first one, and I'll control our progress. There is a slight, persistent downward slope for the mile to our destination. Keep your head flat against the sled, as the rope will be traveling in two directions about a foot above you."

Baumberger sat down on the sled, swung his legs around to rest near the far edge, shot a quick look back at Garret, already in position, then lowered his head.

The sled moved off with a jolt.

"Seventeen minutes," Garret said as they drifted to a stop. "Not a world record, but definitely not shabby."

He helped Baumberger stand upright. The ceiling, all earth and rock, was at least ten feet high. Now Baumberger could breathe freely.

"Okay, Doctor. We've arrived and must now climb into ol' Friendship City."

Garret took the backpack while Baumberger, his feet shaking, climbed a wooden ladder as the younger man offered reassurances. Baumberger counted seventy-two rungs. He hoped he would never have to descend this rickety ladder into this dank, dark hole.

"Pull down on that rope off to your right. It activates a gear on the other side."

Baumberger obeyed. A large square of the metal over his head lifted up.

"We have arrived."

Baumberger climbed rungs seventy-three through seventy-nine and stepped into what looked like a basement.

Garret confirmed his guess. "The basement to your house while here in the city."

They climbed the stairs to the first floor.

Garret placed the backpack on the kitchen table. "You're all set up for tonight. Tomorrow, someone will pick you up at 8:15 in the morning—"

"Someone? Not you?"

Garret shook his head. "Mr. Ishmael thinks I've become too visible. You'll be picked up by a man posing as a Friendship City police lieutenant. He'll drop you off at the medical center around 8:50. A male nurse will take you up to the floor where Sandra Garvey's room is located. I was told that Ishmael gave you detailed instructions."

Baumberger nodded.

Garret left.

Baumberger reached into the backpack and pulled out the large manila folder Ishmael had rushed to him the day before with detailed instructions as to how the contents were to be used. He ripped open the top of the envelope and dumped most of the contents onto the table. There were six pictures, each with a number written on the back: the first, a young Sandra with her mother and father, followed by two of an older Sandra with her mother in the kitchen, cooking; one of her father, Nick, in police uniform; finally, two of Sandra roughhousing with her beloved uncle Joey.

Uncle Joey would be the key to tomorrow. Sandra had apparently misplaced her memory of that event. The pictures would hopefully restore that past to her.

Failing Sandra remembering and reviving her hatred of Nick, there was the last item in the envelope to be used as a last resort. He shook the envelope. A kitchen carving knife in a clear plastic bag fell out.

The knife had Nick Garvey's fingerprints on it.

63

$\diamond$

Owen looked left, then right, before allowing even a hint of a smile. He was alone in the CDC lab.

The chemical formula retrieved from the carved eagle was a pointer in the right direction. The plague could be stopped. He wanted to call President Allison right then, but she had insisted he use only encrypted communications. He would have to wait until he got back to the apartment.

He poured bleach into the three beakers he had used, then rinsed them and returned them to their shelf. No handwritten notes had to be shredded nor any computer files erased. He had a photographic memory and would record the immunization steps on the device the president had provided and give it to her in the morning.

Owen double-checked every slide and the one microscope he had used and wiped them clean a second time. Satisfied that all traces of his progress had been accounted for, he pulled on his overcoat and left the lab, locking the door behind him.

What Owen couldn't know was that locking the door activated the small transmitter embedded in the microscope, capable of storing and forwarding up to six hours of video and audio.

6 4

◆

Ishmael stabbed the off button on his cell phone. His technician at the CDC lab had informed him that less than an hour ago, Owen Pendleton had completed an experiment that appeared to neutralize the plague sample the team had been working on for over a week.

Ishmael pushed back in his chair. Seven of his scientists, including Dr. Horatio Baumberger, had assured him that the ability of the plague molecules to morph whenever attacked would preclude any controlled destruction for years. He shook his head. *So much for self-assured scientific advisers.*

Time to expedite.

Ishmael punched in Garret's cell number. "Take the protective antidote tonight. Tell Lutz. On Friday the tenth, the plague will be released. Per our previous discussions, we will have assembled a special audience, two of which will be your responsibility."

He next called his White House insider.

"I'm moving up your schedule to tomorrow. A limousine will be at the gate between noon and 12:30. Make sure President Allison gets in and rides off. Take the antidote tonight."

Next, Ishmael returned his CDC technician's call.

"Tomorrow morning, you are to keep tabs on Owen Pendleton before he leaves his apartment. I'll have a limousine at your disposal. You will contact them when Pendleton goes for his morning walk using the number I'll send in a few minutes. The antidote should be taken tonight."

One more call.

"Donovan, I have your first assignment. Be ready at ten in the morning. A limousine will pick you up." Ishmael terminated the call.

Satisfied the accelerated schedule was off to a good start, he reached to take his own antidote.

6 5

◆

Owen's clock over the kitchen sink read 8:12 a.m. On last night's encrypted call, President Allison had said a limousine would pick him and the electronic notepad up at 8:30. There would be no normal morning walk today. He smiled.

No long walk. Maybe just a ten-minute walk.

He stepped out of the complex at 8:17. Looking to his right, he figured he could walk the block and three-quarters to the main cross street and back with a couple of minutes to spare.

Owen started off. He reminded himself that even though he was far from being in his twenties, half that speed at his age wasn't bad. When he got to the cross street, he checked his watch. 8:22.

Not bad by a long shot.

He turned and was surprised to see the limousine pulling up to the curb. A uniformed man stepped out from the passenger side and opened the rear door. Owen waved, walked over, and climbed in. He never noticed a second limousine pull up in front of his apartment building.

66

---◆---

D ropped off at the Valley Regional Medical Center at 8:49 a.m., Dr. Horatio Baumberger nodded to the police lieutenant, who had talked nonstop during the trip—mostly bragging about his exploits in Friendship City—and stepped out of the sedan and into the hospital. He was met in the lobby by a male nurse, escorted to the elevators, taken to the neurology floor, and told that visitor hours did not start until 9:30, another half hour.

The nurse ushered him into a vacant room, then left, returning with a white doctor's coat.

Baumberger took off his jacket and slipped into the coat, attaching the hospital name tag handed to him. He pulled the pictures and knife from his jacket and placed them in the coat's deep pocket. The nurse handed him a stethoscope, which he hung around his neck. Then he guided Baumberger down the hall, pointing as they passed Sandra's room. They continued to a desk two rooms down, where the nurse checked Sandra's chart and schedule of medical visits.

"All clear for at least the next forty minutes."

Sandra was seated in the cushioned chair on the far side of her bed. Wrapped in a blanket, she looked awake but not yet alert.

"Hello, Sandra," the nurse said. "Dr. Charles Johnson has requested additional memory tests be performed. Dr. Baumberger here will be checking specific sections of your recollection. He'll feed his assessments back to Dr. Johnson."

Sandra's eyes blinked shut for at least two seconds.

"I'll try to be quick," Baumberger assured her.

Sandra shrugged. "Okay."

The nurse left and closed the door.

As he passed the foot of the bed, Baumberger grabbed a second chair, hardback, and pulled it around to face Sandra. He took the pictures from his pocket and sat.

Sandra just watched.

Making sure he had the pictures in sequence, he pulled out number one and extended it across to her.

Sandra frowned and reached out slowly. She studied the picture for several seconds, then looked up at Baumberger with a questioning expression.

"You were almost two years of age," he said. "Those are your parents, Judith and Nicholas, each holding up one of your arms as you walk into the living room of your home."

Sandra shrugged a second time and returned the picture.

He handed her the two pictures of her with her mother. "I think you were about six in the picture where you are helping your mother put cookie dough on the tray. In the other one, maybe almost nine, helping your mom put stuffing in that turkey."

He saw no reaction other than a slight pursing of the lips. He retrieved the two pictures and handed her the photo of Nick Garvey in his police uniform with new sergeant stripes. She glanced at it and returned it quickly, before he could tell her it was her dad.

When he passed over the two pictures of her with Uncle Joey, he noticed the beginnings of a smile. He reached over and pointed at the one in her left hand. "Playing a board game while arm wrestling at the same time, maybe the same day you helped bake the cookies."

The smile broadened a bit.

He pointed to the picture in her right hand. "Playing catch with Uncle Joey."

Sandra clasped both photographs to her chest.

"Was that in your backyard? Or were you throwing to your uncle in some park?"

She shook her head. "Backyard."

"You loved Uncle Joey, didn't you?"

Sandra nodded.

Although he couldn't see any tears, he watched her wipe her eyes with the back of her right hand while still holding the baseball picture. A faint triple knock rapped on the door. He had five minutes to wrap up.

"Whatever happened to Uncle Joey?" he asked.

Sandra again held the two photographs tight to her chest. Her smile was gone, her lips sucked inward. She didn't answer.

"Is he still alive? I've heard that he isn't. That he died a long time ago, shortly after that game of catch." He pointed to the picture she held close.

Sandra shuddered. "He was shot."

Baumberger waited until she was looking at him, then shook his head. "I was told that he was stabbed."

Sandra shook her head, a defiant look in her eyes. "Shot."

"Stabbed." He held up the bag-wrapped knife, turning it so she could see it. "The New York Police Department had this in their evidence lockers." He pointed at the handle. "It's a kitchen knife with your dad's fingerprints on it." Baumberger made sure Sandra was staring at the knife. He pointed at the blade, his finger resting against some light-brown smudges. "Lab tests"—he pulled out a folded paper—"document that these discolorations are dried blood." He paused, letting his words sink in. "Your uncle's dried blood." He watched the veins in her neck pulse. Mission almost accomplished. "Uncle Joey's blood on the blade. Dad's fingerprints on the handle."

Sandra's eyes looked like they were on fire.

Baumberger dropped the bagged knife onto her lap. He was about to congratulate himself on a job well done when the nurse burst into the room. The young man was waving his arms above his head in wide arcs. "We have to evacuate! Bomb discovered. Now!"

Baumberger checked his watch. *Right on time.*

He tapped Sandra on the shoulder and gestured toward the door with his head. "We have to go. Hold on to the pictures and the knife. I'll help you up."

Sandra, a confused look on her face, put everything in her left hand, grabbed her blanket with her right, and strained to get up. Baumberger reached over and steadied her.

The nurse guided them out and motioned toward an exit sign.

Before they could take a step, a voice behind them shrieked, "Where are you taking my mommy?"

Baumberger turned. He recognized Sandra's daughter, Nicole, and two boys, from photos shown to him.

"Is my mommy okay?"

The nurse approached the three children. "There is a bomb threat. We have to evacuate."

"No way," said the younger of the two boys. "Not in the lobby. They wouldn't have let us come up early."

Baumberger sensed the plan falling apart, especially when he saw a female nurse come from behind the counter. She stopped beside the three youngsters and held a hand to her ear, mimicking receiving a phone call. "The alert just came through. We all have to get out."

"What about the other patients?" the older Hispanic boy asked.

"More nurses are coming to help me move them out." She motioned to Baumberger. "Follow the doctor, and he will lead you to safety."

He returned the nurse's gesture with a thin thank-you smile.

Baumberger marched to the stairwell door and opened it. "Quickly," he said, then pulled the door closed and led them down to the hospital's rear entrance and into the waiting limousine.

67

---◆---

I t was 9:00 a.m., and President Allison was ready to start her staff meeting when a chief of staff assistant motioned to come in. President Allison waved permission. The assistant handed her a folded note. She opened the note, and with each word, she felt a shudder.

"Something's wrong," Vice President Carter said. "What is it?"

President Allison motioned for the assistant to leave. "Owen Pendleton missed his scheduled pickup and isn't in his apartment."

"What scheduled pickup?" asked Serena Clayborn, HHS secretary.

"He had discovered a disruptor to the plague. He phoned me last night, and I told him I would have him picked up with his data and brought here. He was to be picked up..." President Allison glanced at her watch. "Thirty-two minutes ago."

"Did he transmit any data?" Clayborn asked.

"No. I ordered him not to. I'll have to go down and lead the search."

Carter shook his head. "I'll go. If he's been taken by anyone, it's not safe for you to be down in Dallas."

"I appreciate your offer, but he has complete trust in me, and I know his hideouts on the slight chance he's in hiding."

Carter's jaw clenched tight for a moment. "I request that you wear the in-your-shoe location device I gave you yesterday. That way, if you go missing as well, we'll know your last position."

"I'll wear the device."

"I still would prefer you allow me to go in your stead. If Owen isn't hiding and was captured, whoever tries to find him could also be captured."

"Again, I appreciate your offer, but I'll have Secret Service protecting me."

Carter shook his head. "Remember how that worked out for my predecessor and the four men protecting him. We all know how that turned out."

The president felt she had contained the fleeting wince, but Vice President Carter's raised eyebrow look told her otherwise. "I'll wear your device. You'll keep tabs on me. I'll have my men report to you every half hour after landing in Dallas."

Carter shrugged and shook his head.

President Allison stood. "Obviously, there's nothing more important than finding Owen and his data. The staff meeting is over."

*****

Air Force One touched down at Dallas–Fort Worth International at exactly 11:00 a.m. Dallas time. President Allison clicked her watch, shifting its display back from noon, DC time.

Two of the six Secret Service agents guarding the president were the first to descend the wheeled-up stairway. Upon reaching the bottom, they dismissed the runway personnel, then moved quickly across the sixty yards to the hangar door. They opened it, went inside, and after three minutes, waved for the next two agents to descend and stand at the bottom while they scouted around the sides of the hangar.

The middle two agents reached the pavement and took positions halfway to the hangar. After another minute, the first two agents returned to the front of the hangar, each giving a thumbs-up signal.

President Allison descended the stairway two steps behind the last two agents. The jet's exit door closed.

When all three were down on the tarmac, the two agents turned and gave the president a quick salute. When the two agents turned back, automatic gunfire erupted. The two agents closest to the president fell immediately. President Allison looked up and saw gunfire blasting from atop the hangar. Before they could react, the two agents stationed midway to the hangar were taken out. At least a dozen men rushed out through the hangar door, rifles blazing. The first two agents fell before getting off a single shot.

Engine roars off to her right caught the president's attention. Two black sedans were speeding toward her. The fact that she was still standing and had not been hit told her the killers had other plans for her. She gritted her teeth. She would stand her ground, as long as there was ground on which to stand.

The two sedans pulled to a stop, the nearer less than ten feet away. The rear driver's side door opened.

Whatever awaits, she told herself, *don't give them the satisfaction of flinching.*

President Allison stepped in and pulled the door closed.

Both sedans roared off.

6 8

◆

Nick was halfway through a very late breakfast when McKenna rushed in through the front door. "Your daughter has been kidnapped."

"What? Are you sure?"

"Daniel just called me. Said Warren was outside the back of the hospital this morning and saw several men push her into a black sedan. He said Warren saw Nicole, Nathan, and Half-Penny also shoved into the car."

Nick froze for a moment, not knowing if he should charge out the door or get his pistol. "Where is Warren now? Did he follow them? Did he—"

"He's in the hospital himself: intensive care. He was shot. Daniel said the doctors told him that Warren will probably survive." McKenna shook his head. "Probably," he snarled.

Nick went to the breakfront, unlocked the center drawer, and pulled out his Glock. McKenna grabbed his keys.

Twenty seconds later, they peeled off to the hospital. McKenna kept his careening around corners down to no more than five out of every six. Seven miles in nine minutes. Nick didn't feel even Henry and his Dart could have done much better.

Daniel was waiting in the back, requested by Nick's en route call. "Warren is on the operating table," he said, his breathing heavy. "Doc said he has an excellent chance."

Before Nick could even utter the words, Daniel answered the question he must have seen in his eyes.

"Warren told me as they were taking him inside that your daughter and the three others were not visibly harmed. 'Visibly' was his word choice." Pointing, he continued, "The limo turned right, leaving the lot."

"What's down that way?"

"Matamoros," Daniel said. "Sorry. The part of Friendship City that was Matamoros."

"No problem," Nick said. "Hop in."

McKenna sped to the end of the parking lot and ripped a right. Nick's cell rang. "Yes?"

He didn't recognize the voice until just before the speaker introduced himself. "Am I speaking to Nicholas Garvey?"

"Yes," Nick said as he flipped the cell to speaker mode and waved McKenna to pull over, which he did, leaving the motor running.

"Vice President Carter Johnson here. We just received notification that President Allison has been kidnapped and multiple Secret Service agents shot. The FBI—"

"Where did this happen?" Nick interrupted.

"Dallas. Love Field, to be exact."

"How long ago?"

"Within the last ninety minutes."

"Who notified you?"

"One of the agents who'd been shot. He described the van the president was forced into. We called medics in immediately."

"Have you traced the van yet?"

"Police found it on the tarmac of Love Field. The plane she was witnessed being forced into had a scheduled landing in Dallas–Fort Worth International. That landing was confirmed. The mechanic at Love Field who saw what happened said a bunch of people were hustled out of the van and into a small jet, which took off within two minutes."

"Has there been any sighting of the plane's path?"

"None. The mechanic thinks it went directly off a runway, which he said headed to the south. I sure wish the systems we had thirty years ago were still operational. We'd know exactly where it was every moment."

Nick bit his lower lip. "Did the plane bank or turn after taking off?"

"Just a moment. I have the mechanic still on the line."

Nick heard his question repeated.

"Straight line until disappearing over the horizon."

Daniel nudged Nick's shoulder and whispered in his ear.

Nick nodded. "Was the runway the only long one that cuts across the others and points almost due south?"

Again the question was repeated.

"That's the one."

"Keep me informed of any updates."

"Will do." Vice President Johnson paused for an instant. "Is everything okay on your end?"

"No, sir. My daughter has been kidnapped from the hospital, along with my granddaughter and three others from my household."

The noise he heard over the phone sounded like Carter Johnson grinding his teeth. "I'll definitely keep you informed of any changes. And you keep me informed of any updates on your end."

"Agreed," Nick said, then hung up.

"Where to?" McKenna asked.

Nick looked back at Daniel. "My guess is there's an airport in Matamoros."

"Matamoros International. Abandoned for the last twenty or so years."

"Are the runways still in reasonable shape for a jet to land?"

"I've never been there but have been told they were in excellent shape twenty years ago."

Nick decided their destination. "Matamoros International."

*****

McKenna eased off the gas pedal and turned left off Route 101 and onto the road heading to the airport. The road itself was in reasonable shape, though littered with rocks, sheets of plywood, and twisted pieces of metal that looked like old rain gutters. McKenna eased the car around, in and out, or over each item.

The main airport building resided just beyond a rectangular parking lot blocked by more plywood sheets and discarded lumber. Nick motioned McKenna to make a left toward some service trailers and small buildings.

The road split as they approached the trailers, most of them rusted and falling apart. To the right, they could see the runway five hundred yards ahead. Halfway, Nick saw the rear portion of a jet beyond the old terminal building. He nudged McKenna to slow down.

They passed a maintenance building on their left. The road made a right turn just after, approaching the back side of the terminal. McKenna paused. The jet was now fully visible, no movement of any kind to be seen. What caught Nick's attention was the limousine Warren had described to Daniel.

Daniel was already pointing. "That's it! That's the car!"

Before Nick could suggest any course of action, six men carrying automatic rifles exited the terminal and pointed their weapons at McKenna's car.

McKenna's first reaction to speed away backward proved fruitless as two semitrucks emerged from the maintenance building. The first headed in their direction, the second parked astride the road they had just traveled, blocking any attempt to escape.

The first semi pulled up right behind their car. Two armed men stepped down and walked to the front doors on either side.

The man on Nick's side tapped his window. Nick lowered the glass.

"We missed you," the man said. He wore an armored vest and the biggest smirk Nick could remember having encountered. "One of our vans stopped by his house," the smartass said, pointing across at McKenna, "but no one was there." He motioned for the three of them to get out of the car and head to the terminal, where the six men with rifles awaited.

Nick took the lead.

The six men surrounded Nick, McKenna, and Daniel. The two who had ordered them out of the car walked up to a large, shuttered door. Nick watched as Mr. Smirk-Face entered a six-digit code. There was a noticeable click, and the door came open from the inside. The six men pushed Nick and the other two forward.

Inside, another eight men with automatic rifles guarded several prisoners. The first familiar face Nick spotted was that of President Allison. Next, Owen Pendleton. He looked around, trying to find Sandra. He didn't see Nicole, Half-Penny, Nathan, or Julia Ramirez. He began to wonder if he'd made some kind of mistake.

"She's over there." Another grinning man pointed around a partition.

Nick followed the man's finger and found Sandra, still alive. *For how long?* he wondered.

Two more armed men stood guard to assure Sandra and the other captives seated in a small circle next to her remained in their assigned places.

They all looked in reasonable condition: no bruises, no cuts, no blood.

Yet.

6 9

◆

Nick looked sideways at his still-smiling armed guide. The man nodded that Nick could approach his daughter, pointing with the rifle tip to the point where he could stand and no closer. Nick counted off his steps. Seven. Too many to spin around and disarm the grinning thug.

"Are you okay?" He bent forward as far as he could without stepping closer.

Sandra nodded. "A bad doctor kidnapped me and the others."

He remembered Daniel passing along a nurse's aide's description of a tall, stocky man with a coat as white as his hair.

Sandra held out a handful of pictures. "He gave me these pictures. I didn't remember Uncle Joey until I looked at them."

Nick glanced over at the thug, who nodded he could take the items. Nick accepted them. Family pictures. The two of Uncle Joey suggested the message the bad doctor had given his daughter.

Sandra's breathing became labored. "He told me that Uncle Joey is dead and that you stabbed him." She swallowed. "I remembered he'd been shot, and I told him so. He dropped a knife in my lap." She opened the folds in her coat, revealing a knife with blood on the blade. "Said it has your fingerprints on it." Her eyes welled up with one single question: "You didn't stab Uncle Joey, did you?"

He managed to shake his head "no" as the thug waved him backward with a flick of his rifle. "Can I just check on my granddaughter?" Nick pointed at Nicole. "Thank you," he said after the permissive rifle wave. He took only two steps, making sure he kept the same distance as from Sandra. He looked at Nicole first.

"Is Mommy okay, Grandpa?"

Nick nodded.

"She looks very sad."

Nick nodded again, then looked at Julia. He watched her take a deep breath.

"The kids are all okay. I told them we're all being held hostage and that we'll be released when the ransom money is paid."

Nick glimpsed Half-Penny rolling his eyes. Nathan's frown suggested he had his doubts as well.

Another wave of the rifle forced Nick to turn away from Sandra and the others and head back to Owen and the president. Two other thugs took over. Neither showed a trace of a smile. They motioned him to sit on one of three chalked X marks, each the size of a human head. He complied. He was facing both President Allison and Owen.

"We meet again at gunpoint," the president said. "It definitely does not strike me as a friendly get-together."

Nick agreed.

"Did any of my agents survive?"

"One that I know of," Nick said.

President Allison frowned and shot a look of hatred at the nearest rifle-wielder.

Nick turned to Owen. "Find the answer?"

Owen shook his head. "Yes and no. Yes, I found the solution. No, I don't have it anymore. I put the details on the pocket device that was taken from me."

Before he could ask any more questions, four riflemen approached the steel entrance door in response to six beeps. Two of the men pulled the door open after waiting for a loud click. The four riflemen stepped aside as two tall men entered.

Nick had to twist a bit to his left to see them in detail. The first was a smidge or two over six feet with a lean-but-muscular frame. The second man, tall with a light beard, was—*Jeremiah! Or Ishmael.* Nick noticed that President Allison recognized him. She had seen many photographs of Jeremiah in connection to the hunt for Ishmael, so Nick figured she wouldn't be surprised to see him.

Two men removed the partition shielding Sandra and the others from view.

"Good afternoon, everyone," Ishmael said. "Looks like we're all here."

Looking at Ishmael, Nick guessed where all the rifle thugs had found the pattern for their ugly smiles.

Ishmael paused for a moment, looking at the group. "Correction," he said. "It looks like we are *almost* all here." Ishmael waved his left hand at the other man. "I would like you to meet Bart Donovan."

Nick noticed only the trace of a smile on Mr. Donovan's face.

"Bart Donovan," Ishmael said, waving his right hand at all those sitting on the floor, "will be joining all of you."

Donovan's trace of a smile vanished.

Ishmael took a step forward. He motioned to Donovan. "Have a seat, Bart, on one of these two vacant chalk marks."

Donovan shrugged, took a deep breath, and sat to the right of Nick between him and Owen.

Nick looked at the floor to his left, then up at the smiling Ishmael. *Still one more X to be filled.*

70

———◆———

Nick looked at the newcomer. He sat still without moving or glancing in any direction. Nick noticed both hands were clenched into white-knuckled fists. He checked farther to his right and saw President Allison trying, unsuccessfully, to avoid glancing at newcomer Donovan. Then he looked up as Ishmael conferred with several of his armed, smirking minions.

After a few seconds, Ishmael gave a "whatever" tilt of the head, then turned and walked toward the squatting group. "Seems we'll be delayed a few more minutes," he said. "I was hoping to include everyone as I described your collective future."

President Allison gave a sarcastic laugh. "Maybe you should tell us about *your* future," she said, her voice laced with venom. "Assuming you have one."

Ishmael chuckled. "I will definitely have a future." He took one step toward the president. "Longer than all of yours put together."

His step toward the president didn't bring him near enough for Nick to attack, but it did reveal to Nick that Jeremiah had a Glock tucked in his waistband on the side nearest him.

"So tell me, Jeremiah Burner, what does your future hold?" Nick asked, deciding to drop the Ishmael crap.

A second chuckle. "Congratulations. You know my full name. Puts us on an equal footing."

Nick chuckled back. "Next to yours is not quite where I'd like to put my foot."

Jeremiah wagged a finger at him. "Don't be too colorful, Nicholas. Remember"—pointing the finger at the three youngsters—"there are children present."

Nick offered a "You've got me there" tilt of his head as he noted the locations of all the minions. He had no doubt that if these pieces of crap weren't taken down, he and the others, children included, wouldn't make it through the day. He counted six thugs plus Jeremiah. Two thugs appeared to follow Jeremiah's every move. The others continually scanned the room, as he would have expected.

"Seriously, Jeremiah," Nick said, returning his focus. "What do you hope to achieve? Jason Beck is dead, and so is the World Council."

"Wrong on both counts. The World Council is limping along at the moment, but I will help bring it back to full strength." Jeremiah paused as a sneer formed across his mouth. "As for Jason Beck being dead…" Jeremiah shook his head. "You and President Allison know how untrue that is. You both think he's in a sanatorium in upstate New York." He paused again, the sneer turning to a satisfied smile. "Jason Beck is not dead. I'll always remember him. He was my mentor, my role model, my guiding light."

President Allison didn't give Nick time to respond. "Make that 'blinding light.' Blinding you to everything decent and worthwhile in the world."

Jeremiah took one step toward President Allison, then stopped. He shot her a condescending smile. "You started this Friendship City thing where there is no guiding light, no proven principles of workable government, no adherence to established law. It was Jason Beck's goal—and mine—to demonstrate how mistakes like this will be the first to implode."

The two minions just inside the door turned and pulled it open.

"We should now be completing our guest list," Jeremiah said, his satisfied smile broadening.

71

---◆---

A woman entered. Nick immediately recognized Elise Carpenter.

Three steps behind strode Garret, the uniformed man from the airport who had led him to Friendship City, with a revolver in his right hand.

Jeremiah turned to face the door. "Felicia!" he said in an announcer's voice. "Felicia, dear sister. Welcome!"

It was obvious to Nick that Elise did not welcome being referred to as Jeremiah's sister.

She walked halfway to Jeremiah, then stopped. "Since when have you given even one thought about family?" she said with obvious hostility.

"Dear sister, I always give thoughts about family."

Elise heaved a sigh. "I stand corrected. Make that even one *positive* thought about family."

Jeremiah extended his hands as if calling for a spotlight. "I've always had positive thoughts about family."

"Like the time you killed our father?"

Nick looked around. The whole sitting group was wide-eyed, as if expecting an explosion. He glanced at the rifle thugs who were still in position, looking bored.

"That was a very positive thing I did. He was about to sabotage a world-changing medical experiment, at least two of the seven deadly sins."

Elise gave a derisive laugh. "That same world-changing medical experiment that you plan to loosen onto the world and then watch as millions die?" She took one short step forward and glared at Jeremiah. "I would normally say 'Spare me,' but I know that isn't in today's plan. You don't plan to spare anybody."

Nick caught a look of indecision crossing Jeremiah's face, as if he was mulling plan A versus plan B.

He nodded to himself and sneered at Elise. "You were always the perceptive one." He motioned to Garret. "Bring her here," he said, pointing down at the remaining X on the floor.

Garret nudged Elise forward. She stood fast.

Nick sensed it was time. For what, he didn't know.

Jeremiah gave Garret a closed fist bring-her-here-*now* motion. Garret placed his left hand on Elise's left shoulder and shoved her forward.

What happened next happened in a flash, but it seemed like slow motion to Nick. Garret was still pushing Elise, whose right toe seemed to catch on the concrete floor. She pitched forward as her right knee buckled. Garret reached under Elise's left arm to keep her from falling. Elise's right arm went to the side of her face as she fell, pulling Garret off balance. As her right knee hit the floor, she twisted up to her left with something glistening in her right hand.

Nick recognized her earring.

Garret's chin jerked upward as Elise's right hand swept across his neck. Blood spurted out from Garret's throat. From the corner of his eye, Nick saw Jeremiah pull the gun from his waistband. Elise grabbed Garret's revolver, collapsed to the floor facing Jeremiah, and fired one shot. Jeremiah sank to his knees and fell backward, his pistol clattering to the floor.

Nick jumped to the gun as Elise fired three more shots to the door guards' foreheads. A fourth guard raised his rifle and pointed it at Elise. Nick matched Elise's forehead accuracy.

Donovan charged the nearest dead guard, retrieved his rifle, and took down the remaining two thugs, suffering a bullet in the shoulder for his effort.

Nick looked at the three youngsters. Half-Penny was shielding Nicole and Nathan. Nicole was wide-eyed; Nathan pumped his right fist repeatedly with the thumb way up.

President Allison was already standing and helping Owen up. McKenna and Daniel rose, relieved looks on their faces. Nick glanced at Jeremiah and saw that he was dead. Then he crossed to check on Julia and the kids. Donovan, McKenna, and Daniel went about retrieving each guard's rifle, then checking for any signs of life. They returned with the six rifles.

"All dead," McKenna said.

President Allison told Donovan to sit down on one of the three chairs. "You've been shot. It may not be in our contract that I provide first aid, but I deem it appropriate."

"Thanks." Donovan winced.

Nick motioned the group together. "We still have fifty-plus killers waiting outside for Jeremiah to emerge with victory written across his face." He motioned President Allison to join Julia and the kids and to shield them from whatever happened.

The two women herded the youngsters behind the partition in the back.

Nick turned to Owen. "You too," he said. "You have the secret we need to protect above all."

Nick, McKenna, Daniel, and a still-wincing Donovan walked quietly to the door. They knew that without windows, they would be forced to come out shooting.

Nick checked each man. All nodded their readiness. He reached for the door's lever.

Shots, twenty or thirty, caught their attention, the bullets hitting the door, followed by even more. After a slight pause, another round of shots rang out with more dents showing in the door.

7 2

◆

Nick waved the other three men back to where they would each have an angle to pick off many of the killers who made it through. He didn't give them any chance of surviving, but he knew each would take out every killer who entered right up to their own last breath.

The shooting stopped.

Nick and the others braced themselves. The door lever completed its rotation. Nick checked the group behind him. They too were ready to face eternity.

The door cracked open. Barely. A pole with a white handkerchief poked through. Nick waved the others not to respond. After almost half a minute, a second pole poked in. A marine camouflage jacket hung from the end. Knotted through a buttonhole was a cord holding a cell phone.

Nick walked to the jacket, pulled out his knife, and cut the cord. He stepped back and pressed the home button. A close-up of their bullet-dented door popped onto the screen. There were slight vibrations, which indicated to Nick it was a handheld view.

"Sorry," came out from the phone's speaker. "Got it backward." The image flipped. The face of Vice President Carter Johnson snapped into view. "To whom am I—" A broad but uncertain smile crossed Carter's face. "Nick Garvey! Are you okay? Are you in control in there?"

"Yes. In control here. Finally. You? Can you scan around? Just want to be sure."

"No problem," Carter said and slowly rotated the phone, varying the view elevation as required. Nick was able to see a huge contingent of military, the closest a man without a jacket, and a great number of dead scattered on the ground. The panned shot ended up focused on the outside of the door, where splatters of blood shared real estate with the bullet dents.

Nick grabbed the lever and pulled the door on his side open, then turned and gave everyone a giant "okay" wave.

Carter Johnson was the first through the door, followed by at least thirty marines.

Nick held out the camouflage jacket to its owner, who thanked him.

President Allison shook Carter Johnson's hand. "Damn good job, Carter," she said. "I knew I made the right pick."

Carter chuckled.

Six or seven medical personnel entered and headed toward Julia and the youngsters. Nick directed one to Donovan, who was sitting on a box. McKenna and Daniel appeared at Nick's side and gave him hearty shoulder pats.

"One hell of a day," McKenna said.

Daniel just smiled said "Thanks," and walked outside into the afternoon sun.

Nick waited as each of the other former prisoners pulled themselves up and went outside.

When Nicole approached, he smiled at her, reached down and took her hand, and started to lead her outside. She held tight, then paused for a moment and reached to grab Sandra's hand.

"I told you we would make it, Mommy," she said.

Sandra nodded and smiled. Nick hoped he was included.

President Allison and Carter Johnson stood beside a crusty old Jeep, gesturing at a clipboard Carter held. Two marines brought Owen to them. The three of them talked for about a minute before President Allison looked over at Nick and motioned him to join them.

"Owen said he can gather all the chemicals he needs to disable the plague from the hospital," the president said, pointing at the map on the clipboard.

"I checked with my brother," Carter said. "He's pretty sure Valley Regional has whatever Owen needs."

"I assume you want me to get Owen to the hospital," Nick said, casting a concerned eye in Sandra's direction. "I plan to take Sandra back to have your brother check her over."

"Good," President Allison said. "Carter's crew caught Baumberger trying to climb down into one of the tunnels. We'll be interrogating him to try and locate any and all plague containers in Friendship City."

"And outside of Friendship City," Carter added.

A limousine pulled up. Nick got his full crew: Nicole, Sandra, Nathan, Half-Penny, and Julia into the back. He eased into the one empty middle seat while Donovan was tucked into the front passenger seat. Everyone clicked their belts, and they were off.

Nick was somewhat relieved the driver was not Henry swinging wild three-sixties in a 1969 green Dart.

73

---◆---

D
r. Horatio Baumberger was shoved to a straight-backed wooden chair. President Allison motioned for him to sit. A Secret Service agent cuffed his hands to the chair's vertical spines.

McKenna and Daniel were requested to watch from behind an observation window.

President Allison stepped right up to Baumberger. "We have a few questions to which I am sure you have the answers. How forthcoming and productive your answers are will determine whether you're able to leave under your own power."

Baumberger's Adam's apple bounced up and down.

The president smiled. "Don't get too worked up. Yet." She glanced at Carter Johnson, who was glaring at the seated doctor, then turned her attention back to Baumberger. "Give us the location of any and all containers of the plague in Friendship City."

Baumberger squirmed. "I have no idea where they are. I think Garret Marshal knows where both are, though."

"Not much help since Garret Marshal is dead. How did you know him?"

"He brought me through the tunnel into Friendship City."

"Why do you think he knew where—you said 'both'—containers were located?" The president's smile was gone, her teeth now clenched.

Baumberger flinched at the change in her expression. "While we were driving, he told me Peter Meddleson had attached a small transmitter to each of the two containers. Said they shot out a five-second string of clicks every five minutes and…" Baumberger shuddered.

"And what?" the president snarled, leaning in almost nose to nose.

She had to wait while Baumberger weathered three convulsive breaths.

"He told me he'd removed the two transmitters and turned them over to someone else."

"And who would that be?"

Baumberger shook his head. "I don't know his name. All I know is that he's wearing the uniform of a city police lieutenant. He took me to the hospital when…when we picked up the girl."

"Does he know where the containers are?"

"Yes. Said he had Marshal retrieve them so Meddleson couldn't find where the canisters had been stored. He was called to the portal to vouch for Meddleson. He chuckled when he described Meddleson's expression when he dropped the transmitters in his hand. That was last Saturday, the day all those fistfights broke out."

"What time on Saturday did this lieutenant meet Meddleson at the portal?"

"He didn't say. I assumed it was before the fights."

President Allison watched Baumberger turn as if afraid she would punch him. His reaction, she concluded, indicated he was telling the truth.

Carter Johnson stepped in closer to Baumberger. "Did he say anything about similar transmitters being attached to containers outside Friendship City?"

President Allison gave a "good question" nod.

Baumberger took two more slow breaths. "Not in so many words."

"In *what* words?" Carter asked, stomping a foot.

"Not in any words. He gestured, waving both hands in a circle over his head. I took it to mean there were transmitters with each container." Baumberger's shoulders sagged, and his head tilted down.

President Allison placed her right hand under Baumberger's chin and raised it up so he was looking straight at her, eye to eye—

one set blinking, the other glaring. "I assume you know that your future—or rather, if you have a future—depends on how truthful you're being." She released his chin so he could nod yes.

He nodded.

Carter walked out of the interrogation room with the president. "We have interesting information that leads us nowhere."

President Allison agreed.

McKenna and Daniel joined them.

"Daniel just told me about his son's science project," McKenna said. "It may help locate the two containers."

"How?" the president and Carter asked in unison.

McKenna turned to Daniel. "Tell them."

"My son built a project in his science class to detect transmissions from space. He would leave it on, and it would record transmissions for later review. Since it didn't have an expensive dish device, it also picked up local signals. Signals like remote controls opening garage doors and the like. One of the signals matches the one described by Baumberger. Five seconds of electronic pulses every five minutes. My son kept a log of all signals for a two-week period."

President Allison and Carter Johnson looked at each other, then at Daniel.

Before they could ask a question, McKenna stepped forward. "The project has been running and recording all signals for the past two months. Uninterrupted."

74

---◆---

D onovan was rushed from the limousine first. The others extracted themselves at their own pace. Nick focused on Sandra. She seemed to be handling the day's events much better than he would have imagined.

Dr. Charles Johnson met them at the front desk and guided them to the waiting area just outside his office. He took Sandra inside.

Ten minutes passed. Nick tried to stay calm. He looked across at Nicole sitting to Julia's right with Nathan and Half-Penny on her left.

Fifteen minutes.

Julia said something to Nicole, who got up and took the empty seat next to him.

"Mommy is going to be okay, Grandpa," she said, taking his hand in hers. "The doctor just has to do his job."

He gave her hand a squeeze and returned Julia's smile.

Seventeen minutes.

Dr. Johnson opened his door and walked out with Sandra. He gave everyone a thumbs-up.

Nick knew where he was needed. He told Nicole and Julia he would return as soon as possible. They knew where he had to be and assured him they would keep in touch with him about whatever the doctor said.

"Thank you both," he said, and headed for the door.

7 5

◆

Three Secret Service agents, along with Daniel Perez, brought his fourteen-year-old son, Carlos, to the science lab at Escuela Mariano Elementary in Matamoros. President Allison decided that neither of the technology experts she had brought in would touch Carlos's still rotating "Space Transmission Capture" project.

Daniel and Carlos followed the agents outside to the rear of the lab, where Carlos's project was clamped to a small but sturdy table.

Nick arrived less than a minute later, and the president briefed him.

Daniel handed off the log papers to one of the tech people as Carlos went to the counter where his machine slowly rotated.

"Is it still capturing?" the president asked.

Carlos nodded.

"When was the last time you took data?" asked the tech expert holding the log papers.

"Three weeks ago. Almost four."

"In your project proposal, you stated that you can play back up to a month of recorded data."

"That's true. I wouldn't write it down if it wasn't true."

President Allison stepped in. "We believe you. We just wanted you to reassure us that you can offload the data stream for detailed analysis. We're very impressed by your project."

Carlos blushed. "Thank you."

"Could you explain how your machine actually records transmissions?"

Carlos pointed to the four metal arms, each the size of a thermos bottle cut in half, fanning out from a vertical metal axle that slowly rotated clockwise. "I programmed the four receivers to make one complete revolution in exactly one hour. As you can see, the leading faces are concave and are the edges that capture any signals. All captured signals are recorded on the attached computer drive."

"Most impressive." President Allison encouraged Carlos to help those in the group understand how he offloaded and analyzed the captured data.

Carlos demonstrated quickly and in detail, his face beaming with excitement.

It was obvious to President Allison that Carlos was most comfortable interacting with her. "We're interested in an event from last Saturday, May fourth," she said. "Can you download all transmissions starting the day before? Say starting around noon and going right up to now?"

Carlos started typing on the keyboard he plugged into the front of his box supporting the metal axle and the four receivers. "It will take only about a minute for each day."

President Allison smiled and shook her head. "I know I'm repeating myself, but I'm definitely most impressed."

Carlos finished typing and took a step back. "It was fun reading what had been done in decades past to see if there were other civilizations on other worlds trying to contact us."

"I gather you really enjoy your science classes."

His eyes widened. "What's not to enjoy about science? Every teacher from my second grade was always excited when they talked about mathematics and science. They were also excited when they talked about history, but I couldn't *do* history. I *could do* science."

President Allison chuckled to herself, remembering her own passion for electrical engineering and the constant imagining of how it could be made to improve everyone's life.

"It's finished," Carlos said, offering the president a pair of headphones.

"Can you play it back so we can all hear?"

Carlos nodded, replaced the headphones, and threw a toggle switch. A constant low level of white noise flowed from two speakers.

President Allison pointed at the small video screen to the right of the support box. Below a digital clock showing the recorded date, hour, minute, and second, a bright yellow line was slowly sweeping clockwise about the middle of the screen. "What is that showing?"

"The position of receiver number one. That's the receiver I selected for playback. The other three are also recorded, and the data is almost identical. The numbers are on the back of each receiver."

"It shows the line starting at the bottom of the screen. Does that represent the actual position of receiver one at that time?"

Carlos nodded.

Everyone in the yard watched and listened as the yellow line continued moving and the white noise, although constant, encountered random clicks.

Daniel Perez was the first to catch the five-second sequence of clicks. "Those are the ones!"

They waited silently for the next group of clicks.

After five minutes, Carter Johnson raised both thumbs. "Ten clicks across five seconds."

President Allison agreed. She turned back to Carlos. "Can you advance the scan recording so we can hear only the next five seconds of clicks, skipping most of the signals between?"

"You want to hear if the same clicks are heard by the same receiver while it is rotating and scanning throughout a full hour?"

President Allison nodded.

Carlos keyed for about ten seconds. "I set the data file to skip from each five-second group to just before the next group."

"Fantastic!" President Allison said.

The playback of the next four series of clicks showed a very slight, but noticeable, decrease in volume from the previous set. The volume across the next set of six-click series showed a similar, very slight increase in volume as receiver number one returned to its position of one hour earlier.

"The strongest set of clicks appears to be the last," Carter Johnson said. "One before the first one we heard."

President Allison shrugged. "Let's be sure." She turned to Carlos, who was already working the keyboard. The bright yellow line on the video screen snapped to its original position, then switched counter-clockwise to the most recent set of clicks that Carter was sure was a bit louder. The yellow line twitched back and forth between the two click sets. All agreed the final set was, indeed, slightly louder than the first set.

Carlos stopped the bright yellow line at its "slightly louder" position.

President Allison turned to face where the yellow line was point-ing. "We have a direction, but not how far from Carlos's scanner." She turned back to Carlos. "Can you—"

"Move the data up to where the transmitters were brought to the north portal?"

President Allison was taken aback but nodded.

"Mr. McKenna and my dad told me about them being taken to the portal."

President Allison shook her head. *Tough to keep ahead of this young scientist*, she thought.

Carlos's fingers raced across his keyboard. "I'm setting the start point up to 9:00 a.m. last Saturday." He looked up at President Allison. "I left the quick-skip feature in. Okay?"

The president gave Carlos a smile and a nod.

The first compressed two minutes of click sets had the same intensity as the earlier sets, indicating the transmitters had not been disconnected. The intensity of the click sets remained unaltered until the clock read *05-04-2058—15:05:06*. The minutes and seconds skipped almost too quickly to sense the passage of time as the clicks became somewhat fainter, indicating the transmitters were moving away from Carlos's scanner in a northerly direction.

The clicks continued to indicate their move to the north until the clock's hours and minutes read *15:30*.

"Three-thirty in the afternoon," Carter said.

The next three click sets maintained the same intensity, then became slightly more intense.

"The transmitters have changed hands and are coming back," Nick said.

President Allison waved back her two technical experts, deciding to give Carlos first crack at determining relative locations. "We were told the exchange happened just inside the north portal. Can your scanner project where the starting point was?"

Carlos paused, then nodded. "We know how far away the US portal is and its direction. Using this information, we can project the starting distance of the transmitters. The direction is a bit more difficult, but we can do it."

"You keep saying 'we.' Do you mean you and the scanner?"

Carlos pointed past the president's shoulder. "By 'we' I mean myself and those two scientists." He nodded toward the two technical experts. "They probably have much more experience in estimating direction and distance than I have."

President Allison waved the two experts, a man and a woman, forward.

They shook hands with Carlos, and the three of them put the scanner recorder through additional back-and-forth steps, while the two experts jotted number after number into their small notebooks.

After ten minutes, they approached President Allison.

The female tech expert, Roberta, handed the president a slip of paper with two times written down. "The transmitters, if exchanged at the US portal, were handed off between 3:32 and 3:42 Saturday afternoon." She turned to her partner, Jerome, and to Carlos.

Jerome motioned the president's attention to Carlos, who handed her a Friendship City map with a red circle drawn in the lower, Matamoros, half. "We all calculated that the starting point of the transmitters is inside the circle," Carlos said.

Jerome waved a finger above the red circle. "It's the best we can estimate. We're a bit more confident of the angle from this scanner than we are of the distance. We are, however, very confident the target is within that circle."

President Allison thanked them.

Carlos went to secure his computer.

Roberta and Jerome told the president that Carlos had engineering skills comparable to a university graduate.

"Carlos is outstanding," Roberta said. "While we were doing our calculations, he described some of his classmates' projects. Science and engineering colleges should recruit down here."

"Or *up* here," Jerome added.

President Allison smiled, shook their offered hands, and patted Carlos on the shoulder. "Thank you all. You just might have saved millions of lives." President Allison turned to go, then turned back. "Don't tell anyone about what the three of you have accomplished. We need to keep this secret until all containers are under our control."

Roberta, Jerome, and Carlos nodded.

President Allison turned to Carter Johnson and Nick. "We have two missions: find the containers and find our rogue police lieutenant."

76

◆

Robert McKenna stood quietly as Mayor Patrick Riley introduced him and Carter Johnson to the three data technicians supporting the security contingent attached to the US portal.

Mayor Riley approached the lead portal guard. "These gentlemen have been granted access to the video recordings from camera seven for a specific, limited time frame. Am I correct that camera seven records the area just inside where whoever vouches for a newcomer is required to stand?"

They assured the mayor he was correct, and he stepped aside and motioned McKenna forward.

"Excellent," McKenna said. "I have two video technicians with me who will download the required data to our device." He pointed toward Roberta and Jerome.

He waited as the three data technicians took their time stepping back inside the portal door. McKenna finally gave them an almost polite "hurry up" wave.

The full ten minutes were downloaded and the time, 3:36 through 3:40, noted, when a single police lieutenant came on screen and approached portal security. One of the guards produced a paper for the lieutenant to sign. McKenna noted that two of the data technicians were in the background.

The recording next showed a well-dressed man being ushered through the portal. The man and his sponsoring lieutenant exchanged a few words.

McKenna nodded to Carter and Mayor Riley that the lieutenant had indeed dropped something in the other man's hand.

"No need to bother Baumberger for verification," Carter said.

"None at all," McKenna replied. "Especially when we could make out his badge number."

Mayor Riley pulled out his cell phone and pressed a single digit. "I'll have Chief Rojas confine the lieutenant before he can notify anyone."

McKenna crossed two sets of mental fingers, hoping they could pinpoint where in the calculated circle the plague containers were. He crossed his real fingers in the hope that the containers were still within the circle.

7 7

◆

Nick, Daniel, and Half-Penny stepped out of the military van and walked the thirty yards to the intersection. Three of the five Secret Service agents followed halfway. Warren, the bullet removed from his shoulder, remained inside talking to McKenna on his cell. Owen, beside him, was checking the medical bag containing the three versions of his antidote.

Nick looked around. Single-level houses as far as he could see. "The estimated search area starts three blocks down," he said, turning back to Daniel and Half-Penny. "It runs down for about another six blocks and is estimated to start two blocks wide, stretching out to four blocks at the end." He glanced back down the search area and shook his head. "I don't see us searching every house and building in that area inside of three days."

Half-Penny walked across the street, pulled out a pair of binoculars, looked down the street for about a minute, then returned. "Five blocks down, I think I made out a group of men or boys milling around what looks like a basketball court. Can't see the whole court."

"Maybe we can start with them," Daniel said. "Ask them if they've seen anything unusual."

Half-Penny shook his head.

Nick agreed. "The people that hid the containers would go to great pains to keep the location secret. If those men know where they're hidden, they're part of Ishmael's group and would never reveal the location."

Warren joined them. "McKenna said we have to disarm the containers in the next six hours."

"Disarm? What the hell!"

"McKenna said our lieutenant buddy smirked throughout his interrogation. Said he was the one who removed the transmitters but wasn't going to tell where they were located. Said we'd learn the location in six hours when the timer he attached went off and released the gas in both containers. He even replayed some of the lieutenant's actual words, describing how the containers would 'spew a certain death sentence in six hours to all Friendship City,' his exact words, the bastard."

"We have no choice. We have—"

Half-Penny moved to Nick's side. "I have an idea. Don't know if you'll like it though."

"Spill it. There's no time to hold back."

"Near that basketball court down there, I should escape from a police car after 'stealing' Warren's cell phone."

"And that would accomplish what?"

Half-Penny offered a quick scenario, during which Nick's expression changed, first to "somewhat catching the drift," then to "the plan has possibilities," and finally to "no time to waste!"

Nick and Half-Penny apprised the three Secret Service agents of the plan. The agents displayed Nick's same initial quizzical expression. Then they moved to implement the plan by waving all police and military vehicles to back up and leave the immediate area.

78

---◆---

The police sedan was racing down the street when, just past the basketball court, it suddenly swerved, barely avoiding a tree as the brakes slammed on. The engine choked and went silent.

All basketball activity stopped as the six players watched every move. Violent swinging of arms between two passengers could be seen in the rear seat. The rear passenger-side door was flung open, and a young Latino man jumped out and raced for the nearest alleyway.

Half-Penny pretended he was almost out of breath but continued his simulated dash for freedom. Pursuit was slow to develop. Glancing over his shoulder, he was satisfied that at least the first twenty seconds were going according to plan. He would have to find several streets and alleys where he could zigzag. Then, when the police gave up the chase, he would double back to the basketball court.

He darted around a building corner and halted for a quick look back. He saw a Friendship City policeman emerge from the front passenger seat, holding his head as if trying to soothe a painful bump. Half-Penny smiled and resumed running. The policeman lumbered after him, still holding his forehead.

Half-Penny whipped right into the alley and charged full steam to the next intersecting street. At the cross street, he shot a quick look over his shoulder as the policeman turned into the alley.

Two more alleys and cross streets, and Half-Penny was no longer being pursued. He turned left and trotted to the next street. He calculated that he was now one block away from the cross street, which led right for another two blocks to the park with the basketball court. He remembered there were a few shrubs and trees, perfect for being seen scouting the enemy.

He continued to the next street and turned right. After almost a block, he slowed to a calmer but purposeful stride. As he approached the rear of the park, he saw six high-school-age boys tossing a basketball around.

Half-Penny slowed to a stroll. When he was sure he had been spotted by a couple of the players, he cut over the grass and behind a row of four-foot-high shrubs. He stooped a bit and duck-walked toward the front of the park bordering the street where the police cruiser had careened past just minutes before. He could hear the basketball bouncing and the verbal back-and-forth along the court about fifteen yards off. He raised his head to scan the street.

The police car was gone.

The basketball was no longer bouncing, and there were no verbal taunts.

Half-Penny turned and saw all six boys walking toward him. He didn't move.

"Hey, Pretty Punk Boy," the obvious leader called out. "What you got goin' with the blue boys?"

Half-Penny blinked. He hadn't heard "Pretty Punk Boy" since he worked the streets of Manhattan. The term denoted a Hispanic boy whose street creds remained to be verified. He hoped this Mexican gang leader hadn't met him before his jail time.

The six stopped ten feet away, then formed a semicircle around him.

Half-Penny decided to offer his own Manhattan street lingo. "I got nothin' going with them pro-cops."

"Pro-cops?" the leader asked. "You're a long way from home, Punk Boy. Not sure yet if you're pretty or not, but"—he swept his right arm in a semicircle, indicating the other five—"we'll find out."

Half-Penny shrugged acceptance.

"Who did you work for in pro-cop land?"

"El Camino."

The leader's eyes widened. "What was your job?"

"Rescuing babies from people who couldn't take care of them."

"And?"

"And giving them to someone who could take very good care."

The leader nodded. "You were a kidnapper." He swung his right arm in a semicircle again and paused for several moments. "How long did you have that job?"

"Three years."

A low whistle. "Three years! That's superlong."

"I was fast: in, grab, hand off, then run like hell."

"Apparently." Another slight pause. "Why did El Camino let you go? You hadda be a super asset."

Half-Penny could see that the answer to this question "hadda" pass some kinda test. "He was killed almost a year ago."

"By a pro-cop?"

"By a traitor."

"Traitor to El Camino? Anybody else?"

Half-Penny nodded, aware he was on thin ice. "El Camino and Jason Beck."

"You appear to know a lot of what happened up in New York. Why'd you leave and come down here?"

"My grandma was down here, and the pro-cops were after my ass."

"Where does your grandma live?"

Half-Penny gave him McKenna's address, then decided to play his ace. "But I gotta get going. Gotta keep my grandma alive and safe."

"Alive and safe. Your grandma? Is she sick?"

"Not yet. Someone wants to make her very sick and die."

"Who wants to make her sick and die?"

"Someone your cops captured. Someone who wants to give us all some kind of bad plague." Half-Penny sensed he had everyone's attention.

"How does someone release a plague?"

"By a timer attached to a container which he set to release an airborne pathogen."

"He? Who's this 'he'?"

Half-Penny pulled out Warren's cell phone. "Let me play you something. I ripped this away from one of the cops in the police car. That's why I hit him and ran out of their car. I had to stop the plague from killing my grandmother. I had—"

"Play the damn thing!"

Half-Penny tapped the speaker button, then hit play.

79

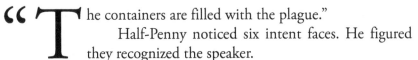

"The containers are filled with the plague."

Half-Penny noticed six intent faces. He figured they recognized the speaker.

"You'll learn where the container is in about six hours. I put a timer on one tub, and when it goes off...whoosh! No one will survive. It'll spew a certain death sentence after those six hours across all of Friendship City."

Half-Penny hit the off button. The six basketball players stared open-mouthed at the cell phone.

The leader gritted his teeth. "That bastard! He—"

"You know him? If you know anything, tell me so I can save my grandma. She's all I have."

"His name is Lutz. Supposed to be a cop, but he's working for somebody outside the city. He told us we were guarding some special kind of...he called it sacred oils. Said we'd get a big payoff if we kept it safe."

"You know where they're located?" Half-Penny could tell he had hit a home run. "Take me there. I gotta see if I can disconnect the timers."

"We're not going anywhere near. We're getting into the last tunnel out of Friendship City. It's just a few blocks away."

Half-Penny raised his hands and pressed the palms together. "I pray for my grandma. Just tell me where the containers are, and I won't do anything until you've had time to get through the tunnel." He glanced around at them. "Do any of you have any family you'll be leaving behind? I'll definitely—"

"I'll take you there," the shortest of the six said. "To the tubs, I mean."

The leader looked first at the short volunteer, then at Half-Penny. "Both of us will take you there." He turned to the other four. "Go to the tunnel and wait for us."

Half-Penny and his two guides retraced the streets he had used to get to the park. Ten minutes and just over a mile as a crow might fly, they stood in front of a two-story house.

"In the basement," the leader said. "You can't miss them. The tubs are in the center of a totally clear concrete floor." He tossed Half-Penny a padlock key. "Do I have your word you won't try disconnecting anything for at least ten minutes?"

Half-Penny nodded. "You have my word." He knew it would take at least that long for the experts to arrive and assess the situation.

After they had left at a run, Half-Penny went to a metal door on the side of the house, unlocked the heavy-duty padlock, lifted the door, and stepped into the basement. Two tubs were parked in the middle of a clean basement as described. He unclasped the flat microphone from his belt buckle and spoke into it.

"The tubs are here, as I was told."

The tubs were spaced at least ten feet from anything else in the basement. He checked for trip wires anywhere from his feet to above his head. There were none. He slow-walked around the tubs. What looked like a cell phone was attached toward the bottom of the tub farthest from the steps.

He spoke again into the microphone. "There's a type of cell phone attachment clamped near the bottom of the tub. The screen's dark. Should I turn it on?"

"Don't even touch the tub or the phone," Nick said. "We'll be there in less than a minute."

8 0

◆

Nick descended into the basement and gave Half-Penny a thumbs-up. "Super job, young buddy."

Nick waved three military bomb experts to review any electrical connections between the tub and its cell phone. After ninety seconds they too gave a thumbs-up.

Nick spoke into his cell phone, then motioned for a fourth military man to approach the tubs. The man carried a flexible metal tube with a suction cup at one end and a glass canister at the other. Another flexible metal tube, shorter and narrower, came from the other side of the canister, with another suction cup on its end.

Owen, Daniel, and Warren came down into the basement.

Nick took a couple steps back and watched the man run his hand slowly down the side of the tub.

The man nodded and held his hand in place. "The liquid starts just above here." He placed the suction cup against the tub wall about an inch below where his hand had stopped and pressed it inward to make a seal. He pressed a switch on the canister. No sound.

"It's cutting a two-millimeter hole with a laser." After about a minute, he turned the switch off.

Owen stepped forward and placed the canister's shorter metal tube and suction cup against the top of a glass jar. He tested the seal, then nodded. The military man pressed another switch. Nick watched as Owen's glass jar began filling with a clear liquid.

"Now," Owen said as the liquid filled half the jar.

The man turned the second switch off. Owen took out a syringe, attached its leading suction cup to the jar top, and gently plunged.

The clear liquid in the jar turned gradually purple. Owen removed the syringe from its suction cup and inserted a second syringe. He plunged again. For about two seconds, the color remained purple. Then it flashed suddenly to a bright green.

Owen looked over at Nick. "It's the plague," he said. "The liquid antidote works." Relief was written all over Owen's face. He pulled out a smaller jar and connected its suction cup to the hole left by the syringe. He nodded to the military man. The man pressed another switch. The small jar was emptied after five minutes, and the switch turned off.

Owen retrieved yet another jar, connected it, and watched as clear liquid filled it halfway. Nick was about to ask why the liquid was clear when Owen switched to another syringe and injected its liquid into the jar. The liquid remained clear.

"Yes!" Owen said. "We're okay. The plague in this tub has been neutralized."

Nick let out a sigh.

Owen and the military man repeated the procedure on the second tub. After ten minutes, its contents had also been neutralized.

Owen nodded with satisfaction. "Now, how to locate the other tubs and do the same."

There was only one problem: they didn't know how many tubs there were.

A fleeting thought caught Nick's attention. He pulled out his cell phone. "I took a couple of pictures of the tubs. I'm going to send them to George, the Secret Service agent guarding my old partner, Tim. If Tim recognizes them, we may have at least two in Manhattan."

81

———◆———

N ick wasn't the only frustrated person in the room. President Allison, Elise Carpenter, and all the others sitting around the table could only shake their heads at each suggestion of how to locate an untold number of plague-filled tubs.

Nick's cell phone beeped. He held it to his right ear. He listened intently and nodded several times. "Thank you," he said and pressed the off button. "Guess there are two tubs somewhere in Manhattan."

"Tim recognized them?" President Allison asked.

"Not a doubt in his mind. Now, how many others, and where?"

"One in New Bedford," Elise said.

"Why New Bedford?"

"That's where Melville's Ishmael didn't want to sail from."

"Your brother would follow someone else's script?"

"He thought of himself as Ishmael. Melville was just an inspiration, but there were details that Jeremiah made part of his own sick world. If there was one spot he would have liked to wipe off the map, it would have been New Bedford."

Nick shrugged. "New Bedford's on the list."

"That makes three," McKenna said.

"So far," President Allison said. "I think we should follow both leads."

"Agreed," Nick said. After a moment, he added, "We still have to determine how many other tubs exist and where they're hidden." He turned to Elise. "Didn't Jeremiah say something about the country being destroyed by seven sins?"

Elise paused, then gave a slow nod. "Yes. The seven deadly sins. He often said most people were guilty of each and every one."

"So the number seven had some significance to him?"

Elise chuckled. "I remember when he was a teenager, he insisted his shirts must have exactly seven buttons down the front."

President Allison stood. "I think we should work with the premise of seven tubs in all and try to find them."

The others nodded.

President Allison continued, "I'll head to Manhattan with a special military squad while our smirking lieutenant is interrogated further here. Hopefully, some mind games will trip him up."

"I'll head to New Bedford with Half-Penny and Carlos's signal-tracking setup," Nick said.

"I'm coming along too," Elise said. "I can try to match Jeremiah's fantasies with actual locations."

8 2

◆

May 10, 2058

N ick did his best to get at least three hours of sleep during the two flights and three limousine drives it took to get him, Elise, Half-Penny, four Secret Service agents, and one of the copies of Carlos's signal tracker to New Bedford. They arrived at their hotel just off Walnut Street and MacArthur Drive at 3:30 a.m.

Nick went into his room, took a shower, washed the sleep from his eyes, and met the others in the lobby at 4:15 a.m. They piled into the limousine and headed to Homer's Wharf, where they set up the signal tracker in the trunk.

At 5:00 a.m., Nick and Half-Penny decided there were too many nearby signals and moved the setup two miles west to Buttonwood Park. Fifteen minutes after setting up there, they recorded the first set of target clicks. The limo began a slow and steady sweep. Twenty-five more minutes gave five more recordings of varying intensity.

Half-Penny used the sound intensity to calculate their distance from the tracker. Using the table supplied by President Allison's engineers, he came up with between 5 and 5.5 miles. The loudest click set suggested the direction to be almost due north.

Nick checked his map. As he showed the map to Elise, he pointed at New Bedford's regional airport with its notation, *Abandoned: Not Functional as of 2042.*

"At least sixteen years," he said. "We'll have to be careful. Probably be spotted a half mile away."

After conferring with the four agents, Nick concluded they should get back in the limousine and head north on the still-traveled Route 140. The plan: see if there was sufficient cover to get out and set up the tracker near their presumed target.

Nick's concern that they would be conspicuous as the only vehicle on the highway was eased when they encountered a beat-up sedan headed in the opposite direction. As 140 made a wide curve around a runway, even more beat up than the sedan, he saw there were plenty of shrubs to provide more than enough cover for the whole team.

Nick had them stop just above the north runway. He and Half-Penny set up the signal tracker. It took only two sets of clicks to establish that the old airport was the source. Another three click sets indicated that in a line of four hangars, the two on the right were the most likely candidates.

They got back in the limousine and reversed course on Route 140 until they reached a section of trees and brush far away from any buildings. They stopped, got out, and headed into the covering branches.

The trees ran out at a two-lane roadway behind the set of four hangars. Far to the left was the longest runway heading off to the northeast over Route 140. To the right, beyond the hangars, was what appeared to be a furniture dump yard of desktops, crunched office chairs, and myriad pieces and sections of other junk.

One of the agents aimed a heat detector at the hangars, starting with the leftmost. The second hangar showed three body signatures.

The team discussed several scenarios for approaching the hangar without alarming the individuals inside and chose the least risky option. Nick and Elise were to emerge onto the roadway, carrying a blanket and a picnic basket. They jerry-rigged a basket from the case holding the tracker.

Nick and Elise waited as the others maneuvered to the trees on the opposite side of the target hangar. Nick gave the others more than enough time to position themselves, then reached for Elise's hand. They emerged from a shallow clearing onto the crusted and cracked roadway. As they crossed onto a wide patch of dry, sunbaked dirt, they paused and gave each other a hug.

From their spot about forty feet from its corner, Nick was in position to observe the two windows at the rear of the hangar. They held the hug for almost two minutes before he glimpsed a face in the near window.

"We're being watched," Nick said. "If any of them come out, we'll stop the hug."

Elise tilted her head back and smiled. "If you insist." She gave a tighter squeeze.

The nearest rear door of the hangar opened, and two men stepped out.

"Hey! What are you two doing here?" The men walked halfway to where Nick and Elise stood, still hugging.

"What does it look like?" Nick hollered in return, releasing the hug.

Elise lowered her arms and turned toward the men. "We just finished an early lunch and were planning some scrumptious dessert time in the clearing over there on those," she said, pointing to a distant pile of abandoned mattresses.

The first man shook his head. "Sex should be to work up an appetite, not work it off."

Elise shrugged.

"Not here, not now," the first man said. As he took a step toward them, shots rang out from inside the hangar.

Nick waved his Glock at the two men. "Drop any and all guns on the road. Now!"

The two men complied as Half-Penny and one of the agents emerged from the hangar, both giving two thumbs-up. Nick and Elise marched the two men back into the hangar.

Half-Penny and three of the agents stood around the single tub, exactly like the two in Friendship City. The fourth agent was tending to a man lying on the floor in a small but growing pool of blood, applying bandages to the man's chest and shoulder.

The lead agent, a muscular black man well over six feet tall, stepped forward. "He was by the door," he said, pointing at the bleeding man. "When he saw us, he raced toward the tub. I shot him."

"Good decision," Nick said. "Since you're not wearing a name tag, I don't know how to thank you directly."

"Captain Robert Yager."

"Thank you, Captain Yager, for your quick action."

Something about Agent Yager, maybe his constantly moving eyes that gave the impression their owner missed nothing, looked familiar, but Nick felt there were more important questions to be addressed than where he'd seen him before.

Yager pulled out his cell phone and notified the group in Manhattan that they should be careful: that the New Bedford tub was protected and would have been set off had they not caught the group off guard.

Half-Penny and one of the agents got to work following Owen's procedures. Within fifteen minutes, they verified the existence of, and neutralized, the plague solution in the tub.

Nick glared down the barrel of his Glock at the presumed leader of the group now handcuffed to a floor-to-ceiling pipe. "Maybe you didn't know, but had you activated those tubs, you would have been dead in twenty-four hours."

"We knew."

Nick saw Elise tug at an earring, a scowl across her face.

"Not worth it," Nick said. Then, so Elise's potential target could hear, he added, "He's just a dumb follower who spouts some ordained line but knows nothing of his superior's world and what lies ahead. He's a minion, nothing more."

"You're the dumb one," the man said with a sneer. "You're the one who thinks he knows it all. The one who will lose it all."

"Not after we find all the tubs. Even if we have to run down a million of them."

The man laughed. "You couldn't even track down seven tubs, let alone a million."

"Thank you. We thought there were only seven but weren't sure. Thanks for verifying the number."

The man's eyes widened with a look of alarm.

Nick smiled. "I'll take that expression as a 'You're welcome.'"

8 3

◆

Nick, Elise, Half-Penny, Captain Yager, and the other three agents arrived just off Manhattan's Battery Park via seaplane from New Bedford.

Nick received word from President Allison that a single tub transmission was coming from the old New York Stock Exchange and that they were now just west of Trinity Church and ready to plan the next moves.

The seaplane motored farther up the west of Manhattan, discharging the seven passengers just below Battery Park City. They crossed the strip of West Thames Park on foot and walked the four blocks to Trinity Church, just two blocks from the stock exchange.

"How did it go?" Owen asked.

Nick gave him a big grin and pointed to Half-Penny. "You taught him well."

"He's a quick learner."

Nick looked down the main aisle to the altar in the distance with the biggest stained-glass window he had ever seen arching high above.

President Allison came up to them. "We've tracked the tub's signal to the stock exchange. The trick will be getting inside without alerting those guarding it."

"How many guards?"

"We haven't been able to come up with a confirmed number. We have heat signatures for two but suspect there might be more. When we were first setting up the heat sensors, the technician said something about a third person walking toward the rear of the exchange.

We've been unable to reacquire that signature." She paused, then added, "So what's next in our bag of tricks?"

Nick had difficulty conjuring up a surefire way to get into the exchange without alerting the two or three guards who had only to tap their cell phones to release a death cloud across New York. He told the president.

She clenched her fists. "There has to be a way."

Nick tried to remember his only previous visit to the exchange. The interior structure took shape in his memory. "We keep the three heat sensors focused while we get a team up on the roof," he said. "It hasn't been used for almost twenty-five years, but I remember thick piping just below the ceiling and another set of pipes below that to support video hardware no longer there. If the team is ready to head out, we should go. We don't know if there's any time limit like we had in Friendship City. We can wait a little bit, but not all day."

"Seems to be the best—"

A breathless young agent raced in the front door of the church and up to the president and Nick. He had obviously been running hard. "I… I just…saw…" He paused and took two measured breaths. "I just saw a third man enter the back of the exchange." Another two slower breaths. "He entered a rear door from where we…where we figured he left. He was carrying a bag with four big S symbols. I didn't—"

Yager waved him silent. "Were the letters brown on the outside and red and green on the inside?"

"Yes."

"Lunch bag from Sam's Super Sub Shop."

"Are you sure?" President Allison asked.

"Definitely. I was undercover in this area almost a year ago. Assignment lasted for over a year."

Nick blinked, remembering Yager in a council guard uniform in the detention center where he had been taken the night he planned his own arrest to free Owen. "I remember you," Nick said.

"And I, you. I'm glad I wasn't assigned desk duty that night. It would have been my head you'd have slammed with a paperweight."

Nick and Yager both chuckled.

"Are you two finished?" President Allison asked. "We've just reacquired the third heat signature." She rounded up a large group of agents, six with sniper rifles, and had Nick and Yager brief them. "That's if the two of you can put aside your reminiscences of fun times together and come up with a plan."

After some debate, Nick and Yager communicated what they considered the most workable approach. Yager pointed upward, Nick nodded, and they led the group toward the exchange and its roof.

Thirty-two minutes later, the team was on the roof, quickly but quietly unlocking a large air-conditioning vent. They maneuvered a video scope to the outside of the exit fan's left support bracket and lowered it just enough to afford a clear view of about 80 percent of the floor. They lowered themselves over the side to the upper windows. Inside, a catwalk ran along the windows for the full depth of the building.

Yager's cell phone illuminated a message. "They're inside eating lunch, seated about fifty feet from the tub, which is in the center of the floor." His cell flashed a second message. "Snipers have all three in their crosshairs."

The team had finished laser-cutting five windows. Three men at each window climbed in and onto the catwalk. Each team pitched a climbing rope over the nearest pipe about ten feet below, then whipped a wire-thick string around the rope's end. They pulled back the string so the team could secure the rope end to the rope itself, securely fastening it to the pipe for quick descent to the floor of the exchange.

Nick's window had the clearest view of an unobstructed descent to the tub.

Yager smiled at him and nodded. "I'm a few years younger, Nick. I'll go first."

Nick gave Yager a sweeping whenever-you're-ready wave.

Yager grabbed the rope and, pulling up most of the slack and wrapping it in loops around his left arm, executed a short rope slide to the nearest pipe. Steadying himself, Yager unwrapped enough rope—about eight feet—to swing down to the second set of piping.

Nick was impressed with Yager's gymnast-like moves as he gained footing on the lower pipes. Yager adjusted his footing and spooled out another ten feet of rope. Nick crossed the fingers on both hands. He knew Yager's next gymnastic maneuver and hoped he wouldn't injure himself or slam into the tub.

Yager crouched down, then pushed forward and propelled himself out horizontally, then swooped down with the rope's ten feet extended. He swung back, almost disappearing below the catwalk.

Nick leaned over and saw that Yager had already released the remaining twenty-five-plus feet of rope. Yager slid down the rope on his forward sweep. The end of the rope brought him close to the tub. Nick tightened his crossed fingers as Yager let go of the rope.

The three eating lunch dropped their subs as Yager landed less than two feet from the tub. He had his pistol already drawn.

Nick uncrossed his fingers. He knew the guards couldn't see the nine snipers who had them in nine crosshairs, but they couldn't miss Yager's Glock.

Military personnel and Secret Service agents poured through all of the exchange's entrances. The guards raised their hands above their heads.

Nick and several of the snipers moved to the descent ladders at the front of the catwalk and made their way to the exchange floor. President Allison was already apprising the situation. Owen, Half-Penny, and Elise were not far behind.

Owen and his ever-present agent, whom Owen affectionately referred to as "my drill sergeant," got to work neutralizing the tub contents.

Nick turned his attention to the three guards. They proved to be committed loyalists to Ishmael's cause. Each refused to say word one.

Owen and his drill sergeant completed their job. Owen smiled and gave a thumbs-up.

President Allison gathered Nick, Yager, and the others together. "We surmised there were at least two tubs in Manhattan. There's still one to find. I've been told there's a complete absence of any further click signatures. Any suggestions?"

Elise raised a hand and nodded. "It's just a guess, but…"

"Guesses are all we have," President Allison said. "Go ahead."

"Saint Patrick's Cathedral."

She was greeted by quizzical looks.

"Jeremiah always claimed that since they preached about the seven deadly sins, the Catholic Church actually promoted the sins and should be taken down. If we know there are two plague tubs here in Manhattan, St. Patrick's would have been his first choice."

8 4

───◆───

Within twenty minutes, limousines brought them to the rear of the still-maintained Rockefeller Center, where a huge Christmas tree used to be installed and decorated, a block west of St. Patrick's Cathedral.

They set up the signal tracker and switched it on. After fifteen minutes, no signals had been captured.

President Allison gathered Nick, Elise, and Yager. "The cathedral is open twenty-four-seven," she said. "Maybe the transmitter has been removed."

Elise shrugged.

"The only way to find out is to go inside," Yager said.

"I agree," Nick said.

A plan was worked up within a minute. Per Nick's strategy, he and Elise would pose as religious tourists. Yager would have the forty agents surround the cathedral. Some agents in civilian clothes would enter several minutes after Nick and Elise.

*****

Nick pulled open the cathedral's Fifth Avenue door and was about to wave Elise in ahead of him but shook his head and went in first.

The central aisle with dark wood pews on either side was guarded by magnificent pillars reaching to merge with a fantastic arched ceiling. In the distance stood the main altar. The few people in the cathedral occupied the front four or five pews.

Nick and Elise took one of the back pews on the left and sat down. Nick, barely moving his head, scanned first to the left, then to the right. Between each pillar, there was a small altar in a niche. No people were lurking in any of the nearest four niches on either side.

After three minutes, Nick motioned to Elise. They stood, moved to the end of their pew, stepped into the left aisle, and stood still as if looking at the niche altar in front of them.

Six of the agents entered the cathedral and split up. Two took seats in the back pew. The others split up again, then walked down each side aisle to take seats four or five pews behind those in the front.

Nick and Elise circled back to the rear of the cathedral and returned to the central aisle. Nick stood for several moments, trying to remember if he had ever seen churches like the two he'd been in that day. He had married Judith in a neighborhood Catholic church, an edifice far simpler than either Trinity or St. Patrick's.

He took Elise's hand, remembering the churches he and Judith had checked out in the months before the wedding. They had walked slowly down the central aisle just like now. He remembered how happy he had been that Judith had accepted his proposal.

Wrapped in memories, Nick gave the hand he was holding a slow squeeze. Elise squeezed back.

Nick quickly returned his full attention to the present day and its mission. He glanced at Elise. She smiled at him and squeezed his hand again. They moved slowly down the central aisle. Nothing made his neck itch. He chuckled to himself that the second of two detectors had come up empty, Carlos's click sensor being the first.

Nick stopped as they reached the first of the pews. The high altar was just ahead, beyond a short flight of marble stairs. He looked to the left and to the right. Pews on both sides going back three or four rows were almost full with worshipers.

Intent on appearing like a fascinated tourist, Nick gestured high above the altar to the vaulted ceiling with its support buttresses.

Elise followed his gaze. "See anything?"

"No." He motioned to the elevated pulpit on their right. "Let's take the altar walk-around."

They strolled along the marble floor to the right, circling the high altar. Nick stopped at the rear of the altar. They overlooked another marble staircase, this time leading downward. Surrounded by marble railings, the stairs descended away from the rear of the altar, leading somewhere beneath where they stood.

Nick felt the first tingling itch at the back of his neck. He looked again at the staircase. There didn't seem to be anything worthy of an itch—major or minor—just a staircase running down below them. He looked up along the stairs and directly opposite saw two metal doors with sections of glass. The glass sections, seven horizontal panels running top to bottom on each door, showed a very slight illumination from within. He could just make out a handrail heading downward.

Still not enough for a pulsating itch.

The sudden appearance of two men from either side of the altar *was* enough. Both wore robes, suggesting they belonged to a religious brotherhood. Their command to "Keep moving!" suggested otherwise.

Nick scratched his neck and complied, leading Elise back to the pews in front of the altar. They took a pew three rows behind the four agents split between both sides of the aisle. Using agreed-upon hand signals, Nick indicated the presence of two suspicious men on the other side of the altar.

After five minutes, all four agents stood, went to their respective side aisles, and walked to the rear of the high altar. They returned three minutes later with the two robed men in discreet custody. Three of the agents walked the men to the rear of the cathedral. The fourth sat beside Nick.

"The taller one reached inside his robe for a cell phone when we didn't move. He never got a chance to use it, as he never saw the other two agents."

Nick nodded his thanks. "There's a floor below this one. I think they were trying to keep us away. Tell Yager and President Allison we should clear the cathedral and find out what's below."

The agent got up and rejoined the other agents.

It took six minutes for all worshipers, several with canes or walkers, to be evacuated.

Yager, President Allison, Owen, Owen's drill sergeant, and the click scanner were front and center after another minute. Nick and Elise led them around the high altar to the stairs leading down to the two metal doors with the glass panels. Nick looked through the glass panels and saw that his initial view was correct: a handrail led down to another level.

He tried the right door. It was unlocked.

Nick motioned for Elise to step back and Yager to accompany him down. Dark carpeting ran ahead for about thirty feet, then branched off both right and left. Nick chose the left hallway, which was also carpeted. Eventually, they came to a group of burial crypts in three rows, one atop the other.

A young man cowered in the corner, both arms chained to a tub.

Nick's neck itch went full bore. The tub was identical to the ones already neutralized.

"Don't make a move." Yager commanded, pointing his Glock at the frightened young man. "Not *any* move!"

"Don't touch the canister!" the young man cried. "It'll kill us all."

Nick holstered his weapon and raised his hand. "We know there's a plague in there," he said. "We're here to destroy it. We've killed four other plague canisters. Can I approach? We don't want to hurt you."

The young man nodded.

Yager waked back to the steps and waved Owen and his drill sergeant partner down.

This time, it took only twelve minutes to verify and neutralize the plague. It took two more minutes to cut the young man free from the tub.

"Thank you! Thank you!" he breathed. On their way back up the stairs, the young man gushed about how he had been duped into joining the group guarding the canisters. He'd been told they were vessels of holy oil for the church that had to be guarded at all costs, and when he overheard the others calling it a plague, he had tried to leave. It was then that he had been chained to the canister.

President Allison and about forty agents greeted them as they emerged behind the high altar. "Good job, again," she said, shaking hands with the team of four. "Is this young man your prisoner?"

"No, but he should be interrogated for what he may know about the others." Looking across at the young man and his still-strained features, Nick added, "He'll probably need protection, regardless of how much or how little he knows."

President Allison agreed.

8 5

◆

Nick stepped aside as President Allison and a dozen agents ushered the young man into a waiting limousine.

Yager tapped him on the shoulder. "We haven't eaten since what passed for breakfast on the seaplane. In another hour or two, it'll be dinnertime. I'm going for a late lunch. Anybody interested?"

Nick, Elise, Owen, and Half-Penny all raised a hand.

Yager gave the military driver directions. Twenty minutes later, the limousine pulled up two blocks south of the stock exchange.

"Welcome to an old lunch counter of mine," Yager said, giving a flourished wave to the building on their right. Nick and the others looked out and saw the door to an eatery with the sign above proclaiming *Sam's Super Sub Shop.*

Nick wagged his head. "Why not?"

They went inside, ordered their late lunch, and after Yager picked up the tab, sat around one of the larger glass-top tables. Their subs and soft drinks came after a few minutes.

Half-Penny was first to finish.

Nick was next. He wiped his chin and raised a thumb to Yager. "Gotta admit your old lunch counter is pretty good."

"Pretty good?" Yager asked. "Only just pretty good?"

"Okay. I'll put a third word in the middle. Your lunch counter of long ago is pretty damn good."

Yager smirked.

"But…you never thought to bring me one of Sam's Super Subs when I was in your jail cell?"

Yager chuckled. "Not my jail. Not my cell."

"I don't think these should be served to anybody in jail," Elise said, giving Nick's hand a quick squeeze. "People would be committing crimes just to be arrested and have a good lunch."

Nick and Yager chuckled.

As they exchanged comments about the lunch, Nick began a slow, light tapping on the tabletop.

Yager looked across at him. "Something on your mind?"

Nick stopped tapping. "We've found and neutralized five tubs of plague. Where are the others? How much time do we have?"

"We'll find them," Yager said.

"But if we're not close to a tub when it releases, we can't protect the city, let alone ourselves." Nick looked at Owen. "Am I right?"

"You are."

Nick's cell phone beeped. He pulled it out and glanced at its screen. "Yes, President Allison?"

The other four riveted their gaze on Nick. He pressed the speaker button so all could hear.

"The young man you rescued from the crypt has given some very useful information," the president said. "It seems he overheard more than just about the tub containing the plague. He told us that the taller of the two men, whom he believed had had direct contact with Ishmael, told the other that there were three more tubs in the city. The stock exchange was mentioned as well. That leaves the last two to complete the seven."

"Did he tell you the location of these last two?"

"No. But he said the tall one chuckled as he said Ishmael was incensed that Melville was reduced to becoming a customs inspector. And that after a lifetime of creating fantastic worlds, he was just stuffed into the ground."

"Hold on. I'll put Elise on, as she knows Ishmael inside and out." Nick handed the phone to Elise.

"Madam President, did the young man give any other details?"

"No. Other than telling us how the tall man snuck away from the tub and caught him listening, just those two comments. He said they chained him to the tub immediately."

"Do either of these references strike you as familiar in any way, Elise?" Nick asked.

"Yes. Both. Jeremiah often grumbled about Ellis Island, where immigrants used to be admitted, even though he had no idea where Herman Melville was assigned and what his duties were."

"Sounds like Ellis Island has potential. What about Melville being 'just stuffed into the ground'?"

"Jeremiah visited Woodlawn Cemetery when he was a young teenager. He ranted on and on about how there were, in his words, 'fancy schmancy' buildings for everyone except Herman Melville, who created more than all the others combined. Our dad checked out the burial sites, and Melville's was a bit better than ninety-five percent of the others, but not an ornate mausoleum. Jeremiah didn't want to hear it."

Elise handed the phone back to Nick.

"Sounds like we have two excellent candidates for the last two tubs," the president said.

Elise gave a nod.

"If I might suggest, President Allison," Nick said. "We are closer to Ellis Island, and you and the other agents are closer to Woodlawn Cemetery in the Bronx. You have two click scanners up by St. Patrick's. Send some agents down with one, and we'll scout out Ellis while your group checks out Woodlawn."

"Sounds workable. I've been assured that Owen showed several agents up here how to verify and neutralize the plague. Owen's drill sergeant is here with the equipment. If we find anything and shut it down, he'll bring the equipment and me down to you."

"We'll keep you in the loop with anything we find."

"As will we. Good hunting, Nick."

"And to you as well, Madam President," Nick said and hung up.

8 6

—————◆—————

President Allison's crew packed into two limousines. Excluding a short stop at a clothing store and another at a flower shop, it took them less than thirty minutes to reach the southern part of Woodlawn Cemetery. They pulled to a stop on East Gun Hill Road in an alley behind some deserted factories.

They set up the scanner. Within fifteen minutes, the president was confident there was a tub somewhere north of their position. Signal strength suggested less than a mile north.

After they left behind the president's limousine, the vehicle with the scanner reversed course, returned to the east of the cemetery, and drove slowly north. A mile later, it pulled off to the shoulder, and they restarted the scanner.

Over her street clothes, President Allison put on a black blouse and a long black skirt and draped a black veil over the back of her head.

Four agents got out, leaving just the president and the driver in regular driver's livery.

After a call from the lead agent in the other limousine, President Allison gave the signal to enter the cemetery. She texted the senior agent from her limousine to enter the cemetery farther west, using the various clumps of trees for cover.

The agent checking the scanner gave a location he designated as accurate to within a hundred yards.

The president's limousine stopped about ten yards into the given hundred.

President Allison pulled the lace veil down over her face, started to exit, pulled back in to grab a sheet of paper from inside a folder, and finally stepped out with the bouquet of flowers. There was little to no breeze. She felt confident she would not be distracted. She walked along the side of the road with the sheet of paper in her hand, stopping occasionally and glancing down at it as if trying to locate a specific grave on a map.

She estimated she had covered almost half of the hundred yards when she saw a figure exiting a large mausoleum with four pillars on her left. The man headed directly toward her.

President Allison kept walking and pressed a button switch under the paper.

The man crossed the road. "Can I help you?" he asked, stopping about ten feet away.

"I'm looking for the grave of Eli Harrington. Can't seem to find it."

The man took four steps forward and looked down. "You have no map on that paper of yours, just a bunch of text."

She lowered her right hand. He grabbed the paper from her left hand, then reached out and lifted her veil. "You look somewhat familiar. Probably a cop." His hands moved for her throat.

She dropped the flowers and flexed her right palm all the way back, then shoved its rigid heel with all her might up between his arms and into the bottom of his nose, breaking cartilage and sending shards up into the man's cranium. He collapsed into the president's outstretched arms.

There was probably at least one other bastard watching, and she couldn't let him see that bastard number one would soon be dead. The man's body was beginning to feel heavy.

Three agents slipped into the mausoleum.

She heard a single gunshot from inside the mausoleum and let the body slump to the ground.

She remembered Elise and her earrings. "That will teach you not to mess with women."

One agent came out and gave an "okay" wave. The president crossed the road, walked up the paved entranceway, and entered the mausoleum. In the center, a tub. Number six. No doubt.

Two agents were just starting the verification and neutralization procedures. Twenty minutes later, the tub was clamped in the limousine's trunk, and the group was on its way to Ellis Island.

87

---◆---

Nick and the others had just completed their scan from Governors Island, a little less than a mile southeast of Ellis Island.

The small ferry pulled up to the landing on the far side of Governors Island. Nick knew it was President Allison and crew, as they had kept in almost constant contact. The ferry pulled back and made a wide sweep to the south, then arced back to the Statue of Liberty.

Owen and Half-Penny were just wrapping up their distance and angle calculations when the president crossed over to Outlook Hill.

"As you requested, the other scanner is on its way to Liberty Island," President Allison said.

"Excellent," said Nick. "Our first data set confirms the presence of a click generator on Ellis. We'll soon have a second data set."

At that moment, Owen and Half-Penny rushed over. Half-Penny was waving his data sheet. "The clicks come from the southern part of Ellis Island. That's the part with the old hospital."

"There's a bunch of buildings running the full length of that side. Were you able to narrow down to which building?"

Owen shook his head. "Our sensor tracking was in the same line as those of the hospital buildings. The first sensor position had other buildings that spread the readings. We need a third angle."

"You'll have it in—" Nick looked at President Allison, who had her cell phone to her ear.

She held up three fingers.

"About thirty minutes," Nick concluded.

"Damn!" President Allison said.

"What?"

"They just landed and started setting up for the scan. They also set up a telescope. They observed at least six men patrolling outside the full length of the hospital section."

"Gotta assume there are others inside with the tub. Wherever it is."

President Allison nodded.

"Cuts down our chances to drill, verify, and neutralize," Nick said.

"Why weren't the other tubs protected like this one?" Half-Penny asked.

"Maybe this one was the most important. Maybe—"

"I think you're right," Elise said. "Jeremiah had a thing about the US letting—in his own words—'a bunch of nobodies into the country when nearby the great Herman Melville is forgotten.'"

Nick turned to Owen. "You have the cylinders?"

Owen nodded back to where their inflatable boat was tied. "Two there and two in the trunk of President Allison's limo."

Nick motioned Yager and the other agent to join him, Owen, the president, and Elise. "We are going to have to wait for nightfall to cross to Ellis. There are most certainly more than just the six guards we've seen. Our best chance of getting to the tub before we're discovered is at night. Fortunately, there's no moonlight tonight."

"And if we're seen?" Yager asked.

"They activate the plague."

"And...?"

"And we have to use the gaseous neutralizer that Owen has developed."

"And...?"

"And we've never used it against a released but uncontained plague. We've tried the gaseous version in a completely sealed room."

Nick waited for another "And?" from Yager. He received a shrug.

"And it completely neutralized the released plague, but we've never tried it in an open environment."

Half-Penny looked puzzled. "Do we have to go in tonight? Maybe a day from now?"

Good question, Nick thought. "I don't have a good answer. My concern is that somehow, some way, they may find out that the other tubs and their guards are no more. There seems to be little in the way of communication between the groups. Probably by design. If no communication, then no tracing of communication."

Elise raised a hand. "What happens if the plague is released before you can shut it down?"

"We have two cylinders of the neutralizer, and we'll give it all we got. Hopefully, the plague won't be too dispersed."

"But what happens to our men who are spraying?"

"We go in wearing gas masks," Nick said.

"And I've developed a vaccine," Owen said. "It worked in a closed environment on several animals. Each animal ended up protected."

"No aftereffects?"

"Our goal was to administer the vaccine exactly five minutes following exposure. There were some initial reactions, but within a half hour, each animal tested the same as it did before exposure."

Elise rolled her eyes and stepped back.

Nick turned to President Allison. "We'll take the two cylinders in our raft." He looked at his watch. "It's just after five. We won't be moving for another six or seven hours, around midnight. Have your limo driver move the vehicle to New Jersey and back down as close as he can get to the Ellis Island Bridge without being seen. Tell him that if he gets our signal, he's to drive as fast as possible to the island's hospital area on the far-right side."

"I'll also tell him to have his mask at the ready."

"Right on," Nick said. "Now get back in your little ferry. Owen's drill sergeant will take you and Elise to your limousine."

Elise put her right hand on Nick's shoulder. "Please be safe."

88

◆

May 11, 2058

Nick checked his watch: 12:07 a.m., with no moonlight.
He glanced at the two rafts. Owen and Half-Penny were to join him in one, Yager and four agents in the other. Owen's two cylinders and his drill-and-neutralize setup were also in Nick's raft. Half-Penny would fill in as Owen's drill sergeant.

Time for one last review. He gathered them around. "The tub has been pinpointed to be inside the morgue section of the contagious hospital side of Ellis Island. You were each shown the map with the morgue highlighted. The hospital on that side of Ellis has been closed and abandoned for almost a hundred years. Hopefully, you each memorized the morgue location, because no flashlights are joining us on our little paddling expedition." Nick motioned to Yager.

Yager nodded. "As covered earlier, our agents on Liberty Island have forwarded the patrol times and lengths of each set of guards. Remember, there are at least nine guards. At any time, there are six patrolling. Half of them, three guards in total, come out on the hour with the other half thirty minutes later. The on-the-hour half patrols the section right along the Hudson River seawall. The other group covers the walkway on the other side of the contagious hospital complex. There seems to be at least a thirty-second but less than a forty-five-second interval where the team finishing and the team starting their rounds meet in the middle and talk, probably exchanging information." He yielded back to Nick.

"The seawall runs about ten feet in height," Nick said. "The agents on Liberty have observed that the guards covering the seawall side seldom get closer than about ten feet. This will provide cover once we get close. Our plan: climb up at the far end of the seawall during the on-the-hour change and subdue all six guards, plus"—Nick crossed the fingers on both hands—"the three or more inside. Any questions?"

No questions.

Everyone climbed into their assigned raft, with Nick and Yager pushing theirs off from Governors Island at 12:09 exactly. Nick and Half-Penny paddled their raft in the lead. After pushing off, neither of them lifted their paddle from the water at any time, rotating it ninety degrees to allow the backstroke to slip through with no drag. Both rafts reached the seawall at 12:41 a.m. and paddled next to the wall to their goal. At 12:57, both rafts were in position.

Nick had Half-Penny give him an assist up at ten seconds to 1:00 a.m. He cleared the wall and crawled onto the grass at 1:00 exactly. The guards had just met their replacements midway along the wall.

He told Half-Penny to stay with Owen in the raft until he pulled them up.

Nick checked to see Yager and the other four agents had cleared the wall and were crawling into position. He followed suit.

The guards never got to finish their conversation. Six silencers fired one shot each, and six guards fell dead to the ground.

Yager and three of his agents stole quietly through a dilapidated section of the hospital wall. One agent came to Nick's side and helped lift Owen, then Half-Penny out of the raft. Half-Penny had already handed both cylinders and Owen's other gear up to Nick.

Three more silencers fired. Three more guards down.

Nick and the other three took up station on the seawall side of the morgue. Although neglected and falling apart, the morgue's windows were boarded up, preventing Nick from seeing in. The plan was for each of the two groups to station themselves by the front and back doors to the morgue, then, upon a signal from Nick, to sneak or storm in.

A loud siren-like alarm put that plan to rest.

8 9

◆

Nick pressed the preset message triggering all to enter. He went in first with Half-Penny and the agent, each carrying a cylinder, right behind. Owen, with his drilling set and compound, brought up the rear. Yager and his three agents entered through the opposite door.

Both groups stood still, many rifles raised but not fired.

A thug stood on either side of tub number seven. Both also held rifles. What kept them from firing was yet another figure, this one without a rifle. The third thug stood in front of the tub, smiling. He held a cell phone with his thumb resting on its bottom, obviously ready to release. With his free hand, the third thug motioned to his right.

In the corner of the room stood a dark-brown wooden frame around four rows, two wooden doors per row. Each wooden door was about three feet wide by two feet tall. Three of the eight doors were open, revealing a dark nothing inside.

The thug broadened his smile. "Some of the bodies of the immigrants were stored here—those the doctors couldn't save."

Nick's neck itch was in a fury. "You haven't pressed to open the tub. You obviously want something. What is it?"

"Good question, oh perceptive one." He motioned to the corner on his left.

A door led to another room. Its glass panel appeared as if broken decades ago, with only a few shards remaining. The door opened.

President Allison walked in, followed by Elise. The thug raised his free hand for them to stop. Owen's drill sergeant followed them through the door and stopped behind the two women.

Owen muttered, "Oh no."

The drill sergeant carried a rifle pointed at the backs of the two women.

Mr. Third Thug shifted from a smile to an evil smirk. "Oh yes, Owen. He helped you neutralize all six of the previous tubs. His help, however, stops here and now." The thug turned his attention back to Nick. "We had to know if Dr. Pendleton's concoction could possibly destroy the plague, and if it could, how." The evil smirk returned. "Since your drill sergeant explained everything to us in great detail, we have modified this last tub to release the plague when it senses any drilling anywhere from top to bottom. It will also release the plague if I merely lift my thumb from my phone."

Nick shook his head. "All very well planned. One question though."

"Why do we do this?" The smirk widened. "Why are we willing to die for this?"

Nick nodded.

"You, Mr. Garvey, and the others seek your rewards in this life. We get ours in the next life, which is much longer and much more important."

Nick glanced at the other two thugs. The rapid blinking of one and the overactive Adam's apple of the other suggested to him neither was as ready for their eternal rewards as was their leader.

The tub master's smirk widened. "I do have one bargain in which you may be interested."

"Which is?"

The thug pointed to President Allison and Elise. "Allow us time to get those two safely off the island, and we can continue our negotiation."

"What negotiation?"

The thug's eyes narrowed. "Accumulating our rewards. These two women will at least be safe for the near future. Indicate your acceptance by everyone dropping their rifles and, Dr. Pendleton, your cylinders."

President Allison and Elise both refused the offer with quick head shakes.

"Can you assure me that both women will be released safely once off the island?" Nick asked.

"I can assure you that if you don't drop your rifles, I'll lift my thumb and the tub will release its contents, first to you, then to the countryside, then—"

"We won't leave," President Allison said.

"We stay here," Elise said just as loudly.

Nick watched both women turn and advance on the drill sergeant, who raised his rifle and shot over everyone's head. One of the other thugs pushed the two women apart with his rifle butt.

"I guarantee the next shot will take out both women," the lead thug said. "Make your decision, Mr. Garvey." He held his cell phone aloft. "Make it now."

"Okay," Nick said. "Everyone drop their rifles. Me first."

He hunched over to drop, figuring all eyes would be on the rifle as it fell. The rifle hit the concrete floor, rubber butt first, and bounced back into his waiting arms. Nick shot the drill sergeant first, then the other two extremely slow-to-react thugs.

The lead thug lifted his thumb as Nick put a bullet in his forehead. The tub belched a purple cloud of gas.

Nick waved Owen and Half-Penny to the tub.

They emptied both of Owen's cylinders: first into the cloud swirling above the tub, then into the tub itself.

Yager stepped forward, picked up Owen's medical kit, and retrieved the case of fifty preloaded vaccination needles. "I gave injections on battlefields for many years." He injected President Allison and Elise first, then Nick, Owen, Half-Penny, and the other agents. Finally himself.

Within ten minutes, Owen's verification and neutralization procedures assured everyone that disaster had been averted.

Yager grinned at Nick. "I guess their next life rewards won't be per contract."

Nick chuckled and shook Yager's outstretched hand.

President Allison shook Nick's hand as well, then Yager's. "Good job. Both of you."

Elise rushed in and wrapped her arms around Nick. She said nothing, just held tight.

9 0

---◆---

When everyone was buckled in their seats, President Allison nodded to the copilot. He unlocked the cabin door, went inside, and relocked. Air Force One started up three minutes later. They were airborne within another ten minutes.

Their seats were situated around an oval table in a conference room, six seats in all, occupied by President Allison, Nick, Elise, Yager, Owen, and Half-Penny. A glass of well-earned wine rested on the table in front of five of the six. For Half-Penny, a glass of well-earned soda. Four Secret Service agents sat in the main cabin.

"We'll touch down in Friendship City in just over two hours," President Allison said. She turned to Owen. "This plague has been put to rest, thanks to you. But do you think some variation could have been engineered? Perhaps put on the shelf for a future threat?"

"Not a chance, Madam President. This plague was so engineered that the molecular-level splitting and modification were accomplished in a very specific way through a very narrow technology window. Doesn't mean there can't be a natural plague-type of sickness grab hold of many people, but the chances are low. We'll be prepared, as we have been most times in the past for any natural sickness, recurring or not."

"Thank you, Owen." She turned to Half-Penny. "And thank you for learning the critical skills needed to replace our thankfully departed drill sergeant."

They laughed.

"Nick, where did you get a rifle that bounces back to you like that?" President Allison asked.

"Special order."

More laughter.

Yager asked Elise, "What *are* the seven deadly sins?"

"Pride, greed, lust, envy, gluttony, wrath, and sloth."

"I'm guilty of only four," Yager said.

"Only four?" Nick asked. "I would have guessed all seven."

"Pride can't be a sin if it's well earned. Envy isn't in my playbook 'cause there's nobody I could possibly envy. Finally, gluttony in moderation is definitely not a sin."

They all raised their glasses.

9 1

———◆———

Air Force One landed at Matamoros International, whose runways had been brushed clean just an hour before.

Nick, Elise, Owen, and Half-Penny were met by a limousine carrying two military agents, one of them at the wheel.

President Allison asked Yager to stay aboard for the trip to Washington, DC.

Nick and the others were driven to McKenna's house just in time for dinner. As they entered, Nathan was helping McKenna at the gas grill on the deck as Nicole set the table and Sandra sat on the sofa with her feet curled under her.

"Where's your aunt Julia?" Nick asked Nicole.

"Out for a drive."

Half-Penny looked concerned. "She doesn't drive."

"Uncle Henry is driving," Nicole said. "In his real fast green car."

Nick had to ask. "How do you know his green car is real fast?"

She didn't get a chance to answer.

"He took her and Nathan for a ride about two hours ago," McKenna said, bringing in a tray of at least a dozen hamburgers from the grill.

Nathan followed, all smiles. "He took us all around Matamoros. It was super fun," he said, excited.

McKenna put the tray down atop a trivet with rubber legs. "Dinner's ready."

Everyone moved to the table.

McKenna looked at his watch. "I told them to be here—" The sound of a car engine roaring to a stop outside cut him short. "Looks like they made the curfew." He glanced at his watch again. "Barely."

Everyone took their seats as Julia and Henry came through the front door.

Julia, sporting a broad smile, waved. "Just like riding in Dad's old car."

Henry pulled out his pocket watch. "Only one minute over. Hope I'm not sent to my room."

They went to wash their hands.

Elise winked at Nick. "Looks like they both enjoyed the ride."

"I'd understand if her dad was a race car driver."

"I'd second that," McKenna said.

Nathan looked at Half-Penny, who was already halfway into his hamburger. "Was your great-grandpa a race car driver?"

"Not that Grandma ever told me. She never mentioned her dad even having a car."

McKenna offered Half-Penny a second burger. He eagerly accepted, as his grandmother and Henry emerged from their respective rooms.

McKenna turned to Nick. "We were told all of the plague has been destroyed. True?"

"All seven tubs neutralized one hundred percent," Owen said and reached for a burger.

"Does that mean we're all safe?" Nicole asked.

Owen beat Nick to the answer. "Yes, we're all safe. The plague has been broken apart to where it can't hurt anyone anymore."

"What if someone did catch it and is carrying it?" Nathan asked.

"We have a vaccine that works, also one hundred percent. The plague was designed to produce symptoms within a half hour. Nobody we know of caught the plague."

Elise held up her glass of water. "Here's to our fantastic and successful plague fighters."

Sandra slowly raised her glass to join the toast. Nick's heart felt like it skipped a beat when she looked at him and smiled. He guessed

Elise must have noticed. She rested her hand atop his. It felt warm. He left his hand where it was.

"More burgers, anyone?" McKenna asked.

Two takers that time.

"Can't save them forever," McKenna said. "By the way, this coming Tuesday, there's a full Friendship City citizen meeting, celebrating the one-year anniversary of the city's incorporation."

Nick blinked. "A year already?"

"Yup. May 14, 2057, to May 14, 2058." He looked at Elise. "I'm sure you remember."

Elise nodded.

"What's on the program?" Nick shifted his gaze from McKenna to Elise.

They shrugged.

Everyone returned to their hamburgers.

9 2

◆

May 12, 2058

On Sunday afternoon, Nick, Elise, Sandra, Nicole, and Nathan went for a walk in a nearby park. They were enjoying the walk; watching wild ducks wading in a pond; bending over to sniff, then snap a photo of some colorful flowers; picking up a fallen tree branch to use as a cane; and listening to hundreds of birds calling. Nick liked seeing Sandra engrossed in every detail, her spirit more bubbly with each encounter. His only daughter was no longer estranged but greeted each brush against one of her senses as an exciting experience.

Nicole rushed about, constantly waving back to her mom to check out some new flower or colorful bird.

Nathan spent his time following ducks as they waddled ahead of their ducklings. Once, he charged after a squirrel that darted from a tree, across the grass, and up another tree. He never got close to the squirrel.

Nick noticed Elise's attention darting about like the squirrel. She chuckled when Nicole pointed at a bird on a branch, which flew away before Sandra could take a picture. Elise gave him a slight nudge whenever Sandra waved at him.

Monday Afternoon: May 13, 2058

McKenna, Julia, Half-Penny, and Henry joined them at Los Pinos, a park wrapped on three sides by the Rio Grande River.

McKenna shuffled along behind Nathan and Half-Penny as they headed left to check out the river. Nick could barely make out the two boys as they pulled up their pant legs and swished their feet around in the slow-moving water.

Nicole joined Julia and Henry walking straight ahead to the northern point of Los Pinos. There were trees and stretches of sand. Several times, Nicole brought some item back to them to inspect.

Nick, Elise, and Sandra sat down at a wooden picnic table with benches.

McKenna's cell phone rang. After a brief conversation, he excused himself.

Sandra looked toward the river. "A nice day and a nice spot," she said. "And nice company," she added, looking at Nick and Elise.

"I'll second that," Elise said.

Nick reached across the table and rested his right hand atop Sandra's left. "I love you, Sandra," he said, just managing to hold back tears.

Sandra smiled back at him and placed her right hand atop his.

Monday Early Evening: May 13, 2058

Nick and the others returned to McKenna's house about an hour before dinnertime. McKenna still hadn't returned.

Julia, Nicole, and Sandra went into the kitchen to cook. Henry followed. Nathan and Half-Penny set the dining room table. Henry was told he could help by having a seat on the living-room couch.

Nick was about to slouch down into one of two padded easy chairs when he heard the front door click open. It was McKenna, in an overcoat on a warm day. He came into the living room and stopped in front of Nick.

"What?" Nick asked.

McKenna gestured for Nick to follow him into the master bedroom. Nick tagged after him, then, in the bedroom, leaned against the dresser and waited. McKenna closed the door and moved to his desk on the other side of the bed.

Nick's neck started itching. "You're very quiet and"—nodding toward the closed door—"secretive. What was that phone call all about?"

McKenna pulled out a padded envelope from under his coat and gave it to Nick. "I didn't want anyone to see me carrying this. One of the portal agents gave it to me. He told me that Captain Martin gave this to him three days ago, the day Martin said an emergency came up and he had to leave Friendship City. The portal agent said he didn't recognize the name, so he checked the portal entry records and found I was the sponsor."

"Sponsor for whom?"

"For you. Well, for your cover name."

Nick took the envelope and saw the name *Wesley Martin* hand printed in bold strokes.

"I figured the youngsters in the other room may not know all the reasons for your cover," McKenna said.

Nick peeled the tape strip on the envelope's back, reached in, and pulled out a small, clear plastic bag and a thumb drive. "What the hell?" He held the small bag up to the light. "There's a glob of something."

McKenna retrieved his portable computer from his middle drawer and placed it on the desk.

Nick plugged in the drive and hit the play button.

A grainy screen appeared, the sound a choppy gurgle. Suddenly, the view of a room took over the screen. Nick noticed the time code at the bottom right: 97 seconds.

Captain Theodore Martin, dressed in civilian clothes and sitting in a chair behind a desk, waved at the camera. "Hello, Wesley. We both have the same last name: Martin. I know we're in no way related, primarily because I know your name isn't your name. I hear you answer to Nick Garvey. I advise you not to trace my lineage by climbing my family tree. Would be a lost cause." Captain Martin leaned toward the camera and winked. "Let me help you," he said, picking up the small plastic bag. "Like you, Nick, Martin is not my real name." He opened the bag, snorted twice, and spit into the bag. "I'll have this sent to you so that when we meet again, we can call each other by our real names. At least by our real *last* names." He waved and winked again, and the grainy screen reappeared.

Neither Nick nor McKenna knew what to make of the recording, but they agreed not to tell the others.

"I'll give this to President Allison to trace."

McKenna nodded, and they left the bedroom to help with dinner.

9 3

$$\blacklozenge$$

May 14, 2058

Nick, Elise, and McKenna had formal invitations to attend Friendship City's celebration of its first anniversary as an incorporated legal and political entity. When Sandra asked to join them, Nick agreed. McKenna had wrangled one extra invitation for a seat on the stage. Officers of the Friendship City police ushered the four of them to their seats on the stage: front row, stage left. They were about an hour early.

Daniel and Warren had arrived even earlier and were in their assigned seats on stage. Closer to the speaker's empty chair sat President Lenora Allison. She waved at Nick and the rest. Yager sat directly behind her. Nick had passed the plastic bag along to her via one of the agents. Nick gave the president a return wave and, wondering to what position Yager had been promoted, gave a nod to the current, or more probably, ex-captain.

They took their assigned seats: McKenna, rightmost of the four just two seats from President Allison, then Nick, Sandra, and Elise. Nick hadn't seen Sandra so excited about anything since she was five years old and had successfully completed her first solo bicycle ride. He smiled, remembering his own nervousness as he stood back and watched her launch off from their driveway, then turn right and pedal along the sidewalk and, unaided but with him trotting not far behind, around the whole block.

He reached across and placed his left hand atop her right. Sandra looked at him and smiled. He squeezed his daughter's hand. She squeezed back.

As he reminisced, some official at the microphone announced that the ceremonies would begin in a half hour.

President Allison asked McKenna if he would switch seats with her for a minute or two. He agreed, and she sat next to Nick. "Your daughter seems fully recovered," she said, placing her left hand on his shoulder. "I'm so happy for you and for her. And for Nicole."

"Thank you. That means a lot to me."

"I also have some news to pass along to you."

"Could it be about Yager's new position?"

President Allison chuckled. "Are you ever surprised about anything? Captain Robert Yager has accepted my offer to be my lead Secret Service agent."

"Excellent choice. I think Sam Kirby would give him two thumbs-up."

"They knew each other at West Point before the World Council shut it down." President Allison reached across Nick and shook Sandra's offered hand.

"Madam President," Sandra said. "I've read up on the founding of this city, and I was most impressed by your foresight in supporting its creation."

"Thank you, Sandra," President Allison said. "However, President Emilio Lopez of Mexico possessed even greater foresight. He brought the various requests to my attention, so his foresight precedes mine by at least a month."

Nick gestured at a large group of men climbing the stage and heading to the right of the podium. Several of the men wore white turbans, one wore a light-colored yarmulka.

"Who are those people?" Nick asked. "Obviously not citizens."

"I'm not exactly sure," replied the president. "I was aware that several other communities around the world are interested in emulating what Friendship City has accomplished. They seem to have been invited."

Nick shrugged. "They seem friendly enough. They're all up on stage, so maybe a few will be speaking."

"Most likely."

Hearing a sound check, the president and McKenna returned to their assigned seats.

Mayor Patrick Riley stepped onto the stage and went straight to the podium, placed a small stack of papers in front of him, riffled through about five of the pages, checked his watch, adjusted the microphone, and cleared his throat. "Welcome to everyone here. Welcome to the citizens of Friendship City. Welcome to the presidents of the two countries, Mexico and the United States, who were most instrumental in facilitating the creation of this remarkable union of neighbors. This, as you all know, is the one-year anniversary of the founding and incorporation of Friendship City."

Applause welled up from every section of the stadium.

"That applause is well deserved. Friendship City, our city, has grown not only in friendship, but in regard around the world. We have had our problems, but we have dealt with them." Mayor Riley paused and swept his gaze over those in the stadium. "Dealt with them together. Together as a family. I am so proud of you."

More applause. More cheers.

"And on this stage with me are two other leaders who are also proud of you, the citizens of Friendship City. The first of these proud leaders is the Honorable Emilio Lopez, president of Mexico."

Applause and cheers.

Mayor Riley stepped aside and motioned the Mexican president to the podium.

President Emilio Lopez, six feet tall with broad shoulders and a husky build—owed to his early career as an Olympic weightlifter—stepped to the microphone and gave a sweeping wave to every corner of the stadium. The stage spotlights highlighted his full head of dark hair and thick mustache.

"Great citizens of Friendship City, it is true, I am so proud of every single one of you. Before Friendship City, you were neighbors and friends. Today, and for the past year, you are family."

As the applause welled up, Nick looked to his left at Sandra and smiled. She was both the oldest and the newest member of his family. President Lopez's words faded into the background as Nick reflected on Sandra's months of struggle in the hospital to regain her memory and identity. He remembered his own trepidation that if and when she recovered all memories, she would again turn her back on him. The thought occurred to him that he owed Ishmael's henchman, Dr. Baumberger, a big thank-you for presenting Sandra with such a ridiculous and outlandish scenario of her dad killing her beloved uncle Joey that even she could see the truth.

Loud applause brought Nick back to the here and now.

"In closing," President Lopez said, "I am not only proud of you, I truly love every one of you."

More applause and shouts of "We love you too!"

Mayor Riley stepped back to the microphone. "And now, the most Honorable Lenora Allison, president of the United States."

More applause and more cheers as Mayor Riley again stepped aside.

"Yes, citizens of Friendship City," President Allison said, "you have earned our pride in you. You have worked hard keeping families intact, adding remarkable depth to your primary education courses, sharing success stories between neighborhoods, joining forces to confront those who would scheme to destroy you, and in your every action as citizens, converting a world of doubters."

President Allison paused for a moment, lightly tapping her forefingers atop the podium.

"In addition to all those achievements I just mentioned, there is one more thing all of you must do. You must also be proud." She swept a hand from left to right, indicating everyone in the stadium. "Very proud. *Proud...of...yourselves!*"

Almost two-thirds of the stadium stood and cheered, applauded, and shouted, "*We are proud! We are proud! We are proud!*"

President Allison took her seat. The cheering continued for more than three minutes.

Mayor Riley finally stepped to the microphone and waved his hands over his head.

The cheering continued for another minute or more.

"We have more," he said finally. "We have seven groups here on stage that hope to emulate our city. As was the case in Friendship City, these people are not elected officials, military personnel, or bureaucrats. They are residents of countries currently at odds with each other."

Nick watched as the mayor flipped through his speech. It was apparent he had decided to cut himself short when confronted with another round of applause.

"I have asked each group to come to the microphone and jointly accept one of our Friendship City flags. Earlier, I was told that few of them feel comfortable addressing a large group." Mayor Riley coughed, then chuckled. "Can't say I'm always comfortable here."

An assistant handed the mayor a folded flag.

"The first group is from two border towns in Turkey and in Syria."

Two men stood and stepped to the podium, where they received the flag. Before they returned to their seats, Mayor Riley made a stretching-out motion. The two men opened the flag and held it between them. They appeared nervous but smiled when the applause erupted. They held the flag open until Mayor Riley motioned them to their seats.

"Next, we have two border towns in Greece and Albania."

Two men stepped forward and were handed a flag, which they held open for all to see.

After Greece and Albania came China and Russia, Venezuela and Colombia, and China and Taiwan.

After announcing China and Taiwan, Mayor Riley added, "As we all know, China has for many years been creating so-called islands in many places in the China Sea, from the south on up. This particular island, actually almost a bridge of sand, was created in September of 2034, just shy of nine months before the mainland was hit with the devastating plague in June of 2035 that killed over a third of their citizens. These two men hope to merge two nearby villages into their own City of Friendship." The mayor motioned them to join him at the podium.

The two Asian men accepted the flag, held it out, and unlike the others, shook hands.

The applause started slowly. Then, as the two men held their hands without releasing, it grew in volume.

As the applause finally died down, Mayor Riley called up the next two gentlemen. "I am pleased to announce two men from adjacent towns, both in Korea: one North, one South. Hopefully, their City of Friendship can heal long-lasting divisions."

The two men accepted the flag and shook hands.

Mayor Riley motioned to the last three individuals. "We have the potential of a unique City of Friendship: Israel, Syria, and Lebanon."

The three men came to the podium, accepted the flag, and didn't shake but held hands as they circled the flag.

Nick almost covered his ears, the applause was so loud. Even the mayor was applauding.

"Wonderful! Wonderful!" the mayor said. He pointed to the men who stood beside him. "I know you believe you will be creating a sparkling and bright utopia. You probably will, but all utopias require their citizens to be constantly alert, to work hard, to help each other, and to never give up." He shook a forefinger at the men on his right, then turned to everyone in the stadium. "You both think...no, you *all* think the devil is dead and buried. He's not dead. And he can come back if you lower your guard."

The back of Nick's neck felt a slight itch.

Mayor Riley announced that several musical groups would perform over the next two hours. The music—classical, jazz, country, blues, and pop—was well received, generating much additional applause.

Nick's itch continued.

*****

President Allison and Yager joined the party at McKenna's house. There was cheer in their conversations, cheer in the air, and a few bottles of cheer on the table. Everyone wore grins. Everyone except Nick, whose neck still itched.

President Allison put her wine glass down on the table. "Something's bothering you. I can tell."

Nick nodded, then shrugged.

"Your neck is itching?"

He nodded again.

Elise came over. "Is there something I can help with?"

"No," Nick said. "I'm not really sure what—" The itch erupted full bore. "Mayor Riley said at the end, 'You both think.'"

Elise and President Allison furrowed their brows.

"You both think...what?" Elise asked. "All he said at the end was, 'You all think the devil is dead and buried.'"

"Close enough." Nick looked upward, his eyes moving side to side as if visualizing some distant event. "Before I was brought in... where?"

President Allison nodded. "Before you were brought in to be executed."

Nick's itch subsided to a low stuck-with-you-until-we-find-the-answer level.

"Just before you were brought in, Jeremiah sneered and said to us, 'You both think he is in a sanatorium in upstate New York.'"

"Who is 'he'?" Elise asked.

"Jason Beck."

President Allison turned to Elise. "Jason Beck didn't die in a helicopter crash. We faked that. His face was burned beyond recognition. He seemed quite out of touch with reality. We weren't about to put him in a prison where other inmates would know of his condition. We placed him in a secure sanatorium, far away from public scrutiny."

"Maybe too far," Nick said.

9 4

———◆———

T he limousine came to a stop next to the stairs leading down from Air Force One. President Allison exited the plane first, followed by Yager, Elise, and finally, Nick. They took their seats in the vehicle. They had flown from Houston to Boston's Logan International in just over two hours.

The limousine, with three Secret Service agents in the two front seats, throbbed to life and left the airport. The president and the others occupied four of eight padded seats that were split four and four and faced each other across a space big enough that it could have accommodated a small conference table.

Nick hadn't asked the others to accompany him to the psychiatric hospital up on a hill a good drive west of Boston. They had insisted they come with him.

He turned to President Allison. "I hope you understand why I didn't want to verify by phone."

She nodded. "Seeing for yourself is best. There's no other way of really verifying."

An hour and twenty minutes later, the limousine pulled up to the hospital entrance. Everyone except the driver entered the lobby. A male nurse ushered them to three uniformed guards, who checked credentials before allowing the nurse to take them into the office of the chief of staff, where he showed them their seats. "She will be in shortly," he said and left.

"She?" President Allison asked. "When we brought…" She took a deep breath. "When we brought Patient 417 here eight months ago, the chief of staff was a man."

Nick remembered a young man of maybe forty-five who struck him as being in strong physical shape.

The back door to the office opened, and a thirty-something woman with red hair walked in, dropped a folder on the desk, nodded to all, and took her seat behind the large desk. The nameplate read *Ms. Amanda Pruitt*, with *Chief of Staff* in smaller print underneath.

"Welcome, President Allison, and…" Amanda Pruitt looked down as she opened her folder. "Welcome Captain Robert Yager, Detective Nick Garvey, and Elise Carpenter." She looked up and smiled. She glanced back to her folder. "I see you are here to see Patient 417."

"We are," President Allison said. "First, however, a point of curiosity on my part. What happened to your predecessor? We met late last August when Patient 417 was admitted."

"He was killed in a car accident in February. His car skidded on an icy patch on the road, and he crashed into a tree. He was dead when rescuers arrived."

"Sorry to hear that," President Allison said. "He struck me as a professional, honest, and caring man."

"I've heard that he was."

Nick's neck itch jumped a couple of notches. "You never met him?"

"No. I was interviewed a week after the accident. Got the job two days later."

"Does Patient 417 look to be in good health?" the president asked.

Amanda Pruitt looked down at her folder and dragged her right forefinger downward. "Yes," she said, looking up. "Good health."

President Allison's gaze turned into a glare. "I used the phrase 'look to be in good health.' Have you actually seen Patient 417?"

Chief of Staff Pruitt paused, caught off guard. She took a deep breath. "Not required. I am not a doctor or analyst. I'm the chief of staff, not the chief of patients."

Elise shook her head. "Good evasive answer. Is Patient 417 male or female?"

Pruitt checked her folder. "Male." Her voice was a snarl.

President Allison retrieved her cell phone and pressed a button. She cleared her throat. "You said you are not a doctor nor an analyst. Do you have a college degree?"

"Yes."

"In what?"

A look of hostility crossed the chief of staff's face. "I have a BA in English literature."

Nick's itch rose to epic levels.

President Allison paused for a moment and glanced down at her cell phone. "I think it's time for us to observe Patient 417."

Pruitt swiped her folder closed. "Not possible."

"And why is that?"

"Only family can visit."

President Allison gave a sigh. "We do not need to visit. Our need is to observe. You know, watch 417 through the window. Since you acknowledged he is male, we don't have to see him undressed."

Pruitt tapped her closed folder. "Not allowed."

"Not allowed by what authority?"

"By the patient admission document."

The president chuckled. "I wrote that document, and it states that I and anyone in my presence can observe Patient 417. Your predecessor agreed and signed the document."

Pruitt sat immobile.

President Allison picked up the slack. "Check your all-knowing folder there," she said, pointing.

"I repeat, not allowed. Patient 417 has the right to uninterrupted privacy."

"Maybe he doesn't even exist. I repeat, by what authority is viewing Patient 417 not allowed?"

"Mine." Pruitt pressed a button on her phone.

"A degree in English lit won't cut it."

"But this will," Pruitt said, flaring her hand open to indicate the door by which they had entered.

President Allison and the other three twisted in their seats. Everyone waited.

Nothing.

Chief of Staff Pruitt pushed her phone button again.

Three seconds passed before the door opened. Pruitt flashed a smug grin as the three uniformed guards from the lobby entered. Her grin evaporated as the president's three Secret Service agents came in after the guards, motioned them to the back door and followed them out.

President Allison stood. "We will now all go to observe Patient 417."

"But..." Pruitt said.

Yager stood and flashed his badge. "No buts. Take us there now or I take you to federal prison."

"I'm just following orders," Pruitt said.

President Allison motioned for Nick and Elise to stand, then turned to Pruitt. "You now have a new set of orders to follow."

Yager waved Pruitt ahead to the front door and took her out by her arm. President Allison, Elise, and Nick followed. They took the first right and headed down a long corridor. As Yager and Pruitt passed a corridor branching off to the right, President Allison stopped and called the two back.

"Which is it?" she asked Pruitt. "Don't know your own hospital layout, or trying your best to mislead us?"

Pruitt was visibly shaken. "But—" She started and couldn't continue.

President Allison tilted her head toward the right hallway. Yager pulled the shaking Pruitt back and to the right. After fifty feet, the hallway ended with a left turn.

The first patient room on the left was numbered 402, on the right, 401. They all stopped at the window to 417. The venetian blind was closed.

"Have the blind opened," President Allison said.

Pruitt didn't move.

"You have cell phone capability to activate the blind. Activate it."

Pruitt started to shake.

President Allison nodded to Yager, who handed Pruitt over to Nick. After three attempts, Yager kicked the door open.

The bedroom was empty. The bathroom, also empty.

President Allison turned and glared at Pruitt. "Where is Patient 417?"

Nick could almost feel the tremors in Pruitt's neck and shoulders.

The president nodded at Yager. "Have the other agents lock down the whole hospital."

Yager pulled out his cell phone, tapped it three times, paused, then gave some orders.

Nick walked Pruitt over to the chair next to the bed and eased her into it. He turned back to the president. "The lockdown is critical, but I don't think we'll find Patient 417 anywhere."

"I agree. Jason Beck is on the loose." President Allison's cell phone buzzed.

Elise reached for and held Nick's hand. "God help us."

Still holding her cell phone to her ear, President Allison's eyes widened. "God might be the only one who can help us," she said, turning off her phone.

Nick turned to look at the president. "What's the problem?"

The president lowered her head and sighed. "The bag you gave me—the contents triggered a close match. A familial match. A one-generation familial match."

"What match?"

"Our Captain Martin is really Jason Beck's son."

The itch in Nick's neck ceased. He shook his head. What in hell was happening?

APPENDIX

$\blacklozenge$

Bill of Rights and Obligations

Friendship City—Bill of Rights and Obligations

As a joint agreement between Mexico and the United States, the following initial rights have been approved by the five Citizen Councils on May 14, 2057, and must each be approved by 60 percent of the citizens-at-large within eighteen months or any not approved will be eliminated. Approval requires a majority approval by citizens eligible to vote. The vote of citizens not participating will be cast against all listed and specified rights.

01) Immigration:
1. Immigration into Friendship City, initially restricted from either Mexico or the United States, is to be by sponsorship of a current citizen. This sponsoring citizen must have been a citizen of Friendship City for two years or of either of its component jurisdictions for the same period. Exceptions to this restriction must be approved by two-thirds of the current citizens. This sponsoring citizen must be free of convictions for any misdemeanor or more serious violation of Friendship City law.
2. Immigration applies to immediate family only. Immediate family is hereby defined as consisting of

the primary sponsored individual, male or female, who may include the following: spouse, parents, and grandparents of self and of spouse, children, and grandchildren of self and of spouse. Immigration does not include anyone outside this specific group, e.g., cousins, aunts, or uncles.

3. Immigration of the infirm within an immediate family is allowed and encouraged as long as, at application, other family members commit to provide sufficient care and support to the infirm individual so as to not burden the Friendship City health care system. Later, should family conditions change so that sufficient care cannot be provided, care will be provided by the city health system unless the family chooses to return the infirm individual to their home country. If repatriation is chosen, proof of sufficient home-country care must be provided before that individual will be allowed to leave the city.

4. All immigrants below age sixty are expected to learn the basics of the other primary Friendship City founding language. When immigration is extended to other countries, those below age sixty are to learn basics of one founding language.

02) Safety:
1. It is the responsibility of Friendship City to provide for the safety of its citizens as well as any visitors. This safety will be provided by a department of police, a fire department, hospitals (currently six), and funded mental health providers.

03) Taxes:
1. The amount of all monies collected through taxes or imposed fees must be fully transparent. This transparency will cover the various taxation levels.

    2.   The amount of collected funds applied to any and all city obligations will be fully transparent.

04) Education:

    1.   Any family member between the ages of fifteen to thirty without an education equivalent to graduation from high school must pursue one of Friendship City's free learning curriculums provided at age-appropriate levels. The associated classes will be tailored to fit in with an individual's free time and will involve a minimum classroom time of six hours per week, which can be broken up into one-hour increments.

    2.   Children at or below the age of fourteen who have not completed primary education appropriate to their age will be enrolled into Friendship City's public or private schools, both free. As school choice is the cornerstone throughout Friendship City, parents who determine their children will receive a better education in a different school can request reallocation to another school. The city, having wide-ranging services, will assume all transportation costs.

    3.   The costs of college-level education will be the responsibility of the family. As Friendship City will not be providing backup to any loans for education, nor for any other use to keep costs under control, all college fees as well as postgraduation job employment statistics will be made public.

05) Elected Officials:

    1.   Elected officials will receive a city-provided salary no greater than twice the salary of the average Friendship City working citizen.

    2.   No elected official may serve more than three terms in any one office. Should an elected official run for and be elected to a different office, the total number

of terms spent across any and all elected offices is hereby limited to five.

3. Elected officials are the only individuals who can propose any law, which must be voted upon by the citizens.

4. Elected officials cannot propose or enact changes to their salary.

06) Policy Measurement:
1. All policies put in place by elected officials must be measured going forward.

2. Should city financial growth decline by 5 percent for a year or less, the elected officials should be alerted. Should the 5 percent decline persist for a year, a new policy proposal is to be suggested. If no policy modification is made or new policy proposed after two years, the previous policy will be restored.

3. Should city financial growth decline be greater than 10 percent for a year, all salaries of elected officials who sponsored the policy will be reduced by twice the decline.

4. Should city financial growth be negative by 10 percent for two successive years, all elected officials who sponsored the policy will be ineligible for reelection, which must be held within two months.

07) Lobby Activity:
1. No lobby activity is allowed. If any city employee is found to accept lobby inducements, that employee, elected or not, will be terminated and any pension revoked.

08) Official Residence:
1. No elected official can reside inside a gated community. Such isolation impairs their perspective and understanding of citizen issues. An individual who

retains a home inside a gated community can be elected to office if that individual commits to live outside that gated community with rental expenses paid by the city.

09) Bureaucracy:
1. No city employee, elected or appointed, can add restrictions or interpretations to any law passed by the citizens.

10) Religious Affiliation:
1. All religions and their respective beliefs and practices will be accepted and protected by the city as long as they violate no specific criminal law. Criminal law of the city currently refers to those referenced in the separate document: Friendship City Criminal Laws as Selected and Enumerated from the Constitutions of the United States and of Mexico.
2. Lack of belief in any religion will also be accepted and protected by the city as long as no criminal laws as referenced in section 09.1. are violated.

BORO Submissions posted on May 14, 2058

The submissions of the following Bill of Rights and Obligations were posted on the one-year anniversary of the founding of Friendship City. The following eleven BOROs are subject to the same voting process as the initial set receiving approval by the five Citizen Councils on May 14, 2057. Each of the following can be approved on or before eighteen months from their posting. The name of the citizen submitting each posted BORO is listed above.

Name: Timothy Dorr
Subject: Transportation
Transportation will be made available, free to all residents of Friendship City, as follows:
1. Light-rail trains, stations, transfer sites for main city and high-use suburban routes
2. City buses utilized for shorter inner-city routes
3. Share stations—walking or motorized scooters, bicycles
4. Automobile ride-share
5. Streetcar trolleys in applicable areas—high city social areas, lakes or waterways

Name: William Dunstan
Subject: Veteran Benefits
All veterans are entitled to lifetime health benefits, disability benefits if disabled, and pension benefits.

Name: Peter Dillon
Subject: 05) Elected Officials
BORO Submission: All campaign funding comprised of financial donations, material contributions, or public or private services shall be received and accounted or inventoried by the city before redistribution to candidates. All political campaign contributions shall be comprised only of individual donations accompanied by the contributors current voter's registration number. Corporate contributions are prohibited as well as foreign-based sources.

Name: Peter Dillon
Subject: 05) Elected Officials
Crimes of corruption while in office are unlike identical crimes committed by the general citizenry as these crimes can harm large portions of the general population and can be of an inestimable damage or devastating hardship and are therefore punishable at two to three times the recommended current or conventional sentencing as defined by law.

Name: Thomas Mitchell
Subject: Retirement
Any Friendship City sponsored pension will be based on the contribution to Friendship City during the working career. Pension will be 10 percent annually of the taxes you paid. A citizen can begin receiving this earned benefit age sixty-five. Supplementing this benefit by continuing working is allowed and encouraged.

Name: Thomas Mitchell
Subject: Immigration
After immediate family immigration sponsorship, any and all other sponsored immigration candidates must be able to contribute to Friendship City. Under no circumstances will a sponsored immigrant receive any benefits until being a citizen for ten years. The sponsors are contractually obligated to provide social services for the immigrant in any and all cases where the sponsored is unable to contribute.

Name: Thomas Mitchell
Subject: Earned Benefits
If a citizen is deemed competent, both mentally and physically, to be able to contribute to society and they do not, that citizen will not receive any Friendship City safety net benefits (i.e., food distribution). These are earned benefits. If a person is deemed not able to contribute both mentally and physically, they are eligible to receive Friendship City benefits. If you can contribute and don't, you can't take.

Name: Thomas Mitchell

Subject: Pension Funding

All pension funds, public or private, must remain 100 percent fully funded at the start of every year. The most recent actuarial tables for lifespans and the last fifteen-year rate of return of the stock or bond market at the mix used must be utilized. Money cannot be borrowed and placed into the pension fund to make up for lost income or a lower rate of return. Pensions are fully funded as you go.

Name: James M. McArdle

Subject: Universal Basic Income (UBI)

A UBI right shall be provided to each citizen and is always given via electronic payment to a specific account. The citizen must actively move the money to a private account each month or lose it. Their obligation is to take an online course annually on some career needed by the city state like EMS or national guard. They could be called up to serve in a temporary capacity should the need arise.

Name: James M. McArdle

Subject: Gun Rights

Friendship City citizens may own and bear arms. During peacetime, the arms are stored at local gun ranges. Citizens must be a member of the Citizen Guard. They must undergo annual Citizen Guard training in weapons, tactics, riot control, and border protection protocols. Citizens may own personal nonlethal weapons for personal protection.

Name: AJ Kaletski

Subject: Media and Elected Official Interaction

Any Friendship City news network or newspaper can interview an elected official or city employee at the request of either party. The interview must be video recorded, and sections can be broadcast or printed, but the complete video must be made available for individuals to review. If no video is made available, the interviewing entity will be banned from any further interviews of any elected official or city employee.

Name: AJ Kaletski
Subject: Military Emergency
If a citywide military emergency is declared, all soldiers have the right to be sheltered in private homes if they inquire with the citizen who owns the property.

Name: AJ Kaletski
Subject: Bail and Fines
Excessive bail and fines shall not be imposed, nor cruel and unusual punishment inflicted on the first criminal offense. Repeat offenses are to be met with more excessive punishment.

Name: AJ Kaletski
Subject: Education
Students below the age of eighteen are required to attend 180 days of school each year until they finish their eighteenth year of age.

Name: AJ Kaletski
Subject: Education
When in city schools, public or private, students are not entitled to all the rights and privileges they have when they are out of school. (Example: Restrictions on freedom of speech, press, and protest. Lockers and backpacks can be searched with reasonable suspicion.)

Name: Thomas Mitchell
Subject: Politician Pay
Elected Politicians salary is based on a multiplier. Base is 1.0X. If the exceeding Economic and Population Well-Being index, the multiplier can double. If the Economic and Population index fails to meet standard, the multiplier is reduced up to 50 percent. The index consists of the following: unemployment rate, inflation, average lifespan, food insecurity percent, K–12 education test scores.

Name: Thomas Mitchell
Subject: Severe Medical Issues
A citizen with a severe medical issue, or their child with a severe medical issue, will have those therapeutic or curative costs covered by the state. A severe medical issue is defined as having a yearly costs to the family of one-third their income. All intervention strategies, including pharmaceuticals, will be covered. Other, less costly medical issues are handled by the patient or family or their insurance. The goal is to prevent families from having to bankrupt themselves paying for a severe medical issue.

Name: James M. McArdle
Subject: City Website
Friendship City must provide an accessible website for all citizens to check in to get news, e-mail, and notifications of things they need to do. In return, the citizens get their UBI payment delivered to their bank account and perhaps perks when they do extra things identified by the city like getting a vaccine.

ABOUT THE AUTHOR

◆

Carl H. Mitchell has an engineering and computer background and lives in Hillsborough, New Jersey, with his wife, Maryann. They winter in Tarpon Springs, Florida.

Carl was born in Hollywood, California. He earned his bachelor's degree from Stevens Institute of Technology in Hoboken, New Jersey. He worked for IBM for thirty-five years in both the technical and managerial ranks.

He had a penchant for writing from a very young age. He was drawn into the world of fiction as a young teenager by Victor Hugo's *The Hunchback of Notre-Dame*. Isaac Asimov and Ernest Hemingway completed his capture.

Carl writes both to entertain and definitely to challenge his readers.

Visit his website: CarlHMitchell.com.

CPSIA information can be obtained
at www.ICGtesting.com
Printed in the USA
LVHW051033100921
697437LV00002B/167